THE
PERFECT
PLAN

ALSO BY BRYAN REARDON

The Real Michael Swann
Finding Jake

THE

PERFECT
PLAN

A NOVEL

Bryan Reardon

DUTTON

DUTTON

An imprint of Penguin Random House LLC

penguinrandomhouse.com

Copyright © 2019 by Bryan Reardon

LIBRARY OF CONGRESS CATALOGING-IN-PUBLICATION DATA

Names: Reardon, Bryan, author.
Title: The perfect plan: a novel / Bryan Reardon.
Description: First edition. | New York, New York: Dutton, an imprint of
Penguin Random House LLC, [2019]
Identifiers: LCCN 2018035962 (print) | LCCN 2018038361 (ebook) | ISBN
9781524743666 (ebook) | ISBN 9781524743659 (hardcover)
Subjects: | GSAFD: Suspense fiction.
Classification: LCC PS3618.E22535 (ebook) | LCC PS3618.E22535 P47 2019
(print) | DDC 813/.6—dc23
LC record available at https://lccn.loc.gov/2018035962

Printed in the United States of America
1   3   5   7   9   10   8   6   4   2

BOOK DESIGN BY JOY O'MEARA

To Barbara and Joseph Reardon

THE
PERFECT
PLAN

I lie among the trees and close my eyes.

The blackness comes quickly now and memories are the last tendrils anchoring me to this place. It's only fitting that I see my brother. We are young, maybe five and seven. The warmth of the sun touches our hair, giving it the smell of summer and childhood. I run through the woods behind him, looking up through the branches of tall oaks and thick white birch trees. The leaves crunch under our feet and the laughter slips out like it belongs to someone else, or everyone else maybe. It surrounds the moment like an aura of innocence, cradling me like a mother's embrace.

My name is Liam. He is Drew. At that age, he was a head taller than me with a rod-straight back like our dad's and sun-lightened hair. Youth rounded his dark eyes but his face had the angles of an adult. Later in life, we would often be mistaken for twins. Mirror images, they'd called us. Yet those who knew us well, knew us intimately, never understood that. Where they saw lines and edges in Drew, they saw crooked and flat in me. Eyes followed my brother like the moths of summer to a porch light. With me, they passed by without a pause, maybe afraid to make eye contact.

That all came later, though. On that day when we were young, too young for our memories to be trusted, I simply ran behind him, following him deeper and deeper into the woods.

"Wait up," I called.

Our house faded away behind us. Normally, we had to stay in sight, but something felt different. My brother's mood carried us over our parents' rules. It lifted us to freedom like shining white wings. I never turned back. I kept going. Kept following him.

We jumped over fallen trees and scurried down a rock ledge. I had no idea where we were going. I had never been that far into the woods before. The first tickle of fear flashed along my spine. Yet it simply added to the excitement of the moment. And I ran.

He came to a stop on the bank of a small stream. Squatting on his haunches, he picked up a stone and tossed it into the water. I stood behind him, out of breath. I had not even known about the stream then. It felt like a different planet to me.

Slowly, I eased to the ground near him. The gritty soil felt cold against my bare legs. I watched him and then aped his actions, selecting a stone and throwing it into the water. Over and over again.

"You're my little brother," he finally said.

I nodded but didn't really think about it. Instead, I watched a water skipper dance across the sparkling surface. He continued to speak, his words merging with the steady babble of the stream.

"That means that I have to look out for you, forever. I have to teach you how to do stuff. Like how to tie your shoes. Come here."

I got up and moved closer to him. He told me to sit in front of him and then untied my laces.

"See, you make a loop . . ."

I watched him with perfect focus. His hands moved with so much grace. He spoke softly, with patience. I followed his direction, lightly chewing on the inside of my cheek.

"You got it," he said, grabbing my shoulder.

I can still feel the smile on my face, and the sun shining down through the branches.

PART ONE

THE ABDUCTION

1

I watch her, but she has no idea that I'm even here. She's standing over by the back corner of the bar with a bunch of her friends. They are all around her age, in their late twenties. The guys are wearing suits and look like total yuppie tools. And the ladies all dress in outfits at once inappropriate and professional, slacks that press tightly against their thighs and white shirts that fold open between the buttons at the chest. They're all pretty, I guess. In a way. But I'm really not paying attention to any of them. Only her.

Her name is Lauren Branch. She lives at 3509 Clayton Street. It's an old row home that has been subdivided into three units. I actually painted the house next door, or part of it. My buddy owns the painting company. I was just working for the day. But that doesn't really matter, either.

She's short, maybe five three, with black hair that is perfectly straight and glasses that may or may not be prescription. Her legs are crossed at the ankle under the table. I can only see one shoe, an absurdly high heel with leopard print. When she speaks, her hands alternate between tenting under her chin and caressing the wooden edge of the four-top. They all seem to be listening to her every word, like she's the boss. They laugh and nod and frown with interest. And I find myself imagining what she might be saying.

When he's governor, we'll all have great jobs and everything will be perfect and I'll get paid a lot.

My mind wanders. My thoughts distract me. For a time, I picture myself married to her. I imagine Lauren coming home from work to my disgusting trailer, finding me on the couch, or maybe working on some half-finished painting. I hadn't painted in years, since high school, really. Until recently, so maybe that's why the image slips into my daydream. Lauren would walk in completely put together in some expensive work outfit with high-heeled shoes and carrying a nice bag with a laptop. What would she do? Kiss me hello? A laugh bursts out of me before I can stop it. A couple of people standing nearby hear it. They look around, uncomfortable, so I slip to another wall and stare at the floor for a while.

It's not really my fault. Maybe that's why I find the thought so funny. I haven't had the best set of examples when it comes to relationships. My mom and dad. My brother and his wife. It doesn't really matter, though. Marriage isn't in the cards for someone like me. My life diverged from that option decades ago, really.

I close my eyes, trying to picture other paths, ones that I might have followed if things had been different. My old art teacher, Mr. Steinmetz, said I was a pretty good painter. Maybe I would have been an artist. I could have lived in the woods, alone, and the world would have coursed through me, out of me, and onto the canvas. I could have shown the others how I saw things, how sometimes the beauty lay hidden behind what the eye could see. Maybe I could have been famous; immortalized in my art.

Stupid, I think. What a stupid fucking thought that is. Maybe I could have been a damn movie star or a ballerina or something. The frustration of it rises. My left hand lifts, crosses my body. I pull up my right sleeve and scratch at the tattoo on my forearm, a Celtic knot with an empty center. I used to dig my nails in until my skin would bleed. But seeing the blood on my arm, at that spot, was too real. Too close to the truth. Scratching it is my worst habit, though I do it anyway, and try to clear my head, to focus on what I have to do.

I can barely hear the Irish music from upstairs, some guy from Maryland who makes fun of the older people up there and sings songs like "Cockles and Mussels" and "Wild Rover." A bunch of people are stomping on the floor to the beat. It's soothing, though. I feel drawn up the steps. In fact, I'm closer in age to everyone upstairs than I am to the happy-hour crowd down here. But I can't leave, not yet. I need to watch.

See, it's finally going to happen. I'm going to do it. It would be easy to say that I'm being forced, that this is not my choice, my decision. That I can't be held accountable for what I am going to do. But no matter how convenient it would be to have a scapegoat, or even share the blame with someone else, I know this is my choice. I *want* to do it. And I will, soon.

Lauren stands up. Laughing, she tilts her head back just a little and the bank of lights behind the bar reflects off the lenses of her glasses. Her chair leg rattles along the hardwood. She steps away from the table and I lower my head, tilting my shoulders to slip deeper into the shadows. I can't let her see me.

2

When I was eight years old Drew used to walk in front of the television show I was watching, a basketball pressed against his hip. He looked from me to the television screen and back.

"Come on. Let's shoot hoops."

I jumped up. I'm sure I was smiling as I bounced out of the house close behind my big brother. He had just gotten home from his CYO game and was still wearing very long yellow-and-black shorts. I had asked our dad if I could watch, but he said no. I didn't know it at the time, but I embarrassed him around the other parents.

"Me against you," Drew said.

I stopped, looking at him. Where most of his friends at the time still had rounded faces, Drew's had already started to change. Over the past summer, almost like he was made of some kind of quick-drying putty, his chin squared and stretched and his cheekbones popped out below his deep-set eyes. Dark hair had started to grow on his legs. Worse, he was about five inches taller than me and three times as strong.

"Horse?" I asked.

"Nah," he said, smiling. "Come on."

So we played basketball. Although the rim wasn't too high, I still had trouble getting the ball up. By the time the score was twelve–zip, I felt hot, but from the inside out. I turned my back, and my feet stomped on the driveway as I walked away.

"You quitting?" Drew asked.

I remember the tone of his voice. It was firm and low, like I was just expected to listen. Like I was supposed to hang on his every word.

"No," I snapped.

"Cool," he said.

My brother took the ball to the foul line. I stood between him and the basket, just staring at the middle of him, like I might suddenly have heat-ray vision and burn him up. He dribbled between his legs once and then broke for a right-handed layup. What could I do? I was way too short to contest it. I didn't have the weight to block him from the basket. He could just run right through me. So, with my cheeks burning and my teeth clenched together, I shot a foot out, hooking the front of his ankle.

Drew never saw it coming. He had broken around me with all his ten-year-old quickness. On contact, he went down. But when I closed my eyes, it looked different than that. I swear he sort of flew through the air. In fact, as I remember it, I can still see him floating right in front of me, the basketball suspended a few feet from his spread hand. It's like a snapshot at the exact second before he realized what I had just done.

In reality, he hit the asphalt, right knee first. The blacktop burned the skin off his leg and his hand as he skidded and tumbled into the grass. Drew grunted and the ball rolled down the hill toward the woods in the backyard. I stood there, transfixed, frozen for another second. I just couldn't believe I'd done that. There had been no thought, no premeditation. I'd lashed out and now, I knew, I had to pay the price.

"Fucker," he hissed.

It was the first time I had heard that word. Before it left his mouth, though, I was already gone. I tore back into the house, through the foyer, and up the stairs toward the bedrooms. When I reached mine, I slid on the hardwood, swinging the door shut. Pushing off the wall, I lunged back and locked it. Then I stood, unmoving, my hand an inch away from the handle. I was so out of breath, but I needed to stop huffing so I could listen. I had to hear him coming.

I stood there in a haze. My heart thumped against my scrawny chest. And the scene played over and over again in my head. I could even see a blossom of crimson blood on his kneecap. I could see the line of his mouth. I could smell his anger. I swear it.

But he never came into the house. He never came after me. I stayed in the room for a good half an hour but never heard the front door open. Honestly, I thought it was a trap, an ambush. So when I finally eased the handle just enough for the lock to pop, I braced for a sudden impact that would hurl the door open. But that never happened, either. I slowly opened it and skulked into the hallway. I made it all the way to the foyer, and nothing. When I looked out the window, he was still out there, shooting the basketball over and over again.

I avoided him for another half hour. At one point, his friend from down the street showed up. At about that time, I heard my mother's bedroom door open. Her footsteps barely sounded as she moved through the house, closer and closer to me.

I sat on my knees in the family room, back in front of the television. I knew I should turn it off, that if she found me there, she'd send me outside. And that could be a problem. For some reason, though, I just stayed there and waited.

She appeared at the doorway. I looked up and she pressed a hand against the jamb. My mother was a tall woman, almost six feet. That day, she wore white shorts and a sleeveless red shirt. But there was something timeless about it. Especially when her perfectly manicured fingernails, shining at the end of long musician's fingers, tapped on the wood frame. And her thick black hair was pressed under a blue-and-white kerchief. Like some tragic 1960s movie star. I didn't think that then. I was only eight. Back then, though, she was just our mother.

"No TV," she said that day, as she said most. "Outside."

I switched it off. With my head hanging, I walked past her, greeted with the overpowering scent of flowers. I headed into my bedroom, grabbed an armful of my action figures, and pushed open the front door. Drew and his friend watched me walk over to the front shrubs. I lay in the grass and played, acting like they didn't even exist, holding my breath because I felt utterly exposed, which is a strange thought for an eight-year-old to have, I think.

For a time, they ignored me and I played by myself in the mulch. Then, out of nowhere, Drew called out to me.

"Hey, come here," he said.

I turned and he was looking over his shoulder, up the street. That's when I saw my dad's car rolling down the hill. I stood up, leaving my figures in the dirt, and walked slowly toward my brother and his friend. At the same time, the door opened. My mother stepped out into the sunshine. She smiled at me and winked.

"It's your turn, little brother," Drew said.

I looked back at him. "Huh?"

"Horse," he said, tossing me the basketball.

I caught it and watched them both suspiciously. His friend fidgeted as I stepped onto the driveway. I remember feeling excited, too, at being allowed to play with the older boys.

As our father parked the car behind us, I eyed my first shot. It was a midrange jumper. Something easy, because I needed to make it. I needed to prove I could hang with them. I heard the car door open and his dress shoes clicking on the pavement. Then I launched the ball. It sailed in a straight line until it hit the front edge of the rim, hard. The backboard vibrated and the ball shot back at me, fast. I grabbed for it but missed. As I turned to give chase, I saw my dad pick it up out of the grass.

Maybe I felt nothing. Or maybe the look on his face melted me into the asphalt. I don't know, really. What I do remember, though, is that he actually dribbled it, the basketball. Twice. Then he stopped and his knees bent. I really thought he was going to take a shot, something I never even imagined seeing before. I felt exhilarated, like we were at an amusement park. I couldn't even blink, but my insides vibrated. In my head, I kept saying, *Shoot, shoot, shoot.*

But he didn't. My father's eyes lowered from the basket. He looked at Drew's friend for some reason. Then his knees straightened, and so did his back. His thin mouth cutting a straight line across his tight jaw, he took a step and handed the ball to me like it was a piece of smelly trash.

"Hey, Dad," Drew said.

"Drew," he said, passing me.

As I stared at his back, my brother or his friend took the ball out of my hands. I heard them talking, but not the words. Instead, I just watched my dad moving toward the door, toward my mom.

"Hi," she said softly.

I think he responded to her. Then her arms opened. She had a huge smile on her face. Like a second sun right there in the front yard. His head turned as they embraced. I saw his expression. Though he held her tightly, every muscle in his face constricted. Like her touch was worse than the basketball.

3

As the sun rises, I walk across the street toward the second row home on the block, five up from where Lauren Branch lives with her two roommates. The building is recently vacant. A Realtor showed it a couple of days ago, but I'm not worried. I step up and take a seat on the front stoop. That's where I wait, avoiding eye contact as people shuffle out of their homes and off to work.

When her door opens and Lauren walks out of her house, I glance at my watch. It's 5:24. That's about average. The latest I've seen her leave is 5:35. The earliest is 5:14. I glance around the block. Three people are in sight. I shake my head and watch her slip behind the wheel of her forest-green Jetta and roll down Clayton toward Delaware. Once she's out of sight, I walk the ten blocks back to my car. I half expect a parking ticket but the windshield is clear. With a last glance at the O'Friel's Irish Pub sign, I pull out of the lot and onto I-95. Luckily, most of the traffic is heading north and I'm going south.

Still, it takes me almost half an hour to get home. I moved out of the city months ago. I used to live out by the hospital, not far from Drew. But I had to get out. So I rented a trailer down by the Delaware River. I have to drive through a park to an access road at the back end that's really nothing more than two tire tracks through the weeds. It winds through a line of trees back to a swampy field, half a mile to the edge of the water. It's wet but my truck has no trouble with the mud.

My place sits all by itself. The landlord wants me to keep up the yard, but he's never around. So the grass, which is more like hay, really, runs up the sides of the dirty white trailer like thick yellow flames. An old Jeep Cherokee, 1995, is parked on the side where the "road" ends. I have been working on it for a few weeks but it still won't run. I park behind it. When I get out, I give the tire a quick kick and walk inside. I don't even lock the trailer up when I leave. No one comes back here. Even the park out front is a little shady.

The inside of the place is dark and smells like an old, damp towel. My cell phone sits on the table next to an empty pizza box. I left it home on purpose. People can track you when you carry it. That's what someone told me.

I grab it and fall into an old wood-framed chair. It isn't mine. The place was furnished when I rented it. I had been living with a girlfriend and I didn't have any furniture anyway. In fact, the only thing I bought myself, the only thing that really belongs to me, is the easel by the window that looks out toward the water.

Leaning back, I listen to the messages. Three from Grace, the girl I lived with.

"Liam, I know you're there. Just pick up."

"Come on. I'm worried about you. Call me back."

"Seriously . . . Karen saw you at O'Friel's. She said you were acting weird. You need to call me. Today."

I close my eyes, my chest tightening. I hadn't seen Karen last night. My fingers press into my eye sockets. I need to be more careful. So much is at stake.

MY PHONE RINGS. One eye opens and I see the time display on my TV cable box, 3:14. At first, I think it's A.M. That I slept through the day and into the next. Then I notice the sunlight coming through the thin remains of the blinds that were already here when I rented the place.

"Crap," I say, rolling over.

I need to sleep. My thoughts are fuzzy, clouded. And I need to be sharp. Now more than ever. So I let my eyes close as the call eventually moves on to my voicemail. But a minute later, the phone is ringing again.

Lurching up from my crappy couch, I grab the phone off the floor. I recognize the number. And I nearly fall over answering it.

"Liam, it's Patsy." There is a pause. "Drew asked me to call you."

Patsy is my brother's wife. My sister-in-law.

"Hey," I say, trying to think straight. "Is he right there?"

"Sure," she says. "We're at Brew HaHa!"

"Shit," I say, slapping the floor. "I totally forgot."

"Yeah," she says. There is another pause, and I can hear my brother's voice in the background. "How long until you can get here?"

I'm already up, stumbling around the trailer, trying to remember where I left my keys. "Tell him twenty minutes. If traffic isn't too bad. Okay?"

"I will," she says. "Drive carefully."

DRIVING BACK TOWARD the city, I fight the urge to hit myself in the head. How could I be so stupid? Especially today.

Somehow, I totally blanked about this strategy meeting. The campaign staff is meeting with the Jefferson Society, a group of young Democrats. Not the normal ones, though, like the College Dems. These are the young lawyers and bankers, the sons and daughters of the local elite. Lauren is a member. Patsy was when we were younger. I think they're all a bunch of pretentious, spoiled little children, at least this group. But they are important, mostly to Drew. Especially considering how the campaign has been shaping up.

I park and walk across Market Street toward the coffee shop. Honestly, I feel like I'm not really there. Like I am a ghost. She's all that I can think about. And she's going to be there, in the meeting with me. I'm going to have to stand close to her. So close that I can smell that perfume she wears. The new one. The expensive one she started using a few months ago. And I'll have to act like nothing is going on.

I need to shake it off. Act normal. I push open the door and head through the front of the shop. One of the baristas waves at me and I smile.

"Hey, Liam," she says.

"Hi, Jill," I say.

"They're already in the back."

"Thanks."

I nod to a few other people, motioning that I'm late. When I reach the back room, I see all the faces turn, look at me. Immediately, I notice that, along with Drew and Patsy and one or two others, I am by far one of the the oldest people at the meeting. Most are sitting at tables, but Lauren stands in the front, her hands holding a pen as she gives a presentation. I slip into a seat near the back, my cheeks burning hot until all the eyes return to Lauren.

"Not only do we understand just how important your group is; we respect what you've been able to accomplish over the last few cycles. Particularly what you've done by organizing the young campaign volunteers into a block. Now the candidates need to come to you for help. As much as they need the party. That was ingenious.

"Things are changing. The state Democratic Party, the county chair. All the ED reps. They've controlled things for generations. But those days are ending. Their ways are slow. Out of touch."

Lauren keeps talking but I lose my focus. I look around the room, wondering where some of the older members of the campaign are. Guessing that either Lauren or Drew didn't invite them. It feels wrong to me, but then I wonder why I'm here. Why was I invited? Why did Drew care enough to have Patsy call me?

These thoughts consume me. I stare at the back of my brother's head for the rest of the meeting, wondering. Could he know? Or suspect? Impossible. I've been so careful. I've planned it all, every last detail. He couldn't know. He can't ever know.

I spiral so deeply that I barely notice when the meeting is over. People rise from their seats, mingle together. Lauren and Drew converge on Kent George, the son of the state's sole US representative. Neither even looks in my direction. I watch their interaction, though. I see how Kent acts toward my brother. Like Drew is a giant magnet. Like his charisma is an undeniable force, drawing him in, holding him close without Drew saying a word.

Maybe I am just tired. When I stand, I feel like I am engulfed by a cloud. I'm there, but not really. None of these people in their perfect clothes, with their perfect hair, can even see me. I sidle back to the wall, lean up against it, and listen like I am invisible. Like I am his polar opposite.

"Patsy!" someone says. I turn and watch one of the less young but very successful lawyers approaching my sister-in-law.

I can hear their conversation perfectly, but it's like I see right through them. Right through everything. Like I'm floating above it all.

"Hi, Geoff," Patsy says. "It's been too long."

They share a business hug, both leaning forward. Meeting like the roof of a house.

"Since you kicked my ass on the bar exam."

"Yeah, right," she says. "How's the practice?"

He shrugs. "Have you ever met a happy lawyer?"

Patsy laughs. "Grass is always greener."

"I guess so. How about you? Do you think you'll practice after the campaign?"

"I'm not sure yet," she says.

"I doubt your father can see you just being some politician's wife," he says.

Patsy stiffens, but probably not enough for Geoff to notice. He tends to say stupid crap all the time. And never seems to get the clue. It's like he's blind to human reaction.

"He loves my mother," she says. "But you're probably right."

"He probably wants you to run for his old seat. Can you imagine? What a power couple. Drew as governor. You as the state Speaker of the House." He laughs. "I remember that was your plan, right? And his. It was a long time ago, but wasn't that what you said at study group?"

"Yeah, I used to think I would run for something. Working on this campaign, though, I'm not so sure."

"You're not meant to *work* on campaigns, that's for sure. Leave that to the ones like Lauren Branch. She's perfect. Like a lovable pit bull."

"She's great," Patsy says. Her eyes wander around the room. "Drew really values the energy she brings to the table. She's got some unique ideas. And she's really in touch with the younger generation."

"It's the millennials' world now, isn't it?"

"Maybe it is," she says. "It's been great seeing you. I need to get back to Drew. Let's get coffee some morning."

"Sounds good," Geoff says.

Patsy's head turns. Her eyes meet mine. A sharp crackle of guilt runs up my back. I don't know why, but the feeling leaves me drained and empty. For her part, she just scans the rest of the room. Then she is gone, walking straight-backed, chin up, until she once again stands at my brother's side.

4

At seven thirty that night, I'm parked outside a firehouse in Elsmere. I need sleep, and I can tell that my patience is nothing more than a spark. It will disappear in an instant; then I will flame up. So I stop, standing in the middle of the large parking lot behind the building. The wind has picked up and with it a deep chill. My hands are in my pockets. I bring them together, closing the jacket across my chest.

The lot is fairly full, a ton of pickups. Most are nicer than mine, though. I see her Jetta near the front. She would have gotten here early for setup. I keep looking until I see my brother's Mustang. It's a 2016 Ford Mustang Shelby 350, blue with a black stripe. It had to cost him around sixty thousand dollars. He said he wanted a BMW but needed to buy American. It would make him more relatable, which I think is utter horse crap, personally. To me, sixty grand is sixty grand.

A couple, both gray-haired and stooped, enter the building as I stand there in the cold. A warm yellow glow pours out, along with the sound of a large and loud crowd. The smell is strong enough for me to picture the plastic mugs of lukewarm beer and thinly sliced roast beef stewing in its own juices.

"Liam, is that you?" someone says behind me.

I turn and see one of my brother's campaign staff. He's a friend of mine, too. Has been for years. In fact, I think he likes me better than Drew, but he would never admit that. Not even to me.

"Hey, Bob, long time. Thought I'd see you at the coffee today."

Bob looks like the prototypical government employee. He is in his late fifties, with thin, curly slate hair and spreading male pattern baldness. He wears V-neck sweaters all the time and out-of-date tortoiseshell glasses. He single-handedly keeps Dockers in business, but I like the guy. He makes me laugh, even when I don't want to.

"Ha! That Lauren never invites us old guys. Am I right?" His eyebrows rise and I know I'm in for a corny joke. "Hey, I was thinking about you the other day. That day it was raining, you know. Yeah, I looked under a rock, and I thought, 'Where's that Liam been?'"

"Hilarious," I say, but I laugh. For some reason, I get a kick out of it.

He takes a little bow. "Well, thank you." He cups my shoulder and almost forces me to start moving toward the door. "I assume we'll be seeing you more now that the campaign is ramping up. No one pounds a sign like you, buddy."

"You mean I'm the one with the pickup," I say.

Bob waves a hand in a looping gesture over the parking lot. "You're not the only one."

"Yeah, but you can't fit much in the trunk of my brother's car."

"Does it even have a trunk?"

Bob cracks himself up. It is a great sound, deep and rolling and strangely nostalgic, like the ocean or an old movie. I glance at him and I realize that I can't for the life of me remember his last name.

"Is that thing infected?" he asks.

"What?" I ask, before realizing I am scratching the tattoo on my forearm again. "No. It's fine."

"Just noticed you've been worrying on it a lot lately. You okay?"

"Sure," I say.

"You sure you okay?"

I laugh it off. "Of course I am. Yeah. Why?"

His eyes squint behind those thick glasses. "I don't know. I just . . . You two getting along?"

"Me and Drew?"

"Yeah."

I look away. "Sure. Yeah. Of course."

"Like always, right," Bob says, laughing again. But this time I don't like the sound as much.

I STAND AGAINST the far wall and watch her. Not Lauren. She's somewhere in the room. The air stinks of too many people and too much drink, but it doesn't matter. I don't feel like thinking about Lauren right now. Instead, I push off the wall and make my way toward Patsy.

She shines among this crowd of unionized men and hard-eyed women. Where the glaring lights hanging from the high ceiling wash everyone out in an overabundance of detail, they only make her light hair shine like silver. Her neck is so long, so straight, that she can look over the three people grouped around her. Her eyes are raw, like the sky just as the sun has fully set. Yet it is her smile, given so freely as I watch, that draws my eyes, tugs at my chest. Not in its beauty, not in her perfect teeth, not in her warmth. Something else, something darker, something only I can see.

Patsy sees me coming. Her eyes shift to me and then back to the man speaking to her. He is the state representative for this district, a retired auto worker, shorter than my brother's wife but so sturdy that he looks rooted into the floor like a tree stump. I can hear him from a few steps away.

"She can't stop talking about your speech at the United Way luncheon last week. Inspiring. That's what I keep hearing. All the women were so impressed. They keep saying that they wished it was you running for governor."

Patsy laughs politely. "I think we have a pretty good candidate fielding that one already."

"Sure, yeah," he says. "But he's lucky to have you, that husband of yours. He's walking a tight line, if you know what I mean, with all those young people he has working for him. Delaware's a small place. We do things a certain way. Your daddy knows that, doesn't he? He should talk some sense into your husband. That young man's charming smile isn't going to be enough. Let's be honest, half the reason the party okayed Drew's run is because of who his father-in-law is. Great man. Great."

Patsy flares that smile again. I pause, awkwardly, to give her a chance to answer a new version of the same comment Representative Marks makes every time I see him, to anyone associated with Drew who will listen.

"I'll tell him you think that. In fact, I told him I was coming tonight and he asked me to say hi to you—and you, too, Mrs. Marks. I think he misses it all."

Marks nods with soberness that borders on bravado. "It hasn't been the same since he decided to retire from public office. Is he well?"

"He's fighting," Patsy says. "He doesn't know any other way."

Marks's wife, I forget her name, gives Patsy a hug. After, Marks puts out a hand and she places hers atop it. The contrast in their texture is mesmerizing.

"He's a lucky man," Marks says. "Brennan is. And give your father our best."

I step up to the conversation. Marks turns and looks up at me.

"Liam. That brother of yours finally got you to come out again."

We shake hands. I nod to his wife.

"He needs my truck," I say with a smile.

Marks laughs like he's sitting in someone's basement playing poker. Patsy turns away, scanning the crowd.

"That's why I like you. Real as the morning. Keep that brother of yours straight. Got it?"

"Sure," I say. "But that's what most people say to him, about me."

Marks nods. "Yeah, it probably is."

He and his wife walk away, leaving Patsy and me alone. We stand next to each other without speaking. She checks out the crowd again, looking for Drew.

"Does he know you're here?" she asks.

"I don't know," I say.

"Have you talked to him?"

"Not today."

She looks at me. The intimate smile is gone, replaced with something different, more practiced. Seeing the change, I'm caught off-balance, like my head is traveling through time.

"Does he ever talk about our mother?" I ask.

"No," she says softly.

I suddenly feel light-headed.

"You remind me of her . . . sometimes."

Patsy looks away quickly. I shouldn't have said that. I know she wants me to move on. She has work to do, candidate's wife that she is. That label is such a joke, though. And everyone knows it. A year before, she had been running a nonprofit for battered women. The local magazine, *Delaware Today,* had done a huge exposé on her when she stepped down to run Drew's campaign. That wasn't too surprising. A woman who had been dubbed an "under thirty person to watch," the daughter of one of the most respected politicians in the state, running her husband's gubernatorial campaign. Stories don't get more intriguing than that.

A lot can change in a year. People whisper about it. Try to figure it out. But she plays the part well: the good wife, hanging at my brother's side. That work, however, is not the only reason she wants to move on. It's more than that. My proximity makes her nervous, but I can't let it go. It almost feels like an addiction. Like it can take over my actions. I can't give it up just yet. I want a little bit more.

"How are you?" I ask.

"Good," she says, not looking at me. "I . . ."

Something stops her midsentence. She takes the slightest of steps backwards. I follow her eyes and see him, Drew. He's staring at us. Then he waves Patsy over. Her smile returns and she hurries away from me without saying good-bye.

AS THE NIGHT drags on, I can't stop watching Patsy. Everything about her is polished and smooth, like one of those worry stones. She glides among the people, from one conversation to another, and everyone watches her go. She is so distracting that I fail to see him coming over.

"Really, Liam?" my brother asks.

I startle, which really pisses me off. My brother and I are the same height. I look him up and down, the perfectly pressed and tailored pants, the red tie and white shirt, the hair slicked back. I showed up in a pair of jeans and a collared shirt, but I never took off my army jacket or gray hoodie. My hair is longer, darker, and looks like I used my fingers as a comb. His eyes are dark, almost black, and mine are lighter, closer to slate. But we share a blocky Irish face.

"What?" I ask, my voice weaker than I intended it to be.

He checks out the crowd, nodding and smiling at the people there, all of whom paid fifty dollars to his campaign for the privilege of attending. He looks like some king holding court. I have to turn my head to keep from saying something stupid.

"The numbers are still bad," Drew says.

I look at him. "Okay."

"Don't act like it doesn't matter to you."

I see Bob. His eyes catch mine and he walks toward us.

"Hi, boss," he says. "Did Karen get you the numbers?"

Drew's expression changes. A smile appears on his face as he nods and pats the older man on the shoulder.

"How are you holding up? Patsy wanted to make sure you say yes to our dinner invite. A happy wife is a happy life, right?"

Bob laughs. "Definitely, as long as you're not cooking."

"Hey," my brother says, charmingly hurt.

"Just kidding, boss. Back to the numbers, though. It's not as bad as it looks. In the city you're dead even."

"With a Republican," Drew says, slowly shaking his head.

"Well, yeah. But remember what we talked about. He's an incumbent. And he's been around for a long time. As we ramp up and more people see you, things will change. I was talking to Lauren about the new messaging, about you two losing your parents and how you took care of Liam. It's testing well with fund-raisers."

"You mean with the old schoolers."

"They're important, Drew."

"I know. Hopefully, my father-in-law can help there," Drew says.

"We'll see. Lauren mentioned that the two of you were working on something. Something *viral*, she said. Hope it's not catching!" He laughs. My brother does, too. Bob puts an arm around me. "Plus, we have the best signpost digger in the state working for us."

That gets Drew genuinely laughing, harder than it should. My cheeks turn red. Bob seems to notice my reaction. I can see him rethink what he just said, and how my brother took it.

"Not to mention," Bob adds, "the unions love this guy. I was just talking to the head of the building trades and he was going on about how real Liam is. They love that. Real men."

"It's all good," I say.

Drew just stares for a second before speaking. "Can you do me a favor? Can you have Karen call that nonprofit on Orange, the one that helps orphans?"

"Children and Families First?" Bob asks.

"Sure," Drew says. "See if they have an event in the next couple of days that I can attend. It'd be a good chance to see how it plays."

"Karen?" Bob asks. "Not Lauren?"

Drew shakes his head. "I have Lauren working on something else."

"Oh, yeah. The virus. I forgot."

"And, Bob, I want you getting more involved in our social media."

Bob nods. "I'll see what I can do. You ever think about making wacky YouTube videos?"

I laugh. When Drew does, I can tell it's fake, but Bob has no clue. He just thinks everything is fun and games. That everything is just great.

"Gotta go," he says, walking away with a huge smile on his face.

I turn to Drew. He's watching Bob. I have so much to say to him. The words feel like the tide rising inside me, like if I stand here for another minute, there won't be any stopping them. In that moment, I see Lauren Branch. She is across the room but watching the two of us. She heads toward us.

"I have to go."

I take a step but his hand falls on my shoulder, fingers pressing into the fabric of my jacket. I will not turn. I will not look at him.

"Should I be worried about you?" he asks.

I pull away without answering. Because if I did, it would bring with it a tidal wave of pain.

5

When I think about my mother, my mind paints the most beautiful picture. Her face shines so brightly, framed by her dark hair and the full green trees behind her. She's looking down, like the painting of the Madonna I once saw, where she holds her baby and her head tilts. She has this smile on her face. It is something I remember so perfectly. Something I see almost every day when I close my eyes. It was like her joy might jump right off the canvas of my memories, surrounding me with warm arms. Like a shield, it would push everything else back. Together, we could hide in that perfect moment.

It happened when I was ten. It was early in the afternoon and we were in the backyard. Mom knelt in the grass, one hand palm down on the ground. She held the other up and a caterpillar circled the tip of one of her long fingers.

"That's one of those gypsy moths," I said, staring at it, fixated by the way the long hairs on the side brushed against my mother's skin.

"It is," she said softly.

"Drew said they're bad."

She laughed and that smile might as well have controlled my entire world.

"Does it look bad?"

I leaned closer. Slowly, I moved my hand to hers. I pointed and gently touched the soft hairs. The caterpillar's black head turned and seemed to look me in the eye. Then it moved. I felt so many tiny legs crawling onto my skin.

"Not really," I answered as it moved onto the back of my hand. "But Dad told Drew that they kill all of our plants. And they make our yard look like crap."

She touched my cheek. "Can't you think of a better word than that?"

I wasn't sure what she meant at first. I don't even think I could remember what it was that I said. She didn't seem to mind, though.

"They're just doing what they need to do to survive," she said. "That doesn't make them bad."

Her big, light eyes seemed to bore into mine. I was only ten, but even then I felt like her words meant far more than what I heard. For some reason, they made me think about my dad. And the look on his face when my mom hugged him.

"Does Dad think you're bad?" I asked.

"Liam!" she said, her eyebrows furrowing. "Why would you ask that?"

I shrugged and held my other hand out. The caterpillar crossed over onto that palm. I petted its hair again, still surprised that it was so soft.

"Baby, look at me," my mom said. When I did, she touched my face again. "Your father works really hard so we can have this life. This house. This beautiful yard. And he doesn't ask much from us, does he? Sometimes, his face might look upset. Or like he's thinking of something else. But he loves you. And your brother."

"You, too?" I asked.

"Of course," she said. "Me, too."

My mother looked like she wanted to say more. Instead, her eyes lowered. Her hand moved from my face. Her fingernail brushed my palm. Then the caterpillar left me, moving to her painted nail. Her arm lifted back up as the gypsy moth moved across the prominent bones of her wrist.

For a time, she simply watched it. I remember thinking that she was going to take it inside and put it in a jar. We could keep it as a pet and she could watch it like that anytime she wanted. Instead, her hand moved to the grass and she waited patiently as the caterpillar slipped off her and down to the ground below the lush green blades.

Surprised, I moved quickly, trying to scoop it back up. But she touched my arm, stopping me.

"Let it go free," she said.

As I looked into her eyes, trying to understand something that no ten-year-old could, I heard my name.

"Liam!"

I ignored it. I couldn't stop watching her. The halves of so many questions filled my head. For just a second, I thought the woman kneeling beside me was a stranger. That something had happened and my mother had disappeared. Before that day, I saw her only as this shining, perfect presence in my life. One that held me grounded. She was the softness in my life. The carefree moments. The random trips to get ice cream. The long walks along the creek, hopping across the water on treacherously slick stones. She was perfect Halloween costumes and spontaneous Christmas carols.

Staring at her, I saw that something had changed. Either inside of her or inside of me. I sensed secrets. Fears. Danger. The sensation clung to me. Holding me still.

"*Liam!*"

She blinked, and the moment flashed out of existence. At once the start of something and the end of something. What, though, I had no way of knowing.

"Your friend is here," she said, waving a hand. "Go play."

I turned and saw Carter appearing in our side yard.

"Hey," he called at me.

I stood up. I turned back to look at her one last time. But, no matter how hard I try, I can't picture what she looked like in that moment. Did she look like what my mother was? Or what she would become? I just can't remember.

The moment passed, though, and I went back to just being a kid. I followed Carter into the woods. We stood by the rock ledge, kicking at leaves and throwing small rocks.

"What do you want to do?"

"Let's spy on the Smiths, see if they're at the fort."

"Cool."

We got into it, Carter and I, creeping through the underbrush while making covert hand signals to each other. When I heard voices carry through the still forest, my heart thumped inside my chest. A perfectly shaped stick lay on the dried leaves beside me. I picked it up, peering down its length like the barrel of a rifle. In my mind, I became a soldier, a sniper maybe, ready to kill in utter and complete silence.

As we moved closer, I could make out words. Keith Smith was my age. He had his friend Ivan with him, a little kid with a giant chip on his shoulder. Ivan and I had almost been in a fight at the bus stop three times. Carter didn't like him any better than I did.

They appeared below us, working on the fort. Carter moved closer to me so we could whisper back and forth.

"We should attack," I said.

"Yeah."

We broke from cover, screaming, and I swung my stick like a club. Carter roared behind me and I heard his feet crashing through the thick covering of leaves. Keith looked up over the shadow of his shelter and saw me.

"Get out of here!" Keith yelled.

I screamed over him, through him. The stick rose above my head. He took a step back. I feigned a swing at his head and hit the side of his fort instead. The sound echoed around us. A piece of bark flew through the air but otherwise the fort remained intact.

"Get out!"

Carter and I stopped a few feet from Keith. Our bodies twitched with potential as we stared him down. The moment inched by and the dance became a fidget. Neither Carter nor I had thought out what to do next. That's when Ivan finally said something.

"You two move and you're dead."

I looked up and saw him across the creek. He stood atop a small outcrop of stone, his hand above his head. The sunlight danced off sparkling mica dotting the surface of the large jagged rock in his hand.

I laughed. "Shut up. You won't do anything."

"Try me."

I looked at Ivan. He did not smile. Something, though, told me he wanted to throw that rock. And it was a big rock.

"If you throw that . . ." I paused. My mind went blank. I felt weakness in that moment, the sort only a ten-year-old could feel. It seemed overwhelmingly real and permanent. I couldn't back down but I was too afraid to commit. Finally, I said the only thing left to say.

"If you throw that rock, my brother will kill you."

Keith's eyes widened. Ivan lowered the stone. Everyone in the neighborhood knew Drew. I smiled, feeling strong, feeling invincible. My chest puffed out and I licked my lips, over the dry patches and the chapped tip that I tended to bite off. Their fear fed my soul. I basked in it, owning it. At the same time I felt a pervasive envy grow inside me. Why couldn't the mention of my name shake the world?

Then Ivan threw the thing anyway. It was so pathetic, really. The stone flopped through the air like an injured bird and plunged into the creek a good ten feet away from Carter and me. But he did it. I stood in utter shock for a second, and then I ran. So did Carter. We charged up the hill like an army chased us. I could hear Ivan and Keith laughing.

We stopped at the rock ledge, both of us doubled over and hacking to regain our breath. There was no way we could still hear them. They had to be well out of earshot. But their laughter filled my head like they stood right in front of me.

I screamed out in frustration. Looking down, I noticed the stick still in my hand. Spinning, I swung it at the nearest sapling, striking it over and over again. Bits of wood flew through the air with each strike. I just screamed over and over again.

"Jesus, Liam. Chill out."

I turned on Carter. It felt like my eyes were on fire.

"If you're so upset," he said, "go get your brother. He'll—"

"Shut the *fuck up, Carter!*"

I swung the stick. I didn't think it would hit him. I thought he was farther away. But the edge caught him just below the knee. The wood vibrated in my hand. And then I saw the blood blossom on his freckled skin. It reminded me of that day with Drew when I hurt his knee, which made me even more angry.

For a second, he said nothing. Neither did I. I just stared at him and he stared at the stick. Then, as if in super slow motion, Carter looked down at his leg. He saw the blood. And he started to scream.

I hung my head. "Sorry, man. I didn't mean to."

Carter just kept crying and crying. Everything took on a red tint. I felt like my body might suddenly burst inside out. For a second, I felt this burning urge to hit him again. Hit him over and over again, really, just to make the crying stop.

Carter turned and ran home. I sat back down in the exact same spot where I had been standing. My head throbbed, and to be honest, I wanted to cry. But I was silent, and I sat there for a long time.

"Liam."

I knew right away it was Drew. I turned and saw him silhouetted by the sun.

"Mom's looking for you," he said.

"Leave me alone," I shouted, my voice sounding shrill and weak.

He just stood there, staring at me. That same overwhelming feeling washed over me, like my head had suddenly filled to capacity with some sticky, thick liquid.

Drew turned slowly and walked away. And I was left to wonder how long he had been standing there.

MY MOTHER MET me in the foyer when I finally made it home. I'd left my rage in the woods. My mother, however, felt differently. Her cheeks were as red as fresh blood and her eyes looked sunken and dark. She held her new cordless phone in her hand. For some reason, I noticed one of her perfectly manicured nails had chipped.

That wasn't the worst of it, though. Her hands were shaking. Her entire body was. And her eyes were wide, almost panicked.

"What did you do?" she whispered.

I couldn't answer right away. It was like this energy was radiating out of her. Burning me. Making me feel like I wanted to tear out of my own skin. She looked around, like she might run away if she could.

"I didn't mean to. I just . . ."

I started to cry. It just happened. I couldn't stop it. I kept apologizing, over and over again, while I sputtered and sniffled.

"I didn't mean to. I'm sorry."

For a second, I thought she was going to hug me. Instead, though, she brushed past. All I could do was watch as she rose up the stairs and disappeared into her room. I followed eventually, but her door was closed. Feeling lost, and strangely alone for the first time in my life, I went into my room, closing the door as quietly as I could behind me.

I heard the phone ring, and not long after that, the door to the garage opened. That meant my father was home. I grabbed a book off the table beside my bed, flipping through it as he stormed up the stairs. My door didn't swing open. He didn't appear on the threshold with eyes red with anger. Nor did he stand with hands on his hips, disappointment in his eyes.

Instead, the door opened slowly. He stepped into the room, moving closer and closer to me, inch by agonizing inch. He was tall, at least four inches above six feet, and he was broad like a man who farmed or mined coal. But he wore a perfectly crisp white shirt with brown slacks and brown shining shoes. His round glasses barely circled his flat, dark eyes, just like Drew's. His black hair was slicked back, not a strand out of place.

He didn't stop until his chest almost touched mine. Softly, he cupped my chin and tilted my head up so I had to look at him. My entire body felt like it belonged to someone else. Or like it didn't belong to anyone. All of me, all that I could feel, hid inside my skull, shaking and lighter than air.

He smiled. His thin lips barely moving. His eyes not changing at all.

"Are you that stupid?" he asked quietly.

"No," I said. Somehow, that tiny word crackled into pieces as it came out of my mouth.

He laughed harshly. "You must be. You listen to me and understand. This is my neighborhood. I work hard so we can live here. And I'm not going to have the mothers telling stories about my son. Do you understand that?"

"I—"

"Shut up and get your shoes on. You're going to march your ass down to that boy's house and apologize."

"Okay," I whispered. For a second, I thought that would be it. That it would end. And I'd be okay. But I was wrong.

"And when you get back, we'll see how tough you really are."

6

I drive the twenty minutes into Wilmington. The clock in the dash says it is 5:34 A.M. I am early, but that's okay. Cutting it close would be dangerous. I have to make sure nothing goes wrong today. I have to be careful and perfect, about everything. I keep repeating that in my mind until I park my truck behind the squat brick building off Clayton Street. When I get out, I open the back door and reach under the front seat. Even in the dark, I find the roll of duct tape without any problem. I jam that into the pocket of my army jacket. Slipping the hood of my gray sweatshirt up over my head, I look at the pavement as I make my way around the building and onto Pennsylvania Avenue, heading east. It's a good ten blocks or so, but it's quiet and a cold wind whips across the river and through the city. It smells like snow, but it is too early in the year.

Most of the city seems to be sleeping. As I pass houses, the occasional light comes on. I picture someone, maybe a young mom preparing a bottle or someone's grandfather measuring out coffee with a stainless steel scoop. I want to stop and step into their world. Not as myself, though. I want to become one of them. I want to step into their reality, own their life. Wake up at home and pad down the stairs while my family sleeps peacefully above my head. They wouldn't have to be with me. I wouldn't have to see them. But I'd know they were there.

For a second, it's almost possible. I think that if I opened my mouth and screamed as loud as possible, I could swallow these strangers whole, take over their lives like nothing ever happened. But the feeling is gone as quickly as it comes. So I just lower my head to the wind and walk.

The sound of my work boots against the sidewalk echoes until a series of cars pass, early risers heading to their office jobs. I follow them until, still blocks away, I see the yellow glow from the windows at the back of the YMCA. I am close. And it will happen this morning.

I know she's inside. I have taken this exact walk over half a dozen times now. I can picture her car in the same spot in the lot across the street. Glancing at my watch, I know, for sure, that I have seventeen minutes until she comes out. She is a creature of habit. Someone should have warned her against that.

LAUREN BRANCH WALKS across the street, right on time. I am watching from the darker corner of the lot, under a small overhang by the back wall. I recognize her gait immediately, long before I can see her face. Her head rises with each step, sending the tight dark ponytail bouncing up and down. Her chin is lifted, proud, and her eyes are open. She walks like a woman who has conquered some elusive greatness, the kind of thing that only she knows. Yet that walk tells the world that it should hang on, because soon, it will all be clear, and everyone will nod and say they should have seen her coming.

She swings a lanyard in her right hand. It whips in a tighter and tighter circle, the nylon strap wrapping around her finger until her keys slap against her hand. Then she reverses the direction, unraveling the lanyard until it reaches its apex and begins a never-ending cycle back to her finger. Someone should have told her not to do that, either.

I move when she is about five spaces from her Jetta. As I get closer and closer, I hear a soft tune. With another step, I can make out the words. She is singing softly, some new Taylor Swift song, one I heard while sitting in my ex-girlfriend's car right before we broke up. She is off-key and her voice rolls into a fading croak.

Something about this hurts. I see this woman, Lauren Branch, as if time rolls suddenly backwards. Maybe she is walking to her car after a long day of high school. She will go home, do her homework, Snapchat with her friends. Her mom will hassle her about dinner or cleaning a bedroom. I picture her having a family, being a part of something loving and good. Maybe she could live in one of those houses I passed. Maybe we could, together.

The idea tears at me, pushing me back. I reach up and pull my hair, then press in on my eyes. Nothing helps. But it's too late for second thoughts. Everything counts on me doing this right.

I feel like my thoughts should be loud enough for her to hear me. I feel like she will spin around, look me in the eyes, and everything will be ruined. Instead, she continues to bounce along, singing and twirling that damn cord. Over and over. With no clue at all. I hate her for that.

I am maybe four paces away when she stops at the back of her car. As she has every morning, she lets her keys land in her hand and she pops the trunk. It swings open and, so predictably, her keys drop from her palm and fall through the air until they stop with a jerk at the end of the lanyard that dangles from the tip of a single finger.

Two paces away and she swings her gym bag into the trunk. Her voice rises, reaching the chorus of the song, and for the first time I notice she is still wearing earbuds. No wonder she never turned. No wonder she had no idea I stood directly behind her, lifting my left hand, palm out to the arch of her back.

I have practiced this over and over again. I know it has to be quick, like a snap. My grasp has to be clean and tight. I need to push her away from me instead of pulling her toward me. Over and over again I have done it, so much that I think I could do it in my sleep. There is no turning back now. I look at my watch. It is now 6:27 A.M. I commit.

The nylon feels warm as it laces between my middle and index fingers. Like snapping a towel, I send a jerk forward. I feel the lanyard slip from her finger and the strap goes limp against my thumb.

Her head turns. I see her eyes; they widen. As predicted, she flinches away from me, shifting her weight toward the car. Without hesitating, my right hand moves with all my considerable weight behind it. My palm presses her green athletic shirt into the small of her back near her hip. I grunt and the force of my push combined with her own inertia buckles her legs. She teeters, off-balance. That's when my other arm curls up, cupping her left leg. I lift it, her foot rising from the asphalt, and I forcefully bend her at the waist. She tries to stop me, to flex the muscles of her back, but it is too late. And I am too strong. She folds in on herself and I push downward.

Lauren's weight does the rest for me. She flips over the ridge of the trunk. It is surprisingly large. She fits in without any problem at all, even alongside her gym bag. I stare down at her and our eyes meet. Somehow her glasses have stayed on. One earbud has come loose, though, and wraps loosely around her neck. At the same time, I pull the roll of tape out of my jacket pocket.

"What the hell, Liam! I—"

That's all she gets out before I slap a strip across her lips. I see the panic then. The fear she must feel. But it means nothing. I slam the trunk closed just as her foot shoots outward. The kick vibrates up the bone of my forearm. I hear a muffled scream of pain just as I force the trunk down until the latch clicks shut.

When I throw open the driver's-side door and slip in, I hear more thumps. I glance at my watch again as my other hand shuts the door: 6:29 A.M. Two minutes.

I drive out of the parking lot. No one is close enough to hear Lauren. No one gives me a second look. I'm gone before she even knows what has happened.

1

The banging continues. It echoes through the car, endless and savage. I planned everything in advance. Just not that. I never thought someone could have the strength, the stamina. My fingers grip the wheel, trying to crush the vibrations out of my body.

"Shut up!" I scream.

The banging just gets louder. *Could she kick open the trunk? Should I have taped her legs down?*

"Shut up!"

I jam my finger down on the power button for the radio and scroll through the options until I find the metal station I have preset in my truck. A Metallica song comes on, a remake of an old classic. I crank up the volume. The bass rattles the windows. The screaming lyrics irradiate my thoughts, mutating them into something more primal.

The pounding continues. I have to turn off the radio; it only makes it worse. Instead, I focus on the yellow lines and the lightening of the eastern skyline. Day is coming. Faster than I want it to.

Bangbangbang

At first, I picture her in the trunk, her Nike running shoes slamming against the interior of the car. As I weave through the traffic on the interstate, though, something changes. The banging sharpens.

Bangbangbang

As I listen, a cold sweat slides down my face. It burns my eyes. I try to wipe it away and slip out of my lane and across a rumble strip.

"Shit," I hiss.

Bangbangbang

The sound seems to change again. Sharpen, like knuckles on a door.

Knockknockknock

Almost like she wants me to let her in, instead of let her out.

KNOCKKNOCKKNOCK

The knock on my bedroom door was firm but not overly loud. My door didn't open right after it. Instead, I had time to get up off my bed and walk across my room. I felt sick to my stomach as my hand reached out for the handle. I remember thinking how strangely polite the whole thing was, considering.

I opened the door and Drew was standing in the hallway. He was not smiling, not exactly, but he seemed to bounce on his toes as he spoke.

"Dad wants us in the basement," he said.

"I don't—"

"Okay," he said, too quickly. "I'll go tell him."

"No," I shouted. Then more softly. "No."

That's when my brother definitely smiled. It was timeless in that I have seen that same expression on his face dozens of times. And it always takes me back to that moment, the way half of his mouth rose but his eyes remained the same. Just like Dad's.

I followed him down the stairs and around to the cellar door.

"Where's Mom?" I asked.

Drew laughed. "In her room."

When I took the first step down, I reached for the railing. Wet with sweat, my hand slipped on the polished wood and I stumbled.

"Don't be stupid," Drew muttered in front of me.

The light above the stairs was off but the glow from our father's work area was enough to see Drew's hockey stuff, which littered the floor like wreckage. Carelessly, Drew bent and picked up one of his sticks as we passed. He took a swipe at a tennis ball, sending it into the goal by the closet.

"Goal," he said.

When he dropped the stick to the poured concrete floor, the sound rattled me and I startled. My father's voice followed the jolt like thunder.

"Get in here."

Drew's pace quickened. So did mine. We walked into his workroom, my brother's head up. Mine down, staring at the red-painted floor.

Our father sat on a high stool beside his workbench building an intricate model of a World War II battleship. The harsh smell of paint and glue hung thickly in the air, stinging my eyes. At first, he acted as if we weren't there. When I glanced up, I saw him hunched over his work, small tools moving deftly in large hands. When he finally turned to look at us, he pulled off his glasses. Using a perfectly clean black cloth, he breathed on the lenses and cleaned them while we stood there watching him. When he was done, he put his glasses on and cleared his throat.

"Drew, turn on the lights out there," he said, carelessly gesturing to the main room of the basement. "And clean up that mess of yours."

"Yes, sir," Drew said.

When Drew left my father's room, I felt a shiver run through my body. I felt alone and raw, as if the air down there was burning my skin like acid. My father cleared his throat again. I knew I had to look at him. I knew that was what he expected. But I couldn't get my head to move. I couldn't stop staring at the blood-red floor.

"How'd it feel?" he asked.

I tried to ask him what he meant, but I couldn't get the words out.

"Look at me," he snapped.

That was enough. The cut to his voice broke whatever it was that had me paralyzed. My head shot up and my eyes met his, struggling to hold his gaze for more than the shortest of seconds. It felt like he sliced right through me, opened me up and left me naked and unprotected.

"I asked you a question," he said.

"What?"

He laughed, a bitterly judgmental sound. "How did it feel apologizing to that boy?"

"Good," I said, whispering.

"Don't lie to me," he snapped.

"I—"

"I said, don't lie to me."

He rose from his chair. He moved to me. I looked up at him only because I didn't want him to touch me.

"I hate him," I said.

I don't know where those words came from. I don't think I meant them. Or if I did, I didn't know it. But they hung there between our eyes.

He smiled, just like Drew. "I don't care."

My eyes shook in their sockets. I blinked over and over again, forcing myself, fighting with everything I had to keep looking at him. I felt dizzy, disembodied.

"It's ready," Drew called from behind me.

My father walked past me, his shoulder bumping mine, causing me to spin with him. Without looking back, he laid out the rules.

"Three rounds. Taped knuckles. Nothing below the belt."

8

The banging finally stops. The silence does something to take the edge off. I am able to breathe as I exit the interstate and wind through familiar neighborhood roads. I drive her Jetta to the back of an apartment complex, pulling up by the access road. I hear her kicking again as I get out and walk quickly to the chain that crosses the entrance. Releasing the clasp, I get back in and, making sure the headlights are off, drive through onto the dirt trail. I have to stop again, jumping out quickly and securing the chain behind the car. With a quick look over my shoulder, I drive off into the woods.

Slipping deeper into the cover of the forest, I follow the trail more by memory than by sight. After a quarter of a mile or so, I glance in the rearview mirror. None of the lights from the apartment complex are visible, so I switch the headlights on. Though the sun must be rising, the thickness of the woods casts me back into the night. The beams, lower than what I am used to with my truck, pan across the trunks, from dark to light to dark again like silent Morse code.

Eventually, the trees thin and the sky appears above, cast in deep blue and rose. As I reach the top of a gentle rise, I catch the first sight of the abandoned swim park. I look down at the lake, a darker amoeba spreading across the forest floor below. Platforms rise out of the water, farther than they should, as if the lake is slowly working its way underground. The closest has a ladder running up the side with an exaggerated loop for a handrail. A large metal slide sits in the middle of the water. Even in the faint light, it looks as if rust peels away from the frame like the skin of a leper.

I chose this place. I have visited it over and over, night and day, stalking like some kind of predator. I know no one ever comes here, even kids. Unlike me, they have the sense to avoid it and all its nightmares.

I reach the bottom of the hill and the trail runs behind a series of squat, dilapidated buildings. Most are equipment sheds and a pump house but the last two must have been cabins. The one on the right is missing half a wall. A sapling grows through the broken wood, slowly peeling the roof away. The high, narrow windows gape open and the door hangs by a single hinge.

The one on the left is different. The structure is more or less intact, and dark wood shutters the windows. The door is shut. As the car turns, the lights reflect off what looks like a silver padlock. I put it there. And I boarded up the windows and fixed the door.

I park the car next to the last building and get out, leaving the keys in the ignition and the engine running. My footsteps echo on the planked decking of the cabin. I remove the padlock and open the door. The air inside is thick and unmoving, with a hint of putridity. I check to make sure everything is still there, that nothing looks disturbed. The water bottles sit in the corner, next to the tarp I used to cover everything else. Otherwise the place is utterly bare. I nod, focusing on my own movement, the next steps, letting the plan guide me.

When I get back to the car, I stop outside the trunk, waiting. There is nothing but silence. For an instant, I think that maybe I taped her mouth too high, that I obstructed her breathing, and that she's lying inside dead. That can't happen. That would ruin everything.

Gasping for air, I race to the front of the car and hit the release for the trunk latch. The door springs open and I see a leg burst out like it was shot from a gun.

"Shit," I hiss.

In three strides, I am back at the trunk. She's already out. She stands, looking at me, her eyes wide and red-rimmed. Black streaks run under her glasses and down her cheeks and blood drips from a gash on her right hand. Her head tilts when she looks at me.

I don't let her think. Like the old tackling drills we did at high school football practice, I run into her, placing my shoulder into her stomach. She folds over and I thrust upward, lifting her off her feet. Her body hangs limp for a minute, like I knocked the wind out of her, as I carry her away from the car. I rush across the decking and into the house.

Once inside, she thrashes, lashing out at me, striking me in the chest with her knees. Her elbow drives into my back by the shoulder blade. As I try to put her down, a kick catches me in the groin. I grunt in pain and send her staggering into a corner.

"Stop," I shout, as the pain radiates into my stomach.

My hand finds the duct tape in my jacket pocket. She scurries away from me, panic filling her eyes as she looks at me. I follow, grabbing her by the feet. She fights, kicking at me, and my fingers dig into the exposed skin below her calf. As quickly as I can, I unroll the tape around her ankles, pressing them tightly together. When I do a good ten passes, I let her legs fall to the ground. She tries to roll away from me but I am quick. I use my knee to pin her when she is facedown. I hear her trying to scream through the tape. The side of her face, though covered in dust and dirt, looks almost purple.

It doesn't matter. I grab her left arm by the wrist. She throws an elbow with her right but she can't come near me. I hook my other hand between her biceps and her forearm. She fights for a moment as I pull her arms back. Then they go limp and I tape them together at the wrist. Once it's done, I spring to my feet and take a step back, looking down at her. She doesn't move, other than her back rising and falling. Half of her hair has pulled free from the ponytail. Lauren Branch moans softly as I watch her. So I turn and burst out of the house.

I nearly fall off the decking. Stumbling, my feet kicking up gravel from the trail, I lurch toward the woods. My thigh strikes the rear panel of the Jetta and I spin, losing my balance, falling to a knee. One hand braces my fall, small stones cutting into the palm. I try to stand but my legs give out from under me.

I can't believe what I have done.

9

My father went back to his workshop after it was over. Drew turned his back to me and walked over to the hockey goal across the room. He dragged it back into place, the metal frame scraping along the cold concrete floor. Putting it down, he found the stick he wanted and fished a tennis ball out from under one of his goalie chest protectors. After a couple of touches, he shot it, hard. I could feel the slap of the stick striking the ground. The ball fired across the basement and struck the netting, disappearing in a tangle of red nylon.

He wouldn't look at me, not at first. He moved to the net, tapping his stick on the floor over and over again. The sound made every bruise on my body ache. But all I could do was stare at the athletic tape around his knuckles. The tiny dark speckles on the banded white strips.

At some point, he stopped. Drew turned and looked at me. He watched me as I lay crumpled on the cold floor. I remember his head tilting, just a little. Then he turned and watched the door to my father's room. Eventually, he walked over and reached out a hand, helping me up.

"It's okay, bro," he whispered with a glance back toward the workshop. "Sorry."

I took his hand, the same hand that had bruised my face and body as my father watched. Everything hurt. My head. My stomach. My arms and legs. Worse than all of that, though, was when I looked up at my brother. I saw the same thin-lipped smile that had been on my father's face as he stood over me.

When I got to my feet, I let go of his hand. Drew's eyes narrowed.

"What? You think I wanted to do that? Stop getting him mad. Do what I do. Figure him out. Give him what he wants. And make him think it's his idea. Stop frowning all the time, too. I can't protect you forever."

"I didn't mean to—"

His laugh cut me off. "It doesn't matter. Go upstairs before he comes back out."

On shaking legs, I moved to the stairs. I heard his stick striking the concrete—*crack, crack, crack*. Each time, I flinched, but he must not have seen that. And I didn't want him to, so I hurried up the steps.

It had gotten dark and the light was off in the kitchen. I stood at the top of the stairs, catching my breath. Carefully, I touched the side of my face. The skin felt flaming hot and a dull throb ran from my cheek up to my temple.

I don't know how long I stood there. I could still hear Drew downstairs, but the sound softened by the distance took on a different feel. Instead of vibrating through my head, I found it comforting, safe. As long as I heard it, it meant I knew where he was. That he wasn't coming upstairs. I also figured that it meant my father was still in his workshop. Still putting together that damn model.

At the same time, I felt that feeling again. Exposed, I guess, but that's not the word I would have used then. Instead, I built a story around it, like a wall rising inside me, protecting me. I was in a jungle, alone and injured. Something big and terrible was hunting me. If I made a sound, it would find me and devour me piece by piece while I screamed.

I moved through the kitchen, the balls of my bare feet coming down softly on the tile floor. When the floorboard creaked, I froze, listening until I heard the sound of my brother downstairs. Once I did, I took one careful step after another, creeping along the wall and up the carpeted steps to the second floor.

I must have meant to go to my room. I even remember thinking about building a tent behind my bed. I would get my pocketknife from where I hid it under the bottom drawer of my dresser. Maybe a flashlight. With my back against the wall, I could be ready for anything that came for me.

Instead, I passed by my bedroom. And Drew's. My steps grew even more silent and slow. I approached the door at the end of the hallway like it was the tomb of some long-dead pharaoh, expecting every move to set off a series of horrible and deadly traps.

When my hand touched the doorknob, I thought about turning back. My room was safer. Most likely, no one would look for me. I could be alone. If I went inside, and my father found me there, it would mean trouble. Probably worse than before. But my fingers wrapped around the brass and turned. Though my brain told me to stop, to go back, I opened the door and slipped quietly into my mother's bedroom.

Her shades were down. The darkness seemed impossible. Hot air blew against my feet from the vent near the door. The carpet under my toes felt unbelievably soft and warm, like a hug. I took a step and stopped, listening. Just over the sound of the forced air, I heard her breathing, a whisper of hypnotizing life. It drew me forward. I inched closer and closer to the bed.

Slowly, my eyes adjusted to the dark. I saw the gentle rise and fall of the fat white duvet. The shadowed peaks of my mother's hair spread across the light pillow like licking black flames. I wanted to touch it, to know it was real, but I didn't. But I did climb up onto the raised mattress, curling my legs up and facing my sleeping mother. I held my breath, afraid to wake her, until I just couldn't anymore. When I finally took in air, that floral scent was there, but something else, too. A sour smell tickled my nose, like a faint wisp of dead flowers left in the rain. I believe it was the first time I noticed it. Maybe not. Maybe it was always there. But I don't think so. Instead, that night, when it filled my nose, I felt so frightened. Somehow the smell seemed wrong, almost dangerous.

I swallowed my fear, refusing to move. Maybe I just didn't want to be alone. So I lay in bed beside her, listening to my mother's breathing, taking in the closeness like a drug. I let it take me away from everything else. I floated above it all, away from them. So much so that when she spoke, it frightened me.

"Liam?"

I held my breath again. I was so afraid that she would wake up and realize I shouldn't be there. She would kick me out.

"Is that you, baby?" she asked, her voice low and strange.

"Yeah," I whispered.

She paused. When she spoke, I knew I had heard her words before, but this time, it was different. They seemed to come from someone else's voice. Like some horrible beast eating my mother from the inside out.

"They're just doing what they need to do to survive," she slurred. "That doesn't make them bad."

10

I *kidnapped Lauren Branch.*

As I kneel in the gravel, my fingers wrap around the tattoo on my forearm. I squeeze, like I might be able to extract the past, like some viper's poison. At the same time, my teeth grind together. I push back the feelings, the pain and the disgust, and I lock onto the plan. The steps I've laid out. They are all that matter now. Once begun, the game can't be stopped.

I'm a monster. I remind myself of that simple fact. I have abducted a young woman this morning. She went to the gym, starting her day as she always did. And I threw her into the trunk of her own car. Now she's inside this abandoned cabin, her arms and legs taped together. Her mouth taped shut. On the floor, just feet away from that abomination. She's someone's daughter. And I did that.

With a hand on the rim of the Jetta's open trunk, I pull myself up from the ground, absently brushing small stones off my knee. My eye catches her gym bag. I grab it before turning away from the cabin. Slowly, I walk out to the edge of the water. The gravel at the bank crunches under my feet. As I look out over the rising sun reflecting off the silver surface of the pond, I don't realize I am scratching my arm again. When I look down, I see blood on my skin. Not my blood. Someone else's.

Frantic, I brush at it. Willing it to disappear. And it does. Just like that, and I realize it was all in my head. Everything is in my head. And I need to control it. So I stand there, looking out over the large pond as my fingers claw at the legs of my jeans to keep them away from the tattoo.

"Make sure the tape is secure," I say to myself. "Lock the door. Get into the Jetta, and take Limestone to McKennans Church to 48 to Kirkwood. Ninety-five northbound back to the city."

My forearm burns. But the muscles in my arms loosen and I let my hands dangle at my sides as the list continues. I need to focus on the plan. Only the plan. It keeps me centered. Moves me forward, instead of letting me look back at what I've done.

I need to ditch her car. But first, I have to go back into the cabin. I need to make sure that she's secure before I leave. So once I've gotten through the last few steps, I walk up the decking and back inside. I find the idea revolting. I have no desire to see her cowering in a corner. To watch as her eyes avert in fear, maybe submission. I do it anyway, pushing open the door and stepping back inside.

Lauren is in the corner where I left her. She is still bound. Still crumpled on the dirty floor. After a quick glance at the tarp, and the bulge underneath it, I see her eyes. She doesn't look away. Instead, she stares right back at me. Defiance, maybe. Or something different. I can't be sure.

Uneasy, I take a step closer to her. Her expression questions me. I hear her voice in my head. *Why would you do this to me? Why me?* I imagine going to her. Taking the tape off. Would she plead with me? Beg for her life? Would I like that?

Instead, I stay where I am. I watch her with a flat, hard expression on my face.

"I'm going to take your car back to the city," I say. "Then I am coming back here. Don't do anything *stupid*."

I watch her for a second. Then I glance back at the tarp. I don't mean to, but it calls to me. Or what is under it does. It's not time for that, though. So I place her bag carefully on the ground by the door. As I turn to leave her, I hear her phone. I spin back and snatch the bag up. Digging through it, I find it. When I look at the screen, I see a text message from some girl I don't know. I had half expected it to be my brother. He'd do something like that. Text her from his phone, right under his wife's nose.

I laugh and shake my head, but my knuckles turn white as I squeeze the phone. It's smarter to take it with me. It's better if they find me, not her. So I slip it into a pocket, thinking of my brother. And Patsy. For the first time, I want to hurt Lauren. I want to embarrass her. Make her feel weak and powerless. Like the entire world is staring at her and laughing. I want to dig into her skull and drive her as crazy as I feel.

"Don't do anything stupid," I repeat instead.

And leave her behind, alone and bound in duct tape.

11

What was that look on her face?

The thought vibrates inside my head. I've decided that she thinks I'm an idiot for returning her car to the city. She probably wonders why in the hell I'd do that. Why not just leave it at the cabin, hidden. But she's the stupid one. She doesn't know even a part of the truth.

I shake my head and grip the steering wheel even tighter. Rush-hour traffic filters into the city. Every time I have to hit the brake, I feel the skin of my face burning hotter and hotter.

I should have left the car at the cabin. I know that. But that's not what I'm going to do. As I turn onto Pennsylvania Avenue, inching behind a particularly annoying white pickup, way nicer and newer than mine, I glance over at the gym parking lot. I could turn in and leave it there, too. That would make sense, even to *Lauren*. But I keep driving, a tight smile pinching the corners of my eyes.

I crawl down Pennsylvania, getting more and more annoyed by the truck in front of me. When I get the chance, I veer into the left lane. Nearly hitting a black BMW, I swerve back after passing the truck. I hit my brakes and watch as he jerks to a stop. I see his arms go up. I see his mouth open comically wide. And I laugh, more to myself than out loud.

She's gotten under my skin. Without saying a word. I understand this, logically, but I can't stop it. Instead, I picture her back in the cabin. She must be scared out of her mind. She must be wondering what I'm going to do to her. I can't imagine what that must be like. Maybe she is scratching and clawing, bending her body, painfully, trying to find a way to escape. That thought sets me even more afire. I lean forward, barely noticing the guy in the truck behind me. Even though he's about an inch off my bumper.

What if she escapes?

That can't happen. I taped her perfectly. Just like I researched. She won't be able to get free. Plus, I secured the padlock. And the windows are boarded. There's just no way.

But what if?

My head shakes.

Nononono

I don't have time for this. I don't have the luxury. I need to stick to the moves I've laid out. Thought out. It's all too dangerous now to get distracted.

Blinking, I look around. I'm about four blocks from where I left my truck. So I slam my foot down on the brake. The car stops. I see the guy's eyes widen. I hear his brakes locking. His tires squealing, smoking. His bumper hits the Jetta, but not hard.

Leaving the key in the ignition, the engine running, I put the car in park. Then I open the door and step out into the street. Horns blare. More tires skid and cry out. I look back at the line of cars behind me. And I see the guy lurching out of his truck. He is bearded and thick with a cheap white button-down and jeans. Rage burns in his eyes.

"What the fuck is wrong with you, asshole!"

He walks quickly toward me. Coming up on me. I just stare at him for a second. His rage is infectious. It triggers my already frayed nerves. Suddenly, like a light blinking out, the plan is gone. All I see is this guy rushing me. All I can think about is what I'm going to do to him.

He doesn't see it. He keeps coming, thinking that this is going to go his way. For my part, I just stand there, turning my body to the side, just a little bit. Just enough. I know what he's going to do. He'll come in hot. Get right in my face. And stop. Right there. If he was calling the shots, he would start off talking all big. Maybe give me a push. Size me up. Possibly make a move if I showed a hint of submission. But he's not calling the shots. He never was.

When he's about three steps away, still moving at a pretty good clip, I take a step forward and to the side with my lead foot. At the same time, my right hand shoots out, past his head. I see his eyes widen when he realizes that there will be no strutting. No talking. I haven't said a word, in fact.

I hook him by the back of the neck and pull him toward me. I turn all the way to my side, pushing him past me, into the corner of the Jetta. He hits it, hard, right above his knee. He folds over the hood awkwardly. I turn, reaching for his head, wanting to slam it into the car, but hit his back instead. He sort of rolls and tries to bounce up. So I grab him by the throat with my left hand. I squeeze and lean down, putting my body right up to his, pinning him down.

He makes a gurgling sound. I imagine it is groveling. Some pitiful attempt to pay the check his misplaced bravado had written a second before. But I don't want to hear another word. All I want to do is squeeze. To hurt him. To show him who's *stupid*.

Stupid.

The voice I hear in my head is not my own. It's not this bearded asshole's, though. It's his. And when I hear it, my muscles freeze. My eyes open all the way. My breathing sets my chest thrusting in and out. I stare at this man, my fingers on his throat. I don't know him. I never will. And he has nothing to do with any of this.

My grip loosens. I let go of him and straighten. With a quick look around at what I've done, I turn and walk away, leaving Lauren Branch's Jetta parked in the middle of rush-hour traffic.

12

I think I was twelve. Maybe younger. I don't know. But I remember the sound perfectly. A wet crack. And then a dead thump. There was no scream. Not even a moan. Just crack . . . thump.

It happened one day after school. As my bus turned onto our street, I had my forehead up against the window. That's how I saw them. My mother and father standing at the end of the driveway. My eyes widened and a hand came up and slapped the glass. I pressed my face against the smooth, cold surface, trying to get a better look. I was sure it was some kind of mirage that I could blink away. When I couldn't, a strange mix of panic and excitement made me shake.

I was just a kid. To be honest, even as the dread of my father grew deeper and deeper, I still lived in my own world. I had friends. In fact, I had been spending more and more time with them, with less and less supervision from my mother. I didn't truly understand why or what was wrong. But I guess I noticed. That was probably why I reacted the way I did. I hadn't seen my mom leave the house in weeks.

Like any twelve-year-old, though, I barely knew my parents. I certainly didn't understand their relationship. They spoke, sometimes.

We had dinner at the table as a family, though it happened less frequently every week. The reality was that I sensed something awful between them. Something that made me think of my dad's face that day when he hugged my mom. And that sour smell that clung to her now. At the same time, it was all very adult. Very subtle. And I was very young. Very naïve.

As the bus slowed at my stop, I noticed someone else was standing with them. It was the woman who lived across the street. She had kids older than Drew and me. When I saw her, I stood up before the bus came to a complete stop. The driver sort of yelled at me but I ran past him and out the door.

For some reason, instead of heading into the house, I went to them. As I neared, I could see the woman's hands moving as she talked to my mom and dad. Her motion, her liveliness, made my nerves even worse. It was like she was the fuse on some giant, cartoonish bomb, her hands the sparks and her words the droning hiss.

I have no idea what she said. Instead, I stared at my mother. It wasn't windy, but I swear her body swayed. The way she moved reminded me of the fishing hole down in the woods. There were these really long blades of grass, or reeds. I don't know for sure, but even when the water was calm, they moved gently back and forth. Over and over again. I used to stare at them, too, but in a very different way. Those plants always made me feel calm. My mother's unsteadiness had the exact opposite effect.

"That's so . . . really nice," my mother blurted out, interrupting the neighbor.

I started. As much at the suddenness of her announcement as at the sound of her voice. It was thick. Sort of like she was talking through water, which made me think of that pond again. Her face seemed to change. Like I suddenly had to look at her through that same greenish murk.

Something even more frightening happened then. I saw my father smile, a full smile. It might have been the first time. I know I'd never seen anything like it. Because he did it while looking at my mother. It looked so foreign and sad, I guess. He even put a hand on her shoulder.

"We should probably get you back inside," he said gently.

I looked at the neighbor then, expecting her to feel as shocked as I did. Instead, the woman's head tilted a little and her eyes softened. When my mother turned and headed back into the house, muttering happily to herself, the woman touched my father's arm.

"Remember what I said the other day." She looked at my dad with such earnestness. "Anything you need. From any of us. You can't do this all alone. Promise you'll ask us for help. Okay?"

I swear a tear came to my father's eye as he nodded and thanked her.

"Come on, Liam," he said.

He put a hand on me that day, too. A fatherly touch on my shoulder. A gentle guidance back toward the house. I walked ahead of him, feeling so off-balance. When the door shut behind us, I turned to him.

"Is Mom okay?" I asked.

"She's fine," he muttered before grabbing his keys.

My father left without telling anyone where he was going. I hovered, somehow sensing something changed that day. That the neighbor's words had somehow become that first domino. That when they fell on my father's ears, the woman's compassion set off some awful chain reaction. Honestly, even after he returned home and I heard the bottles clanking in the heavy paper bag in his hands, it would take me years to fully understand what he was doing.

THE SOUND HAPPENED a few hours after my father came home from the liquor store. I was probably watching television when it happened, but maybe not. I can't recall anything for sure until after the sound. I heard it and then I was at the doorway to our kitchen. At first, I didn't notice her. For some reason, I didn't look down. I saw the distressed white chairs around our small round table. I saw light reflecting off of Mom's brand-new side-by-side refrigerator. I even saw the wineglass by the sink, empty but for a small ring of blood-red at the bottom. Three empty bottles standing sentry behind it.

She didn't make a sound. Nor did she move. My eyes lowered naturally. And I saw her sprawled on the tile floor. In her fall, her robe had bunched around her hips. And I don't think she wore anything under it. I saw her, down there, and my head jerked away from the sight.

"Mom!"

I stood frozen in place, praying silently that she would answer me. That she would get up and fix how she looked. But there was nothing. So I had to look again. I had to see if she was okay. My head turned slowly and I tried to see her but at the same time look away from where her legs lay prostrated and exposed on the kitchen floor. I focused instead on her beautiful dark hair. It fanned around her head, completely covering her face, the black strands shining as brightly as the pristine porcelain.

I took a step closer, lowering to a crouch. That's when I noticed the blood. It was darker than I would have thought, maybe because it clung to her hair with a gory desperation, matting it, devouring its sheen. When I saw it, the air caught in my throat. My eyes widened and my nose burned. This strange feeling coursed through my entire body, at once setting my nerves afire and freezing my muscles in place. My mouth hung open.

I forced a single word out. "Mom?"

She didn't move. I couldn't even tell if she was breathing. Panic replaced my paralysis. I sprang back to my feet, fleeing the kitchen and screaming.

"Dad! Dad!"

I didn't even know if he was home. But I didn't hesitate, either. I raced around to the stairs leading down to the basement. I took them three or four at a time and crashed down onto the red cement floor so hard that I felt it in my jaw. I didn't stop, though. I ran across the main room, to my father's workshop.

"Dad!"

I rounded the doorway and found him on his stool, his work lamp pulled low over the table, and a pair of tweezers held between two thick fingers. I stopped dead in place. I was out of breath, stunned by how calmly he sat there while Mom lay bleeding and maybe dead in the kitchen.

13

The windows on Clayton Street are dark now. Lifeless. The utopic lives I dreamed behind them have moved on. Gone about their day. Driven to work. Walked to the gym or the small breakfast place at the end of the block. As I approach my truck, I feel the emptiness. It triggers the loneliness I have carried for so many years. Most of my life.

But it's good. Not the emotions. Those I bury down with the rest. The silence, the dark windows, those are good. There are no eyes watching me slip back behind the wheel and start up the engine. No one cares as I roll down Clayton and onto Delaware. At the next two-way street, I head south. From a block away, I can see the snarl of traffic. I can hear horns and even voices.

When I'm thirty or so yards from the intersection with Pennsylvania Avenue, I glance in my rearview. No one is there, so I make a lazy three-point turn and park. Adjusting the mirror, I can see Lauren's Jetta a block away. As well as all the other cars inching past it. I lean back and watch the show for a second, until someone walking down the sidewalk catches my eye. It is a mother with a young boy, maybe six. He is skipping and she is holding his hand and checking her phone.

As they pass my car, my head turns. I stop looking at what I have done, and instead feel myself slipping backwards in time. What would that little kid do in my shoes? If he found his mom on the floor. If he thought she was dying. He would panic. He would cry like a goddamn baby. That's what he would do.

Without realizing it, I'm scratching again. And leaning forward in the seat. I want to chase these strangers down. Scream at them, like they've stolen something precious from me. But they haven't. They have nothing to do with me. I know this. But the feelings are so real. The memories so raw.

They turn the corner, slipping from my sight, and I can breathe again. This doesn't usually happen. I know it is because of Lauren. What I have done to her. What I am going to do. That's what's pushing me over the edge.

So I dig my phone out of the front pocket of my jeans and dial his number. His real number, not the other one. When he answers, I can hear the tightness in his voice right away.

"Where are you?" my brother asks.

"In the city," I say.

I glance back at the mirror. The first police cruiser has arrived. I see the officer stepping out of the car.

"We were supposed to meet up for breakfast today," he says carefully. "Why aren't you here?"

"Sorry. Things are crazy."

More police arrive. One stands beside the Jetta, directing the two sides of traffic around the still-running car. The first officer stands off to the side now. He speaks with a thick man in a white shirt, the one with the beard. I can't take my eyes off him.

"I'm busy, Liam. You know that. I can't afford anything going *wrong* right now."

"It's cool," I say. "Everything's cool. I promise."

"It better be," he says. "I suggest you head home right now."

I keep staring at the car, the police, the guy with the beard.

"I will," I say, and hang up.

14

I stared at my father for a second as he sat on his high stool. My life crashed down around me. Fear gripped me by the chest, crushing the air out of my lungs. While he just sat there with his stupid tweezers, staring at me over those tiny glasses.

"It's Mom!" I finally said.

My father, his eyes devoid of any emotion, stared back at me. Slowly, he put the tweezers down beside whatever model he was working on. Maybe that same battleship. Maybe something else. I can't remember. But I can still see the way he turned on the seat and took his glasses off. He cleaned them carefully with the same black cloth he always used.

"She fell. She needs help."

He said nothing. He just kept making a lazy circle around the lens, over and over again. Sparks crackled inside my skull. I wanted to rush him, shake him until he woke up. But I also wanted to turn and run away, back to Mom, before it was too late. Instead, my feet pattered on the cold cement, as if dancing to my frantic uncertainty.

"She's bleeding. She's not moving. I don't think she's breathing."

He stopped cleaning his glasses but he didn't get up.

"I told you that she's fine," he said.

Then my dad went back to working on his model. I stood there for a second, but all he did was move the lamp down even closer and lean over his work. At first, I thought he didn't believe me. Then, as he continued to work on his model, I started to not believe myself. Maybe she was fine. Maybe I'd made the whole thing up. Maybe he was right about both of us, my mother and me.

I BARRELED BACK into the kitchen, my heart threatening to burst through my ribs. I might have been crying, even. I saw my mother first. She was there, on the floor. Real. So was the blood. I hadn't made it up. She wasn't fine. But then I saw Drew. He was kneeling next to her, his fingers gently touching her head. While I was gone, the blood had escaped the netting of her hair and was pooling on the white tile. It looked so red, like it might suddenly catch fire. I stared at it while Drew watched me.

"Get me the phone," he said.

It took me a second, but I broke out of the daze. I lurched over and grabbed Mom's cordless off the wall mount. I rushed back, my arm outstretched. Drew shook his head.

"No, call 9-1-1. Tell them we need an ambulance."

"You should," I blurted out.

I saw his eyes dart toward the basement door before he said, "Do it, Liam. Do you want her to die?"

Shaking, I dialed the number. When someone answered, the words ran out of my mouth like a flash flood.

"My mom's hurt. She fell and she's bleeding." I looked to Drew. He turned and walked out of the kitchen. "My dad won't come. We need help. Please."

The woman on the line asked me questions. I tried to answer them, but I kept interrupting.

"Are you sending an ambulance?"

"Yes, son. Is there an adult there that I could speak to?"

"No, my dad—"

I never heard him coming. I didn't see him until the phone tore from my hand. I flinched, grabbing for it, and saw my father's eyes. They bore into me, cutting me from the inside outward. One of his large, dry hands struck me on the chest. I pinwheeled away from him, slamming into a chair. It fell to the floor and I followed, landing on my hip.

I lay there, afraid to move. Afraid to breathe, as my father spoke calmly to the woman. He took control. Drew reappeared and my father motioned for him to go to the front door. Then he stood over Mom. He didn't look at her. Instead, he kept staring directly at me. He spoke clearly but quietly.

"I'm going to hang up," he said. "I need to be sure she's okay."

I could hear the woman still speaking as my father turned and walked over to the wall mount, replacing the receiver. Then he stepped up to me, standing over me but not coming any closer. I knew I should keep looking at him, keep eye contact, but I couldn't. So I looked away, right at Mom, at her exposed legs, and . . . everything else. I flinched again and jerked my head. My father laughed, a sound at once shockingly wrong and horribly cutting.

He reached down and grabbed my shirt just below the collar. He lifted me up to my feet. I stumbled, unable to totally regain my balance. This upset him. He sneered and pushed me into the table. I hit the edge hard but was able to put my hands down and keep from falling.

"Get those bottles out of here. Take them to your mother's room. Put them under the bed," he said, his tone flat but his eyes burning with anger, or maybe hatred.

I didn't move. I remember being so totally confused. I couldn't figure out what he'd said. Or why he'd said it. In that moment, I didn't know who he was. What he was supposed to be. It was like I couldn't be sure of anything. Maybe it was all my fault. Maybe this was the way it was supposed to be. Maybe I was being a weak little baby. Being stupid.

Whatever the truth was, my pause simply angered him more. He grabbed me by the shoulder and yanked me to the counter. He pointed at the wine bottles but wouldn't touch them.

"Do it!"

I did. When I walked into her room, the smell was an assault. I recoiled, shaking as I put the bottles under the bed one by one. Then I rushed out of the room. I needed to know if Mom was okay. If she was alive. So I inched out into the hallway, reaching the stairs just as two men in black uniforms carried my mother out of the kitchen. She was strapped down to a bright yellow backboard. A clear mask clung to the bottom part of her face. Thankfully, someone had covered her legs up with a thin white blanket.

I needed to know. I needed to see her. The men stepped through the front door. I took a step toward the landing before my father appeared at the bottom of the stairs. He glanced up at me and then looked away like I no longer existed.

"Drew, let's go," he said.

Drew hurried out of the kitchen. My father put his hand on my brother's shoulder and they rushed out of the house.

I WAS ALONE for hours. The sun set and the streetlights turned on. I paced the living room, going to the window every time I heard a car passing by outside, hoping it was them. After a dozen or so, I stopped, but I couldn't ignore the passing headlights. They tortured me.

At one point, I ended up moving toward the kitchen. I wasn't thinking at all. I just walked until my foot landed on the white porcelain tile. And I saw the dark red stain on the floor, the edges turning a horrid, thick black.

I froze, my stomach turning. I wanted to run, get the hell out of there, but I didn't. I couldn't. Instead, I stared at my mother's blood and everything else simply vanished. The gore drew me closer, deeper, until I could hardly breathe. I wanted to disappear into it, melt into my mother's blood like some vampire in reverse.

At that instant, I heard a car passing by outside. I turned my head. And when I looked back, it was just a bloodstain on the floor, one that scared me and made me feel sick. Swallowing down the tightness in my throat, I went to the sink and pulled free a handful of paper towels. Kneeling down, I wiped at the stain. It felt surprisingly solid under the towels, and when I moved them away, I realized I'd only been able to mop up the very center. The rest remained dark and thick, dried onto the tiles.

I returned to the sink, this time more frantic than the last. I took a huge wad of paper towels and wet them. Sliding on my knees, I bent over and scrubbed at the floor. Pink water pooled around my effort, some seeping through the fabric of my jeans.

"Shit," I said, trying harder.

The more I worked, the worse it seemed to get. So I got up again and grabbed one of my mom's white dish towels. I sopped up the tinted water and continued to scrub at the floor. I was working so hard that I failed to notice my father's car pull into the garage. And I never heard him walk into the house until I looked up and found him standing in the kitchen with me, looking at me through his small round glasses.

I froze again. He said nothing. He just looked me up and down, lingering on the damp knee of my pants, and then shook his head slowly.

I wanted to scream out to him, beg him to tell me how my mother was. It had been so long. I needed to know if she was okay. If she was home. But the words wouldn't come out. Not a letter of them. Instead, I just stared back as all the muscles in my face seemed to go slack.

My father said nothing. He turned and walked out of the kitchen. I heard him head down the stairs to the basement, his basement. God, I wanted to follow him, but I couldn't. He didn't have to yell at me, or even tell me to leave him alone. The space between us simply pushed back at me, buffeting me like two magnets in reverse.

I looked down at the floor. Surprisingly, the stain was almost gone. I took one last swipe with the towel and stood up. I was going to put it in the sink, I think, but I heard footsteps passing through the living room. So I broke into a sprint, rounding the corner in time to see Drew starting up the stairs.

"Hey!" I said.

Drew took two more steps up without even a look over his shoulder. I rushed closer.

"Drew! Where's Mom?"

He stopped. Slowly, he turned. His dark eyes cut straight through mine and I took a step back.

"She's dead, Liam."

AFTER MY BROTHER told me that, I ran. I never looked back. I bolted from the house, through the yard, and didn't stop until I made it to the rock ledge in the woods. I skidded to a stop, my entire body quaking. My foot touched a large stick amid the leaves. I grabbed it and lashed out, slamming it into anything I could, tree, rock, whatever. And I screamed with each strike.

"It's his fault!" Crack. "He wouldn't help her!" Crack. "He did this!" Crack. "I hate him!"

The stick splintered in my hands. I dropped it, and the tears started. I cried as I tried to find another club. I grabbed one fallen branch but it was wet and full of fungus. It snapped in half as I lifted it off the ground. I threw it away, over the rock ledge, letting out a primal yell as I did.

Shaking, crying, coughing out air like I was drowning, I dropped down to my knees. The dampness wicked through my pants. It felt like ice against my skin. But I didn't care. I just cried and hacked.

"I didn't do anything wrong," I stammered.

And I punched myself in the chest, so hard that the coughing got way worse. I sobbed, although I would never tell anyone that. But it happened, and it kept happening until the last bit of energy in my body seeped through my wet legs, down into the cold, dead earth.

Still kneeling, I quieted down. But I didn't move. The soft sound of the woods at night replaced my agony. It calmed my breathing. Stopped my tears. Not in a comforting way, though. Instead, the emptiness pressed in on me, reminding me with each second that she was gone. That I'd lost her. And that she had left me behind. Left me with them.

15

I could have run away. I could now. I imagine someone hearing my story and wondering why I don't. What could possibly hold me here? It's never as easy as that. Nothing is. I've considered it. I've even tried. But I can never get far.

The last time, I almost made it. It happened at the ocean, years before I returned to that same spot. I went to a party right after my brother married Patsy. It should have been a great time. To everyone else at the beach that day, I'm sure it was. When I walked up the boardwalk over the dune, I could hear their voices and laughter rising even before the party came into view. The westward wind carried the smell of Old Bay seasoning and burning wood. And faintly, under it all, I heard the roar of the surf. Even then, I think it was calling to me, as it would when I eventually returned to that place.

When I reached the top of the hill, I saw the party spreading across the sand. The sun had set and the fire of a dozen tiki torches added to the warm glow of the evening. They surrounded a cook fire. Atop a handmade rack, steam rose from four big cooking pots. Even if I couldn't smell it, I'd have known they were filled with seafood—blue crabs and clams and mussels and fresh shrimp.

I stopped before making my way down to the beach, just standing there and watching. This was an annual party, thrown by one of Drew's friends from high school. Everyone who played lacrosse for our high school was welcome, from current freshmen all the way back to my brother's year. I recognized a bunch of the faces but I still hesitated.

To be honest, I almost turned back. If I had, it wouldn't have made a difference. What happened that night could not be avoided. If not at the party, then someplace else, at another time. There are moments in life like that. They are as inevitable as the end, no matter what your gut tells you.

So, eventually, I moved. I merged with the guys and girls. People greeted me. Someone threw me a Bud Light. I settled in, my back to the ocean, and watched everyone drinking and dancing and talking. For a moment, I think I had fun. Or at least, I felt at ease. Almost at home.

"Liam!" someone called out to my right. I turned and saw a kid from my year. His name was Andy, but it took me a second to remember that. We got talking and, as it always did, the conversation turned to my brother.

"Hey, is Drew coming?" he asked.

"I don't know," I said.

I hadn't seen him for a few weeks. His first campaign had already started; I had been laying low. I had just broken up with a girl because she moved away to Lancaster, Pennsylvania. So I was painting houses during the day and drinking at a dive bar just over the state line every night.

"Too much of a big shot, huh?"

I stared at Andy for a second without blinking. "I didn't say that."

"Oh, I was just kidding. It's kind of cool, him running for something. Good to see a lax boy making it big, right?"

"Sure," I said.

And just like that, he appeared at the top of the dune. Andy saw him, too. He sort of laughed.

"He's here."

"Yeah," I said.

"I haven't seen him in years. Who's the smoker?"

This time, I didn't even bother to look at him. "That's his wife."

Andy choked on the beer he'd just drunk. "Oh, shit. My bad. Don't tell him I said that, okay?"

"I won't."

My brother walked toward the party, Patsy on his arm. She was dressed like she had just come out of some advertisement for a swanky cruise. And he had on his most preppy boat shoes and a light-colored collared shirt with three buttons undone.

As I watched them, Patsy's head turned. Then she touched his arm. I saw her smile, her chin tilting up into the air. She moved with such freedom. Like a bird. I stood there, staring, and I pictured her doing just that. Lifting off the warm sand and disappearing into the darkening sky. Without realizing it, I started to scratch at my forearm.

Then Drew smiled at her. He said something but he was too far away for me to hear it. As he spoke, his eyebrows did this very charming thing, dipping just enough. She kissed him then. Leaning in quickly as her hand cupped his jaw. It was fast, but everyone there seemed to see it. Someone whooped to my right.

They broke apart then. Patsy moved away from my brother. For a second, I imagined she would make a run for it. Bolt up the coast. Instead, though, she melded into this group of strangers like they'd come to see her. Like she was the party.

EARLY THAT NEXT morning, hours before the sun rose, I sat in my truck outside their house. I'd left the party just after they arrived. Instead of going home, though, I went there. And waited, watching as they eventually pulled up and walked into the house. The warm glow from the windows as the lights went on called to me. The memory of her body moving like a beautiful dance across the sand haunted me. I gripped the steering wheel, fighting my urges.

It had started to rain an hour before. I remained in my truck, staring out through the droplets of water on the windshield. The world outside became a kaleidoscope. Instead of a rainbow of bright colors, though, it took on shades of gray and darkness. Except for the light behind their window. I felt myself slipping into that world, the one I saw but knew did not exist.

It was like a dream. Suddenly, my door was open. I was out in the rain, moving through the darkness. I crept among the shrubs and small pines until I saw the lights from my brother's back porch. I moved closer, hopping a split rail fence and continuing along a line of expensive-looking bushes in their yard.

After only a minute, I saw Patsy. She walked into the kitchen, right up to the window. She stood with her hands on the sill, and I swear she stared back at me. Without my realizing it, my knuckles dug into my eyes. Droplets of rain ran down my cheeks, under my shirt. My head spun and throbbed. But I opened my eyes again.

Patsy remained standing there, though the rain coating the window faded her details, giving her an otherworldly aura. I moved closer, crossing an open stretch of lawn. I didn't care if she saw me. Maybe I wanted her to. I stopped just off the porch once I could see her eyes again. I fed on that strength, the way she held her chin high, the straightness of her neck.

Over the patter of the rain, I heard him. And so did Patsy. His voice was cold but loud, calling to her. Ordering her. I lurched forward, like I might stop it all from being real. And I noticed her flinch. It was subtle but unguarded.

I moved to the left and saw him. He stood in the doorway to their kitchen. Bangs of hair hung down his face, framing those piercing eyes. The set of his jaw, the line of his mouth; it was all I needed to see. Though the weather and the walls of their home muffled his voice, I might as well have been able to hear every word.

His voice lowered and his expression became more intense. He spoke to her calmly, softly. Every word seemed to chip away at the light behind her eyes. For the first time, I thought I saw her sadness. Her despair. But I also saw a woman trapped. The muscles of her forearm pulsed as she gripped the sill. She did not turn to look at him as he spoke. My brother paused and I saw that thin smile of his, the one I'd known for far too long.

What did I expect to see? My brother lunging for her. Smashing a fist into her face. Kicking her while she lay defenseless on the kitchen floor. Maybe, in a way, I hoped for that. Maybe that would finally be enough for me to act. Seeing that might break the crushing hold he maintained over me. I could storm into the house, grab him by the throat. What would it feel like to press into his flesh, see his eyes bulge as I closed his windpipe? I could look into those eyes and see his pain. I could watch him die.

Instead, I crouched in soaked grass wiping water from my eyes as Patsy stood like a statue in the window, not even blinking. Eventually, his words stopped. He walked away. So did she. The lights went off and I was left in the darkness, watching nothing.

ALL THE OTHER times I ran away, he found me. He'd come to me and his words would slip into my ears, violating my memories. Eventually, in a cold and calculated voice, he would threaten me. Not with violence. No, he would hold our past up to the light. He would remind me of what we had done. His words would flay me, leaving me raw and rough and, as always, under his control. With his arm around my shoulder, I would follow him home again.

That night it was different. I was going to run. To get the hell out of my life. Out of Patsy's and Drew's. I was going to get into my car and drive forever. Never stopping. Never turning around. He wouldn't know where I went. He'd never find me. No matter how many police officers he knew.

I got into my truck and I started the engine. But I never moved. My resolve crumbled as quickly as it had formed. I stared up at that dark window. I imagined what was happening behind those cold brick walls. And something changed.

For the first time, it wasn't Drew's slithering words that drew me back. Instead, it was her. I closed my eyes and I saw her face as it looked through the rain-streaked glass. Somehow, though it should have been too distorted, I saw the bright lights inside her dimming, darkening under his weight. I would try to blink the sight away. I would try to tell myself that she was okay. That she was fine. But even inside my head, my voice would change. It would deepen. Go as flat as death. And I'd hear his words inside. My father's voice haunting me.

She's fine. She's fine. She's fine.

Then her face changed, too. Like some kind of nightmare, Patsy's hair darkened. Her complexion yellowed. And suddenly it was my mother I stared at through that glass. Who I stared at in the darkness. All alone.

I knew that I wouldn't leave. I was still weak. Still hiding behind the weight of my pain. But I knew I would never truly be free. The past is like flypaper. The more you struggle, the more tangled you become. Until you finally just stop trying.

16

I can't stop watching the scene in my rearview mirror. I'm thirty yards away from the police. I could walk out of my truck, walk right up to them, and end all of this. That, too, might seem reasonable. The police are always the answer to those who have never needed them. The rest of us know. We understand. Between me and anyone else, my word loses. And that's a horrid understatement in this case.

As I stare, other thoughts slip into my mind. I picture Lauren back at the cabin. I see her as if I am in two places at once. Time seems to speed up. She wastes away. Parched. Suffocated by the tape across her mouth. Her flesh dries and peels away, leaving nothing but bones. More bones.

Jesus!

I grind knuckles into my eyes, trying to push it all away. When I open them again, look back into the mirror, I see it. The dark blue Crown Victoria with a yellow strip and shield. Although I'm sitting in the city, that cruiser belongs to the Delaware State Police. Less than half an hour and it's already here. Faster than I thought. My brother has a lot of friends in the state police. He worked in the Department of Public Safety for years before getting elected to County Council. There is only one reason they would be responding to a call in the city limits.

Seeing it, I grab the wheel, gripping it so tightly that a bone in the back of my hand crackles. Sitting there in my truck, I'd convinced myself that everything was progressing as I meant it to. But it was a lie. It is always a lie.

As if in answer to my thoughts, a Mustang Shelby 350, blue with a black stripe, appears in the intersection not far behind the police. The sight of it vibrates through my body. To see him so close, so quickly. It is electric. It is contrary. My first impulse is to get the hell out of there, to run away. Never look back. But he is like a star, his gravity tugging at the very center of me, drawing me ever toward him.

My hand is shaking. He's right at the corner. So close. Everyone else, everything else, it all just disappears. It is just Drew and me, careening together at terminal velocity.

"Fuck!" I say, but the word is so soft that I can't even hear it.

The engine roars. I swerve back onto the street and leave him behind. For now.

I'M STILL SHAKING when I roll to a stop outside of the second cabin nestled among the trees lining the old swim club. I try to list the steps of the plan, but they won't appear in my head, not fully. Words dance just on the edges, hard words that hint at unwinnable choices.

I know one thing. Lauren Branch is bound and helpless inside the cabin just outside my window. It is the only truth now. I lift my hand up, hold it before my eyes. I will it to stop shaking. It takes a second but it eventually stills. Once it does, I lean over and pop open the glove box. When I reach it, I immediately feel the cool grip of the Ruger 9 mm semiautomatic pistol sitting above my registration and insurance card. My fingers wrap around it, finding the trigger guard.

Things are moving fast. I need to stay one step ahead of my brother or everything's lost. So I get out of the car, gun in hand, and walk slowly up the decking, to the locked door, the only thing between me and the woman I have abducted.

17

I was twelve. And my mother was dead. That's what he'd told me the night before. I awoke that next morning with Drew's words ringing in my head. Nothing else seemed grounded. I had no idea when I'd left the woods, or how I'd made it back to my bedroom. When I opened my eyes again, the sunlight set my head to throbbing. I felt spent, like I'd run a marathon in my sleep. But a deep and angry restlessness tingled above that, forcing my eyes to stay open.

Quietly, I got out of bed and slipped from my room. The house was eerily still. Both Drew's room and my parents' were empty. So I went downstairs, and found no one in the living room or the kitchen. I sat at the table, my head in my hands, but heard no movement anywhere in the house. I even went down into the basement and checked his workshop.

He wasn't there, so I walked into the cool, dry room, listening to the sound of a dehumidifier rumbling in the corner. My eyes fixated on the model atop the table. It was a navy ship, but I don't know the exact kind. The detail was amazing. Perfect miniature guns bristled across shining decking. The windows of the tiny bridge appeared to be real glass. The red stripe painted at the waterline looked perfectly worn, like the sailors had just returned from traveling across the world.

I stared at that horrid ship, through the plastic and glass and paint and glue, deep into what it truly meant. Time did not slow. Nor did I linger over that thing, troubled by my urges. Instead, the thin plastic of the crow's nest snapped as I grabbed the model and yanked it off the table. Holding it in two hands over my head, I turned and reared back. A primal sound rumbled in my throat and I let it fly through the open door of the workshop, out into the main room of the basement. It clattered across the cement floor, parts flying away like shrapnel.

"It's your fault!" I screamed, maybe for the hundredth time since Drew had told me.

Storming out, I ran at the model and kicked it, sending it jetting through the air and against the far wall. The remaining hull snapped in two. When I drove to give one last kick, I hesitated, losing my balance and falling to the floor.

"Mom," I whispered helplessly.

Pain radiated up my back and into my shoulder, so bad that it hurt to breathe. I slapped a hand onto the floor in frustration as tears filled my eyes. Honestly, though, I didn't cry from the pain. I just sat on the floor and cried for everything else.

YEARS LATER, I would rent the movie *Ferris Bueller's Day Off*. It was funny and I liked it, but when that scene came on of Cameron Frye beating the crap out of his father's 1961 Ferrari 250 GT, I fell off the couch onto my knees. I crawled closer to the television, transfixed, feeling like somehow whoever it was who came up with the idea for the scene had somehow stolen my life away.

I could barely breathe when he kept kicking the bumper over and over again. And the car teetered on the jack. I knew it would topple, that the car would careen through the glass and fall stories to the forest floor. When it did, when it happened, it felt like an awful and wonderful release. I felt at once more normal and more crippled by my own memories.

Later, though, when Ferris and Cameron talked about what happened, and Cameron's neck stiffened as he decided he would stand up to his father, I turned off the movie. And I never watched it again. Because that's not how it goes. Ever.

I was still on the floor in the basement when they came home. I heard the rush of air through the house when the front door opened. Without even thinking about what my father would do, or what I had done, I sprang to my feet. I ran up the stairs, the pain suddenly gone. I nearly slipped on the kitchen floor as well.

For a split second before I turned into the doorway to the foyer, I thought about my father. I thought about what I had just done. It wasn't that I was going to have some penultimate moment of confrontation. There was no way I would stand up to him, toe-to-toe, and rewrite the future. Neither of us had that in us. Instead, what I realized, what I felt, was that I didn't care anymore. My mother was dead. I was alone now. Part of me didn't want to be alive, either.

I had no idea of the concept then, but I do now. It was like the guy who, surrounded by police, pulls his gun and steps away from cover. He walks up to the officers, begging them to shoot. Suicide by police. I think I was committing my own version.

I didn't care, not at all. I remember it so clearly. I grabbed the doorjamb as I rounded the corner. I saw my dad first, his dark eyes cutting into mine, and all I felt was anger as he walked toward me, and eventually past me toward the basement.

I saw my brother next. For a split second, I felt an almost unbearable dread at the thought of living without my mother. Then, like some kind of dream, she appeared behind him. Her back was hunched and a dark stain marred the white bandage around her head. Yet she stood in the foyer looking back at me, her eyes sharper than I'd seen them in years.

"Mom," I stammered.

My legs felt numb. My vision fluttered. I looked to Drew, but he acted like nothing had happened. Like he'd done nothing. Then, shaking, I ran to her.

"Easy," she said, her voice strong and clear.

I stopped before touching her. For a time, no one else existed. Drew vanished. And my mom and I were alone in the foyer.

She moved first. Her arms opened and she hugged me. I buried my head into her chest, feeling every one of her ribs. She ran a hand through my unruly hair.

"I'm sorry," she whispered.

"It's—"

The rest of my words drowned in my father's scream.

"*Liam!*"

The sound of it made both my mother and me quake.

18

_____

I stand at the door of the cabin, my left index finger tracing the curve of the shining silver shackle to where it snakes through the rusting loop above the cabin door handle. I still hold the gun in my right hand. It dangles at my side, the weight a physical reminder of who I am and what I've done.

Lauren Branch exists on the other side of the door. I tuck the pistol into the waistband of my pants at the small of my back. Then I reach into my front pocket and pull out a set of keys. I stare at them for a second. If I close my eyes, I might still see shining silver, the thick brass disc engraved with a Ford Motor Company logo. Now the luster is gone, long covered with a layer of damp, clinging rust. The hair on my neck stands on end.

Staring at these keys, I imagine the part they will play in this. I've staked so much on what they are. On what they represent. Our lives hang in the balance and a simple lie will tip the scale.

Still mesmerized, I pull a plastic evidence bag out of my back pocket. I ordered it from some true crime fan site. I drop the keys in and run my fingers along the seal. With a final look, I slip the bag into my pocket before fishing out the second set, the one with a key for the padlock. I hesitate before unfastening it, partly because I am afraid of what I will see. Not that I think she has escaped. Or that something worse has happened. I'm not even worried that someone found her, rescued her while I was returning her car to the city. Instead, I am afraid to see myself again in the fear that will shine from her eyes.

When I get the lock undone, I pause only a second, taking a deep breath before swinging the door open. Lauren is there. Alive. Flesh and blood, not just dried bone. Her chest heaves and her eyes are open, watching me. In them, I see the fear I expected. But something else, too. Judgment? Confusion? Neither makes any sense. Without meaning to, I glance at the tarp. I wonder if she felt any curiosity. If she thought to drag herself to it. To peel up the plastic and see what it hides.

Turning away, I walk slowly to the far corner, where I left a six-pack of bottled water. Taking my time, I peel the plastic off and take one in my hand. I look at it, even picture giving it to her. Helping her drink it. But I pause.

I don't like Lauren Branch. Not at all. I've watched her for a long time, even before I knew. Even before all of this started. She is a young person who feels entitled to more than she has earned. She uses words as if she thinks they are weapons. As if they are something more than paper-thin speed bumps. Worse, she uses her face, her body, her smell. I've seen her do it over and over again. Like those things represent some greatness. Some accomplishment. Not just random genetic gifts bestowed down a long line of past benefactors.

I don't like her, but I don't want to hurt her, either. Not really. I stand up and turn, looking at her again. I see those same traits, those factors that make her a human, a person. I can't care about those, though. Instead, I need to see a bishop, a knight, or a pawn. I have to move her. Use her. It's nothing more than that.

So I bring her the water.

"I can take that off. The tape on your mouth. If you promise to stay quiet."

Her lids flutter. She looks back at me and I see more. Revulsion, maybe. Or frustration. I hesitate. But her chest is rising and falling so quickly now. And her face turns a dark red. I think she's having trouble breathing, so I kneel down. Lauren flinches again but checks herself. I see the effort for her to remain still as I reach for the tape. I begin to pull it off as gently as I can.

"Just know," I say. "If I hurt you, it'll be your fault."

The tape sticks to her lips. The skin around her mouth turns a burning red. Blood blossoms at the corner. I continue to pull and she yanks her head the opposite way. The tape tears away from her swollen mouth.

"What the fuck!" she screams at me.

I rear back. She is looking at me, but it is most definitely not fear. It is something that, oddly, reminds me of my brother.

"What is wrong with you?"

"I . . ."

Her head tilts like she is speaking to a young child. "You didn't have to be so fucking rough, you know?"

Her response makes no sense.

"What are you talking about?" I say.

She frowns. "He didn't tell you?"

It is all so surreal. I abducted this woman. Doesn't she understand how much danger she's in? Fighting or crying or cringing, I could understand all that. But this. She radiates an air of superiority.

"Who?" I ask.

Lauren Branch shakes her head. "God, Liam. Drew. I'm in on his plan, you moron."

PART TWO

HIS PLAN

1

God, Liam. I'm in on his plan, you moron.

Her words seem to solidify between us, becoming something huge. Like an avalanche falling in my path. All I can do is blink as the dust of her statement settles, searching for a lie among the rubble like I would a survivor.

But it is true. There is no doubt. I see it now, and understand what I had noticed in her eyes since this started. She was confused, frustrated, judgmental. Not surprised. Not overly afraid. All because Drew told her. And she . . . agreed. Agreed to be abducted. Held against her *will*. But what else? What more could she know?

I don't have time to ask myself those questions. There are far more pressing ones. Drew told her. Why? That answer is not hard to guess. He wanted a fail-safe. But why? Against me. Or against my stupidity. That is the true question. The one I can't ignore, even though it may already be too late.

He is playing with me. One way or another. I realize that. To him, everything is a game. And he never loses. I can't forget that, either.

I stare at her, still unable to formulate the words. She could have gone to the police. Set things in motion that neither of us would have wanted. That's what a normal person would do. But he trusted that she wouldn't. My head tilts, and I realize that Lauren knows Drew better than I thought.

For her part, she watches me with an air of control, like she is making the rules. She strikes me in this moment as a young adult who has grown up in a world of untested privilege. Her eyes are so clear, as if surety is a shield to hide her naïveté. Her expression so easy that it belies her reality. I imagine the deck has been stacked in her favor since birth. I can almost see the shadows of her parents hovering over her shoulders, guiding her into a bucolic world of successful mediocrity.

This is not the thought I should have. Instead, I should be wondering how the hell she knows about my brother's plan.

"What did you say?" I ask.

"Seriously." Lauren rolls her eyes and squirms around as if to show me the duct tape around her hands and feet. "Can you take this crap off? I get it, you wanted to be authentic. Which is great. Really. But come on. There's nobody . . ."

Her attention shifts from me, moving to the tarp again. Then she looks back. That confidence slips. Maybe she's not so sure. There is fear there, behind all the rest.

"Why aren't we at your trailer? That's where you were supposed to bring me."

"Things changed. It was too dangerous to go there."

"What's under that?" she asks.

"None of your business," I snap.

We share an awkward silence. I fight to clear my head of all the questions, to avoid looking back at the tarp. At the bulge in the center of the plastic. Lauren, on the other hand, just appears more frustrated. I wish that I had left the tape on her mouth.

"So, what now?"

Once again, I think about running. I don't know if I have the strength to finish this. But I know I don't have the strength to run, either. Not anymore. I turn away. My legs feel so tired all of a sudden.

"Where are you going?" she calls out behind me.

I say nothing. I open the door and walk outside. She keeps yelling as I close the door and step out on the decking. The cool air washes across my face and I just stand there for a beat, taking it in, hoping it might wash away the fear and disgust I feel so sharply now. It doesn't, though.

Slowly, quietly, I walk out to the edge of the pond. The water laps up, touching the tips of my shoes. I watch it, coming and going along with the breeze. For some reason, I think about that model ship my dad used to work on. When I was little, on days I knew for sure he wouldn't be home, I used to sneak downstairs. This is before I smashed it, and I would be really careful when I climbed up on his stool and reached across to turn on the bright lamp he liked. I wouldn't touch the boat, not then. Instead, I would just look at it. I'd take in every single inch of the thing, sitting there until my legs cramped.

I always had this one dream. I would place my hands under that boat and lift it up off its stand. Then I'd slip out of the house, through the woods, down to the stream. I imagined putting that model into the water. And watching it sail away.

A harsh laugh slips out, breaking the silence. As I stand by the water's edge, I can't think of anyone but my father. And I wonder what he would think of all of this. But then he's gone. And I see her. I think of her. And everything else vanishes, for a time.

EVEN NOW, I wonder how she sees me. Does she think I am a monster? Then I wonder. Is the "she" in my head even Lauren?

I turn away from the pond and walk back into the cabin. Lauren is there, her lips tight and her eyes judging. No matter what, it is too late for anything else. But it's more than that. I'm not doing this for myself. If I was, it would be over already. And none of this would have happened. No, I'm doing it for her. Everything is for her.

And as Lauren stares back at me, I wonder how she sees me, too. At first, I thought I was the nightmare in her eyes. The very thing that haunted her parents when she was young. The worst of what she was warned about. It is no longer a matter of who I am. Instead, the question should be, *What am I?*

In truth, though, she sees me like Drew does, pathetic and weak. I want to cry. I feel the years shedding from me like snake skin. I want to sink down to the ground, cover my face, and let out the pain and the fear. I dream of hands, sharp but perfectly manicured, touching my face, running through my hair. I need more than anything to hear her voice in my ear, whispering, telling me that it will all be okay.

I walk back to Lauren, grabbing the water bottle off the ground from where I left it. I bring it to her, kneeling and extending it to her as slowly as I can. It takes me a second to remember that she can't grab it because I've taped her wrists.

"Drink some," I say, moving it toward her mouth.

She hesitates but then nods. Tilting her head back slightly, she parts her lips. Carefully, I let a thin stream of water into her open mouth. When she looks done, I move the water away and turn the cap back into place.

A text hits my phone. I pull it out and see it's from Drew. From his burner, not his real number.

I should have known you'd fuck it up

I stare at the words, wearing their intent like a familiar yet filthy shirt. Lauren, the look on her face vacillating between fear and bravado, nods at my phone.

"Who's that from?" she asks.

"Who do you think?" I say.

She nods. "He must be pissed at you."

I turn to her and she's smiling.

"Shut up," I say, but I know how right she is.

2

———

*L*iam!"

My father's scream churned up the stairs as suddenly as the bile in my throat when I heard it. I felt my mother's body against me, thin muscles tightening over sharp bone. She pulled away from me. When I looked up at her, her head turned.

I expected to hear footsteps storming up after my name. Or a sharp order to come down to face what I had done. I could picture the remains of his beloved model scattered across the blood-red floor. I could see his face, eyes burning with rage, spittle flying from his cracked lips as he screamed. I waited for what had to come but my fear was only met by silence.

My mother moved away from me, toward the stairs. I could hear her soft steps upward as I listened. My father didn't make another sound. I remained alone in the foyer. For a second, I looked to the front door. I thought about making a run for it, maybe never coming home again. But where could I go? What did I know? I was too stupid to run off, to survive on my own. I told myself that over and over again as the urge grew inside me.

My mother disappeared into her room. I had no idea where my brother was. My father had called my name. I couldn't ignore that. The silence that followed simply added to my anxiety. Against my own will, I moved toward the basement. Silently, I made my way down the stairs.

It was as if someone else drove my nervous system, telling my muscles to contract and expand as I drew nearer to my father. When I reached the bottom step, my eyes so wide, I looked around the main room. I couldn't find a single piece of the model, anywhere. I held my breath as my bare feet touched the cool cement floor. Turning, I realized that the pocket door to my father's workshop had been pulled closed.

As quietly as I could, I crossed to his door. I stood outside, the skin at the tips of my ears burning as I listened for any sound, any sign of my father's wrath. Instead, the utter silence chilled me far worse than any word of anger could have.

I don't know how long I stood there outside my father's workshop. The air felt chilled as it touched my damp skin. Something, probably fear, tickled the back of my throat. I tried not to cough. With my knees locked, I felt light-headed. A part of me actually wanted the door to suddenly rip open and my father to lunge at me, even hit me, just to get the torturous anticipation to stop.

That never happened. Eventually, my hand lifted up. My fingers balled into a loose, weak fist. I tapped on the door, lightly. After, my arm fell limp to my side. Then I stared at the floor, waiting again.

Nothing. I didn't hear even the stir of movement from the other side of the closed pocket door. I made a fist again. I even lifted my hand up to knock again, but froze there. Slowly, I backed away from the door, across the basement, and to the stairs. I glided up, gripping the railing as tightly as I could. Once on the main floor, I moved quickly, not caring about noise anymore. I ran up to my room and shut the door behind me.

I sat alone, afraid that even the slightest movement might draw my father's attention. When I heard him coming upstairs, I thought I might faint. I literally shook as the floorboards creaked under his weight, the sound growing closer and closer. I knew I was in trouble. And I knew it was going to be bad, so bad that I almost threw up.

As I cowered on my floor, though, the sound passed my door. My father, instead, went to my brother's room. I heard the soft knock. The door opened and closed. I crawled toward the wall we shared. I was so confused, so surprised by it, that I dared to put my ear against the sheetrock. I heard whispers, not much more than murmurs, really. They went on for a time and then my father left. He walked back down the stairs and probably back to his workshop.

I stayed in my room, still afraid to make too much of a sound. But nothing made sense. I couldn't understand how my father hadn't killed me for what I had done to his model. I couldn't take the waiting anymore. So I slipped out of my room and to my brother's. I knocked on his door like our father had before.

"Come in," Drew said.

I opened the door. Drew sat on his floor. He watched for a moment. His mouth even opened, like he had something to say. But then a change flashed across his face. Like a curtain closing behind his eyes. He leaned back on his elbows.

"What?"

I looked back down the hallway and toward my mother's closed door. Then I whispered.

"What did he say?"

"Who?"

"Dad," I said, a little annoyed.

I was young, but I got the sense even then that he was toying with me. When he smiled, it was like a cat's claw.

"Nothing," Drew said. As he spoke, he stretched his legs out. One foot touched the open door. Through white socks, his toes gripped the edge and jimmied it back and forth. "Much."

I felt my cheeks get red. I wanted to jump on him. Stomp on his stupid smile. But I didn't.

"Jesus," I said instead.

"Watch it," he said back, still smiling.

"Did he say anything about the model?"

Drew arched an eyebrow. At the same time he swung the door half closed in my face. Then he slowly reopened it, still using just his toes.

"What model?" He laughed. "Did you do something stupid again?"

"Shut up," I said.

Drew pushed off the floor with his elbows, like he might get up and hit me. I flinched and he laughed again.

"Ass," I hissed, mostly to myself.

I turned to go back to my room. Before I could leave, though, he called me back.

"Liam?"

I turned. "Yeah."

"Do you know why I told you Mom was *dead*?"

I swear I saw red when he said that. With what I'd done to the model, I almost forgot. That it was him who had lied to me. Someone might think that the only reason I didn't try to hit him is that he would have beaten me pretty good if I had. The truth is, at least I think it is, that I just felt so confused. So off-balance. I had gone from seeing my mother bloody on the floor, to being told she was dead, to seeing her alive. Then I had destroyed the one thing my father loved the most. I felt like my head was going to suddenly crack in two from the pressure inside.

So instead of hitting him, or kicking him, or anything, I just stood there, not saying anything. He stared back at me, his eyes as dark as I'd seen them.

"Because." He enunciated the word like some know-it-all professor on the television. "You're killing her. You know that, right? You're such a fuckup that Mom's drinking herself to death."

My nostrils flared and my throat locked up. I barely forced a single word out, and when I did, it just tasted like poison in my dry mouth.

"What?"

In response, his smile simply broadened. Then, using that god-damn foot of his, he slammed his bedroom door in my face.

3

I knew it wouldn't be easy. I knew what I was getting into when I stalked her. When I pushed her into that spacious trunk of her car. I tried to prepare. To expect every contingency. But I didn't see this coming. It's as simple as that.

Lauren agreed to this. She agreed to let this happen to her. It is the sad truth. I don't understand it. Or maybe I do. Maybe we all do. But what I don't know is how far down the rabbit hole I've fallen.

"What do you know?"

"Jesus, Liam. I know everything. What are you talking about?"

She's so sure of herself. I can tell Lauren is used to being in charge. Particularly when it comes to men. She thinks she's calling the shots. That my brother *delegated* this to her.

"What, exactly?" I ask.

She pauses before answering. I stand a good ten feet away from her, unmoving, like she has suddenly come down with some awful and contagious disease. At the same time, she watches me like a rabbit might watch a dog. She knows she's faster, smarter, but she can't ignore the inherent risk of being this close to me.

"Call your brother if you need to," she says. "I don't care. Just let me out of this tape. It hurts."

"No," I say without thinking. Of course I am not going to let her out of the tape. Not yet.

She looks around the cabin again. The motion transforms her, sheds years from her age. Like she is looking for someone. Like her parent might suddenly appear to hold her hand and tell her what to do. As I think this, I feel a new sensation. Empathy, I think. Then she looks at the tarp again and I remember just how serious this all is.

"It's a stunt," she says, the pitch of her voice rising. "We're just supposed to lay low for a couple of days. Then he'll find me. He'll be the hero. I get not going to the trailer. That makes sense. It does."

A stunt? Is that what he told her? It is certainly not what he told me. Far from it.

"He didn't tell me that you'd know," I say.

"He didn't?" she asks. I can see her brain spinning around, faster and faster. "That makes sense, too. We talked about it. It has to look real. If it goes wrong, everything goes to shit. For everyone."

"Yeah," I say.

I move closer to her. I can sense her questions coming, ones I won't be able to answer.

"So you and Drew have talked about it?"

She snorts. "Of course. Come on, take the tape off. I'm obviously not going anywhere."

"And you were okay with this?" I ask.

Her head tilts. The aura of superiority returns.

"Really." She laughs. "I always thought of you as the tough guy. But you're nervous, aren't you?"

All I can do is stare back at her. She has no idea what she's gotten herself into.

"You need to drink," I say.

I grab the water off the floor and twist the cap. Moving closer, I reach out with it.

"If you take the fucking tape off, I can do that myself," she says.

Her use of the F word bugs me. I'm not sure why. But I have so much I need to do. So many steps before it's all done. I check my watch. The event starts in less than an hour. I'm not changing the plan. That's not going to happen. I won't let it. We need to go.

"Listen to me," I say firmly. She flinches and my voice softens despite myself. "We're leaving. You need to stay calm and quiet. Do you understand?"

"What? Where? To the trailer?"

"Not yet," I say.

"But . . . Liam, we can't get caught. Not now. You understand that, right?" she asks, as if speaking to a three-year-old.

I shake my head, annoyed. "We won't. Everything is under control."

She looks around the cabin, her eyes lingering on the tarp. "I doubt that."

I could hit her. I could slam my fist into her perfect face and watch her glasses break into jagged little pieces. But I won't. She underestimates me. And until I fully understand this new wrinkle in the plan, maybe that's a good thing.

I'm not sure what I'm doing when I reach around behind my back. I slip my fingers around the grip of the pistol and ease it out from under my waistband. When I bring it around, when she sees it, everything changes. I see the fear again, and uncertainty. For the first time, she looks as if she might try to escape. So I turn the barrel in her direction.

"Maybe you think you know me. Maybe you have some ideas. But the truth is, it doesn't matter. I don't care. About you. About anything. So, before you think of doing anything cute, remember this. I'll put a bullet in myself as quickly as I'll put a bullet in you."

My words are like something physical. They change her, syphon-
ing the glimmer of arrogance from her eyes, draining the blood from
her face. But she nods.

"Good," I say.

I slip the gun back into my pants and help Lauren to her feet. We
move to the door. Once on the decking, I glance one last time at the
mound in the corner, then lock the door behind me, checking it twice
to make sure it is secure.

4

————

It happened by accident. Believe me, I never saw school as an escape. I hated it almost as much as I hated being home. Then, in ninth grade, I ended up in an art class. I hadn't signed up for it. My parents never went to freshman-year orientation and I don't even think I knew I was supposed to fill out a course selection form. Instead, some guidance counselor I had never met put together my schedule. I certainly would not have picked art over one of the shop classes. Not back then.

On the first day of class, I sat in the back at a small round table, all by myself. Mr. Steinmetz, this heavyset guy with a dirty-looking goatee and wispy long hair pulled back in a ratty ponytail, was the only teacher who would let you wear a hood in his class. So mine was up. He noticed, I'm sure of it, but never seemed to care.

I pretty much crapped the class on purpose. I'd never done anything even close to art before, and I had no intention of starting. But something changed over the weeks. At home, things got worse. Mom's health, the way Drew treated me after the model incident, and, most of all, how my father used my brother against me. Or, worse, how they had become some kind of horrible team. The physical side of the abuse had waned. Instead, their true art took center stage. Both would ignore me for weeks. Then, when I craved any attention at all, my brother's whispers would start.

You did this.

You're killing her.

That stuff haunted my mind while I sat back there, hiding in my own hood but watching Steinmetz as he demonstrated brushstrokes on a huge canvas.

"Depending on the size of the brush, its bristles, and the amount of pressure you apply, you can create different effects with the same color."

It was this deep blue, the color on his brush, almost black. As he moved, his hand so confident, his movement compact and thoughtful, something new and amazing seemed to escape onto that field of white. I saw dark, cutting texture. Fading brightness. I felt sad and exposed. I leaned forward and slipped my hood down. I think the teacher saw that.

In the days following, he seemed to be speaking to me as he demonstrated technique and color mixtures. When he handed out supplies, he moved an easel up to my table.

"You have room back here. You might like using this instead of the tabletop."

He set up a still life in the front of the class, a strange pile of fruit and books and earthen jugs. For the first time, I tried. I mixed colors; I moved my brush. Quickly, though, I grew frustrated. What I did looked nothing like what sat in front of me. When I looked at other students' paintings, that feeling grew. I withdrew and put my hood back up.

Then, he was there. Steinmetz looked at me and looked at my palette.

"Forget that," he said, pointing at the fruit. He tapped his chest. "Paint whatever's in here."

THAT DAY, I came home to a mostly empty house. I had no idea where my father was. Nor did I give a shit. Drew was at lacrosse practice. I was thankful for that. Ever since the day I destroyed my father's model, Drew had gotten worse and worse. Some days I thought his vacillation between cruelty and utter disregard came from my father. On some occasions, I'd see him watching how Drew treated me with that goddamn smile on his face. Other days, though, when I didn't think I had crossed my father, Drew still wouldn't look at me. Even acknowledge my existence. Or worse, he would come to my door and talk at me, into me, telling me how useless I was. How embarrassing. Those times I wondered if it just came from Drew. If he just hated me that much. So, whenever either of them wasn't home, I felt lighter.

At that point, I'd taken to checking on my mom every day when I came home. So I crept up the stairs and eased her bedroom door open. That smell escaped, fruity and sour, but so familiar by then that I barely noticed. My stomach rumbled from hunger as I peered around the door. I expected Mom to be asleep, like she usually was, and I was shocked to see her sitting up in bed.

"Liam, baby," she said in a gentle slur.

My stomach rolled again, but that time I wasn't sure it was hunger. And it wasn't just her voice. Even from that distance, I could see how yellow the whites of her eyes had become. They almost glowed in the perpetual gloom of her bedroom. When she lifted her hand from the duvet, beckoning me into the room, her long fingers were no thicker than pencils. Worse, flecks of deep red paint dangled from her nails, exposing the jaundice underneath.

"Come here, baby," she said.

I swallowed it down, all of it, and smiled. Moving quickly across the room, I sat on the edge of her bed. Taking her hand in mine, I looked into her eyes, through them at the mother she used to be. The one I spoke to every night in my dreams.

"How was school?" she asked.

"Good," I said, gently rubbing the thin skin on the back of her hand. "Did I ever tell you I'm taking an art class?"

"Yeah," she said distantly. She blinked, and for a second that cloud that hovered on the surface of her eyes seemed to part. A ray of clarity shined back at me and my heart fluttered. "What, what did you just say?"

My smile broadened into something real. "I'm taking an art class . . . at school."

She sat up straighter. "You are? Really?"

I hadn't seen her like that for so long. It was at once hopeful and terrorizing, like the calm at the center of a hurricane. But I needed it so badly that I clung to every second. Unwilling to let it go.

"Yeah," I said. "I like it, I think."

Her eyes changed again. That focus remained, but it seemed to turn back, peering deeply into the past.

"Oh, I loved to draw," she said.

"You did?"

"All the time." Her lips rose into a smile that seemed to match my own. "I still dream about it. Oh, how I just loved Christmas Eve."

At first, I thought I'd lost her. But then Mom continued her story. I hung on every word, not because of their beauty, but because they offered a glimpse into my mother's past.

"I was the youngest of four. So it was like I was always reaching to try to keep things the way they were. As everyone grew up and got busy with school and jobs, they wouldn't be around as much. But on

Christmas Eve, everyone would come home. We'd be together, and it was so much fun."

She laughed and squeezed my hand.

"The thing I remember the most," she said, her voice clear, "was the waiting. Isn't that funny. I loved the party, but it was the hours before, when I was home alone with Mom and Dad. The minutes passed so slowly. I used to get paper out, and my oil pastels. Dad used to call them adult crayons." She laughed again. "He would sit in the living room with me sometimes. And I would spread out the paper right under the tree. The lights would shine down through the pine needles in a rainbow. And I would draw and draw. And Daddy would tell me how much he loved my pictures. He . . ."

No, I remember thinking when her words slowly faded away. The look on her face changed, too. But I needed her to continue. I needed to hear more.

"You were close to your family . . . then?" I asked, desperate.

A tear formed in the corner of her eye. As it spread across her iris, it seemed to drag that cloud back, extinguishing her sun. One of her long, thinning fingers, painted such a fiery red, caught a wisp of free hair and tucked it behind her ear.

"I was," she said.

"But I thought . . ."

"He never got along too well with them," she said so softly that I could barely hear it.

I leaned down, my face not far from hers. "Who? Dad?"

In that instant, she changed, becoming something amazing yet frightening. This woman who sat up looking me in the eye was a stranger. Yet, at the same time, I'd known her forever. I'd felt her under the suffocating weight of her condition. Trying to break free. Trying to survive, to live. Most of all, to love me.

As she looked at me, her hand touched her stomach. "I remember when I was pregnant with you, Liam. I was so happy. I could feel it, even then. Even before I held you. Or looked into your beautiful eyes. I knew what you were going to be like. I knew it." She smiled slyly. "I knew you'd be my favorite."

"Mom!"

"Sometimes we get caught up. Sometimes, life seems to take a turn that we didn't see coming. And maybe people judge that. They wonder how we end up like this. How can we be so weak? But they don't understand. Love makes us weak, baby. Because we stop caring about ourselves. Because we care for someone else so much more. Then . . . we can never be free again."

I felt my entire body shaking. Her words didn't make sense to me. Not completely. But I could feel them settling into the deepest part of me, slowly entering my soul, changing it forever in ways I wouldn't understand for a long time.

She nodded again. And I watched the moment blink out. Her focus faded to nothing. When she spoke next, she sounded worse than I had ever heard her. "I'm tired, baby."

I sat there, needing to know more. At the time, though, it was what she said about our family that grabbed hold and wouldn't let go. I'd never met my uncle or aunts, and had only seen my grandparents a few times. I didn't even know where they lived, actually. So my mother's story came out of nowhere and rocked what little history I had.

"Mom?"

Her eyes fluttered. Then closed.

"Tired," she whispered.

Gently, I placed her hand down on the mattress. Holding my breath, I got up off the side of the bed and left her alone in what seemed my mother's endless effort to sleep it off.

———

I WENT TO the kitchen for a snack next. I was starving, I remember. All I really wanted was an apple. But I knew we wouldn't have any fruit. I checked the pantry first. We had cans of soup, Campbell's Double Noodle. My mother bought it for us when we were sick. It had to be five years old. There were other cans—beans, stock, tuna. Nothing that sounded great. We were out of cereal. In fact, we had been for a while.

I got pretty pissed off at that, actually. I slammed the pantry door and yanked open the refrigerator. There was no milk, anyway. We had some sticks of butter in the back. A pizza box left over from a few days ago. I opened that and it was freaking empty.

"Goddamn it!"

I slammed that door, too. And then I kicked the fridge hard enough that a pain ran through my foot and up my leg. I knew I wasn't really upset about the food. The kitchen had been like that for years. In fact, I ate more at school than I ever did at home. Even in the moment, I knew that it had nothing to do with empty cupboards and everything to do with what my mother had said. I closed my eyes and remembered the clarity in hers. I needed it to come back. Just one more minute. That's all.

Spinning, I rushed back up the stairs. I pushed her door open. Right away, I could see she was asleep. But I moved to her bed, sat back on the edge. I touched her hand as I had before.

"Mom?" I whispered.

Then I noticed how cold her skin felt. I leaned over her, agonizingly closer and closer. My dry lips touched her forehead. She felt like a glass of ice water.

"Mom?" I said, louder.

Her hand shook first. It seemed to run up her arm, into her chest. Her torso thrust up off the mattress and fell back down, shaking more and more violently.

"Mom!"

Her eyes never opened. Her head turned slightly and she vomited onto the bed. The stain it immediately left was burning yellow like the sun. Then she went utterly limp.

"*Mom!*" I screamed.

But no one heard. I was all alone.

5

———

Lauren won't look at me. She sits in my truck with her forehead touching the side window, staring out the glass at the cabin. The early sunlight cuts through the tree branches, reflecting off the shining silver of the padlock. I'm surprised when she speaks.

"Why'd you lock the door?" she asks.

"What?" I say, turning the truck around.

"The padlock on the door. Why'd you lock it?"

I look at her but she's still turned away from me.

"Why does it matter?" I ask in a tone that suggests I have no interest in the answer.

"What's under the tarp?" she asks.

My grip tightens on the wheel as my foot slips off the gas pedal. The truck drifts to a stop on the dirt drive that leads away from the cabin.

"Nothing you need to worry about," I say harshly.

"Huh," she says. Lauren finally turns to look at me. "I somehow doubt that."

I let go of the wheel. My right hand reaches behind my back before I even realize what I'm doing. Lauren sees me and puts a hand up.

"No, I'm sorry. It doesn't matter. Just drive. I'm cool."

I leave the gun tucked into my pants and hit the gas. The truck rolls around the lake and up the hill toward the exit.

"Where are we going, anyway?" she asks.

"None of your business."

Lauren shakes her head.

"Don't you get it?" she says. "I'm on your side. I'm not going anywhere. What do you think I'll do, run to the cops? I would be in as much trouble as you." She shakes her head and smiles. "And Drew would be so pissed. He'd kill us."

I turn, searching her face, looking for some clue. All I find is that same bravado. She probably can't imagine why Drew would trust me. It just shows how little she knows.

"Why are you scared?" she asks. "It seems . . . out of character, considering."

"Considering what?" But I wonder why she thinks I'm scared. What is she seeing?

"All the stuff you've done for him." She laughs, talking about me like I was a character from some movie she watched the night before. "We all know you're his muscle. In fact, I kind of owe my career to you, at least partially. Remember that whole thing with the political signs during the last election, when that dude Steve went"—she makes air quotes—"*rogue* and then disappeared? I helped with the media the next day. That was my big break. I mean, I was killing it before that, but it got me noticed a little faster.

"I heard you were the one who destroyed those signs, and you pinned it on Steve. I heard it was all Drew's plan. That Steve had been talking outside the campaign, about money. And some other stuff. I heard you beat the living—"

"You don't know shit," I say.

"Ha! I'm the one who set up the shoot. I had every reporter from Baltimore to Philly there. Drew, with his shirtsleeves rolled up, fixing his opponent's signs. Pounding them back into the ground. Brilliant, really. The whole thing." She shakes her head, as if proud of her own work, before continuing. "I know you're like a legend. And it's not just the sign thing. Everything else you've done for your brother. And this. It's like the *Mona Lisa*."

Mona Lisa? I have no idea what she's talking about. For a second, I think she's mocking me because I paint. Could she know that? Could she have seen my work? Been to my trailer?

She just keeps going. "It's perfect. Can you imagine his Q score after this?"

"What are you going about?"

"Q score. Q rating. It's this scale of how popular someone is."

"Kidnapping someone will make my brother popular?"

"His name recognition will go through the roof. The numbers will finally turn our way."

My head hurts as the conversation with Bob and my brother comes back. "That doesn't even make sense. A kidnapping is going to make people like him?"

"Like, hate, who cares?" She shrugs. "Q scores test both. Think about it. Two of the highest negative Q scores are Kim Kardashian and Justin Bieber."

"So?"

"I can't name two people who don't know who they are."

"But Drew's a politician," I said. "People hate the Kardashians. No one would *vote* for them."

When she laughs at this, it is the sound of wonder. "Aren't you paying attention?"

I feel stupid, which makes me angry. But I can't afford that right now. I need to find my focus again. But she just keeps talking and talking.

"It's perfect. I mean, nobody trusts the news anymore. Half the people think it's fake already. They always get it wrong. They're just looking for the story that will sell the most subscriptions, get the best ratings.

"He's going to spin it. It won't have anything to do with him. Just some random act of violence against someone on his staff. Can you imagine the pictures? He'll be there with the police when they find me. He and his wife will come to the hospital."

So that's what he told her. That this is all some sort of television drama. That she was "kidnapped." They'd just lay low. Then stage a miraculous rescue right in front of the news cameras. Perfectly executed by the dapper young politician. Maybe his shirtsleeves would be rolled up again.

I close my eyes. "And what about me?"

"You?"

I nod slowly. She looks confused at first. "Oh, no problem. They'll never catch the perp. No way. You were careful, right?"

"Sure," I lie again, thinking of her car.

"It'll all work out. But you know that. Stop playing dumb. I know this isn't news to you."

I want to burst out laughing. Everyone has a plan. Everyone thinks they know exactly what's going to happen. But at least one of us has to be wrong.

I DRIVE DOWN the highway, surrounded by the last swell of rush-hour traffic. A school bus stops beside my truck at a light. I glance over and see three boys staring down at us. They laugh and point, at what I have no idea. Lauren glances over, too.

"You think you should be driving so . . . conspicuously?" she asks.

"Why not?" I say. "Why would they be looking for me?"

"Maybe they're not. But they're definitely looking for *me*."

I picture the police surrounding her abandoned car. Nobody could miss that.

"Well, then, I suggest you stay out of sight."

There is a minute of silence. Then Lauren speaks again, the tone of her voice familiar. One I have heard whenever she is working.

"I heard he basically raised you," she says.

"What?"

"Your brother. After your mother died and your dad ran off."

"Huh?"

Could she be that crazy? I know my brother isn't. He didn't tell her anything. Not really. No matter what she might think.

"It must have been hard," Lauren says, in that tone. "On your own. The two of you. You must look up to him. Like a—"

"I know about you two," I interrupt, my words flat.

That does it. The smile vanishes from her face like it's been burned to ash. In a way, it feels good to see her suddenly off-balance. But I get no joy from it. Not really.

It's Lauren's turn to look away. "What do you know?"

"Pretty much everything. He likes to talk, my brother."

She turns her body, trying to get as far away from me as she can. For the first time, I notice that I haven't taken the tape from her arms or legs.

"I can take that off," I say.

She doesn't answer. I weigh the options I have, and I realize that there is one benefit to what my brother has done in telling her the plan. It locks her in, like she said. She won't even try to run. She's too deep, and she has to see it all through now. So, at the next light, I reach over and pull at the tape. At first, she resists, but I get it going and eventually her hands are free.

"You can get your feet," I say as the light in front of us turns green.

"Where are we going?" she asks.

"To see Drew," I say.

She spins around, her eyes wide. "No, you're not."

"I am," I say. "It's part of the plan."

6

I sat in a chair, looking out a large plate-glass window. Cars rolled in and out of the hospital parking lot, their beams dancing through the night in a kind of perfect rhythm. They had my mother in a room by then, 353. I had stood in the doorway and looked at her but could not go in. Instead, I wandered the halls until I found an out-of-the-way family lounge. And that was where the police officer eventually found me.

He stood over me as I sat leaned back with my feet spread out in front of me. When I looked up, the ceiling light shined from behind his wide Mountie hat.

"Is your name Liam Brennan?" he asked.

His voice was surprisingly high, like the music teacher's at school. I blinked and saw the man wore glasses and had to be about the same age as the paramedic who'd brought me to the hospital. He wore the brown uniform of a county officer, but I didn't know that then. All I knew, without a doubt, was that he was the police. I tensed.

"Yes."

"Can I speak with you?"

I didn't respond. Instead, I looked around, as if searching for an exit.

"Son, it's okay. You're not in trouble. I just want to talk about your mother."

I tried not to say anything. I knew, even in the moment, that I shouldn't. But the officer sat down across from me. He looked me in the eyes as he spoke. He asked questions that, maybe, I had wished people would have asked for a long time. And I spoke to him, eventually.

"How long has your mother been like this?"

"Drinking?" I asked.

He nodded. "An alcoholic."

I looked out the window and shrugged.

"Do you live alone at home with her?"

I shook my head. I wanted to say yes. Maybe I wished I did.

"Does your father live with you?"

I nodded.

"What's his name?"

I paused, but told him.

The police officer leaned forward. "Are things okay? Is anyone hurting you?"

"Me?"

He squinted. I had to look back out the window.

"I'm fine. We're all fine."

He spoke to me for a little while longer, but my guard had risen. In fact, a deep panic set in at the thought of my father learning that I spoke to a police officer about *family business*. I gave him nothing after that. Even before he finished and walked away, though, I started to vibrate. I sat for a moment, staring out into the night. I went through everything, repeating every word I used over and over again in my head. As I did, my cheeks grew hotter and hotter.

Suddenly, I rose from the chair so fast that it tipped behind me. I didn't care. I moved past it to the elevator, leaving my mother in room 353. I slipped from the hospital without a real destination in mind. I just needed to get out.

Maybe I was walking home. Or maybe I was looking for some hidden escape, one that would rewrite the life I found myself living. Or both, I don't know. But I hurried down the dark streets near the hospital, speaking out loud to myself.

"I didn't tell him anything . . . Nothing's going to happen . . . They don't know anything."

I passed a few people. They hurried around me and then stopped, staring at my passing. I grew more and more detached, like my head was one place and my body belonged to someone else. I just kept walking, turning onto whatever street appeared darker and lonelier.

Like so much back then, I really don't know what happened. At some point, a man appeared in front of me. He might have had his hands out, trying to get me to stop. Maybe he just saw a fourteen-year-old boy in distress, a kid who needed help. It could be that something else happened. My chest felt so tight that I could barely breathe. And I kept talking to myself.

"They won't come to the house. That won't happen."

The guy just wouldn't leave me alone. He should have. I don't know how he couldn't see the condition I was in. He had to see the anger in my eyes. The craziness.

He touched me first. I am sure of it. His hand fell on my shoulder, and I snapped. I lashed out, swinging wildly, my arms like gears spinning faster and faster. I drove into him without grace or feeling. He may have swung at me, or not. My face ended up pretty well bruised. But maybe I did that to myself as I unleashed the unbridled rage that had been building up inside me.

At one point, the two of us fell to the sidewalk. I was panting. I felt like I was having a heart attack. He was sort of rolling away from me.

Saying something like "Chill, man." I got to my feet. Somehow, I stayed standing, even though my vision spun and I felt so dizzy.

The guy quieted down when I walked away. Before I knew it, though, I saw red and blue lights again. At first, I thought I was dreaming, or that I was back in my foyer with my half-naked mother on the cold, dead floor. I even thought that they had come to help us.

I heard them behind me. Yelling at me. But I kept walking, anyway. I just wanted it all to stop. I wanted them to stop me. To end it all, maybe.

The next thing I knew, my face slammed into the sidewalk. I felt the weight of men on my back, pulling at my arms. And I started to cry.

"Help me," I whispered.

But I don't think anyone heard me.

1

I park the truck a few blocks from the event. As I'm getting out, I give Lauren a smile.

"I'd stay out of sight if I were you."

Her jaw clenches and I shut the door. It's a risk bringing her here. I know that. But it's the least risky of my options. Maybe she will end this game. Walk into the event behind me. Then we'd all go back to where it started. Back to what life had become. It wouldn't be me giving up. Me losing my courage yet again. It would be her.

So I walk east, leaving her behind and heading toward a building that houses a dozen or so nonprofits. I'm running a few minutes late, so I'm alone as I push through the revolving door and into the lobby. A receptionist there smiles at me. I think I've seen her before but I can't remember her name. So I just smile back.

"Hey, Liam," she says.

"Hi," I say. "How are you?"

"Are you going to your brother's talk?" she asks.

"Yeah," I say.

She points me in the right direction. I give her a wave and head back to a conference room off the lobby. My brother's already up at the podium, which I assumed he would be. I stand where he will eventually see me.

"Some of you may not know my story. Maybe you think I'm just here shilling for votes. I get it. It's that time of year, right?"

The crowd laughs with my brother. And he feeds on their energy.

"The truth is, I'm an orphan. And when I think about all the work you do for children and families in this state, it means that much more to me. Because I know that there are people . . . families out there that need help, and have no idea how to find it. Families like mine."

Drew pauses dramatically. He looks out at the fawning crowd, taking them in like drugs from a needle. Then his eyes meet mine. They widen, for a fraction of a second, but I see it. Then he moves past me, on to his next political victim.

I look away once his gaze passes. I see Patsy. She stands between two reporters. One whispers to her. When she turns and speaks to him, it is as if he devours her words. I turn back to my brother and watch him work the crowd in much the same way.

"As Americans, I think that we all need a villain for every story. Our hero needs to vanquish the bad guy . . . or lady in the end. In a way, a story without one, without a clear villain, can be the scariest story of all. Because we know that it can happen to anyone. At any time.

"Our story had no villain, at least not one that I could understand. I grew up in a home with both my mother and my father. We lived in a safe, beautiful suburban community full of bicycle rides and basketball with our friends. As far as I knew, we never hurt for money. But a poison seeped into the very foundation of our lives. A silent killer that didn't stop until it took everything and left us broken and alone.

"My mother was an alcoholic. I didn't even know what that meant

at first. I noticed the little things. She would disappear in the after-
noons. Then in the mornings. She got thinner and thinner. She smiled
less and less. But I was a child. My father, her husband, he faced it
alone for so many years. He loved her. He did everything he could for
her. But in the end, it was too much. He watched her die one day at a
time until he was left a shell of himself, almost as dead as Mom.

"Her illness broke my family. It tore us apart with an agonizing
and slow hunger. It left us in pieces, vulnerable. At seventeen, with my
parents decimated by alcoholism, I found myself alone with my
younger brother. Suddenly, our perfect suburban home was without a
mother, and without a father. What choice did I have but to sacrifice
everything to raise my brother? What else could I do?"

He pauses again. This time, he looks right at me and nods. I feel a
current run down my back, melting my feet to the floor.

"I thought I was alone. I thought I had nowhere to turn. But now
I know that I did; I just didn't know where to look. That's why, when
I'm governor, I promise that I won't stop fighting until I've tripled
funding for Children and Families First, and other organizations like
yours. I won't stop fighting until we find every family out there that
is suffering in silence. We'll bring the help to them, not hope that they
can find it themselves. I promise that we won't leave one child behind."

The crowd in the room devours his words, leaving nothing but
their applause behind. I stand there, my brain turning so fast that the
truths seem to be flung to the sides, stuck there by the centrifugal
force of my brother's reality. I claw and scrape at them, needing them
to come to my rescue, convince me that what happened did in fact
happen. That I am right and he is not. The truth shouldn't be like
that. It should be easy. Black or white. Right or wrong. Instead, it is
a bog, sucking me in and suffocating my thoughts until my legs
feel numb.

I think this is all I have to endure. That it can't get worse, until he sees me again. That half smile slowly forms on his face, one that haunts every day of my life.

"Thank you, thank you," Drew says. "But I mean what I say. It's personal for me. And for my brother, who just happens to be here today. Right there, in the back." He points at me. "My brother, Liam. Like me, he knows how important this is. For us it's not just politics, or even passion. It's simply life."

Everyone in the room turns as one. They look at me. I see the pity in their eyes. I feel their misguided attempts at empathy. The attention burns like acid, pulling bile up my throat. My cheeks burn. I am sure they take it as embarrassment at my sudden fame. But the truth is, I feel only an unbridled and barely contained rage.

My brother seems to milk the moment. He stands on the stage, his face changing, the charm returning to his grin. He lets the seconds tick by. He knows what he's doing. He knows what this is doing to me. I imagine that the crowd around me has vanished to him. That his focus bores into me, feeding on me like a succubus.

A woman beside me moves closer. Her whisper fills my head.

"You and your brother are so strong."

I have to fight everything inside me, otherwise I might turn on her, lash out with the truth. And maybe I should. Maybe that would change everything. But even as I think of the possibility, I know it's too late. The plan is in place. The steps have been taken, and I am going to see it through to the end.

"We have work to do," my brother announces, breaking the crushing pressure around me. Attention returns to him and I can breathe again. "It's not going to be an easy fight. But I know the stakes. For that reason, losing is not an option. My brother and I struggled. We fought and clawed our way through the hard times. But what we never did was give up. That's my promise to you. I will never stop fighting. I will *never* give up!"

I take a step back as the crowd erupts around me. It makes me sick, really. But the moment has passed. I am in control again. I am refocused. I see Drew looking at me and I believe he can see that on my face. Maybe his smile slips, just a fraction. If it does, only I would notice.

AGAIN, I FIND myself watching her. Patsy works the crowd. She moves among the people, touching them, laughing at their tiny jokes, slipping in and out of grave conversations like they are small talk. I see the lawyer in her. And the leader. Everyone knows her in this crowd, mostly due to her years running the nonprofit. But others, particularly the reporters in the room, won't leave her alone. She is like the drug that has been taken away. Their withdrawal bleeds from wide, sycophantic eyes.

"Hey, Liam, I didn't expect to see you here."

Bob's sudden approach startles me. I rip my attention from Patsy.

"Bob," I say, off-balance. "Hey."

"Hey," he says with a soft laugh at my discomfort. "I'm glad you're here. It's about time your brother got you more involved. Patsy, too, huh? She's back to working? The reporters are hilarious. I swear, I think she could sell them typewriters if she wanted to.

"It's great, though," he says, shaking his head. "Having her energy back. I don't really get why she stepped back to begin with, but . . ." He glances over at my brother. "Whatever. Maybe she's just filling in for Lauren today. But it's great. And everyone's talking about it. I hope he hears them. Considering . . ."

"Considering what?" I ask.

He shakes his head. "Things aren't looking too hot. I got the final count from the beef and beer the other night. Not enough money, Liam. Nowhere near enough. That, and the polling numbers, there's blood in the water. I just heard from the campaign that a bunch of staffers are jumping ship. They're heading to Greene's campaign, for Christ's sake."

"The guy running for state rep?" I ask.

Bob nods.

"But he has, like, one full-time job to hand out. What are they thinking?"

"I have no idea," Bob says.

"That's a bad sign," I say.

"You're telling me," he says.

I want to say more. I want to tell Bob what my brother is really planning. What he's truly capable of. What he'll do to get what he wants. I owe this man that. He's good and innocent. That consideration is moot, though. For as we sit there, each lost in our own thoughts, Drew approaches.

"Why the long faces, gentlemen?" Drew asks, but he is staring at me.

"Bad news, boss," Bob says.

Drew ignores him for a second. "I was looking for you, bro."

"I'm right here," I say.

"That's true." He smiles. "My brother. Always reliable."

We continue to stare at each other. Though that charming smile shines, his eyes try to rip the truth from me. He needs to know how far my disobedience has spread. Not showing up to the trailer. Leaving Lauren's car in the middle of the street. Letting the police find it so quickly. So conspicuously. Could it be my "stupidity," or something more?

I do my best to stare back at him as if nothing is wrong. As if his plan is moving ahead without a hitch.

"I swung by your trailer today," Drew says. "Did you forget we were supposed to meet?"

"No," I said. "I just lost track of time."

"Is that it, huh?" he asks.

To my surprise, Bob jumps in.

"That doesn't surprise me," he says.

We both turn to him. He is smiling, his face like that of a misbehaving child.

"He lost track of time with that brunette he has waiting in his truck."

It's like the ground suddenly disappears under my feet. Though I stand frozen in place, I feel myself plummeting. I just stare at Bob. I can't look at my brother. But I feel Drew moving closer to me. Almost touching me. When he speaks, the tone is flat and perilous.

"A brunette, huh?" he asks. "Anyone we know?"

I shouldn't have brought her here. I had planned to be in and out. Bob wasn't even supposed to be here. And I parked a good four blocks away. Too risky. But it was a mistake. How big, though, I'm not sure yet.

Oblivious, Bob laughs. "I didn't get close enough to tell. Maybe you should ask your brother."

I know Drew. I can guess what he's thinking. It's one thing if he didn't know where Lauren was. Even if he didn't trust me. Even if he could give me enough credit to think that maybe I have my own game playing out. He couldn't move on me. It would be too risky. But now, he could hold me here and call the police. They'd find Lauren in my truck. That, paired with her car being parked in the middle of the street. The description from the guy with the beard. It would be enough. Lauren would play along and Drew would send me to jail. I changed plans on him. I put him at risk. I know my brother can't stand for that. And I want to hit myself for being so freaking stupid.

I spit words out like they are shards of glass. "I have to go."

My brother's fingers seize my biceps. He squeezes, the pressure like a vise grip, slowly tightening to the point that I might never get away.

"Wait up," he hisses close to my ear. "I think we have some things to talk about."

Bob notices. He takes a step back, obviously uncomfortable. I fight the urge to pull away from my brother. I can't make more of a scene. I just need to get out of here.

"I'll leave you two to it," Bob says.

He turns and walks away, leaving us alone. This was planned. This is why I came, to talk to him, to make him wonder. But Bob saw Lauren; he told Drew about the brunette in my truck. That wasn't supposed to happen.

"You brought her here?" he hisses.

I don't answer right away. "I had to," I say. "The police were all over the place."

"Of course they are," he says. "You left her fu . . . her car right in the middle of traffic. What did you expect?"

"It wasn't my fault," I say, stammering.

Can he not see what I am doing? With Drew, I never know. I just need to play my game. And hope it is better than his.

"I'm taking her to the trailer now," I say in a soft whisper.

Drew nods. He looks around, making sure no one is too close to us. Then he moves in, that half smile back on his face.

"This is about Patsy, isn't it?" he says.

My voice cracks. "What?"

"I saw you last night. The way you were looking at her. The way you stand when you talk to her. I've seen it since the day you met her. You're always staring at her. Practically drooling." He laughs. "But you know what, Liam? She thinks you're a total loser. She thinks you're disgusting. That trailer of yours. Your pathetic jobs. I try to tell her you're okay, but she just laughs at you."

My cheeks burn. I turn, looking toward the door. I need to get the hell out of here. I need to get away from him. I wish I had never come. And he senses all of this. He latches on like a pit bull.

"Oh, wow. You really thought she might be into you. What? Did you think she was going to leave the future governor for *you*? Come on, bro."

He grabs my shoulder, his fingers digging in to the bone.

"Look, we're almost there. It's so close I can taste it. We just need to stick to the plan. When the story breaks, we'll be right there to lead the search. I'll"—he makes little air quotes—"put the campaign on hold. Her life is more important than anything. It'll play like a damn cute kitten video."

He gets even closer. I can feel his breath as he speaks.

"And once it's done, once I win, you won't have to worry about anything. I'll get you whatever job you want. You know how hard I've worked for this. You know what we've been through together. Just stick to the plan, okay? Just do what you need to do, this one last time, and everything will finally work out. We'll be together. You'll finally be safe."

He pulls back. He looks into my eyes. I try to play dumb. I try to look the way he needs me to look. Not because I am scared of him. But because I need more time.

"Liam," he says. "Don't . . ."

Just then, a woman appears through the crowd. She is sharply dressed in a deep blue suit and wears stylish glasses. Her steps are compact and quick as she greets people. I see her first and then Drew does. His grip immediately loosens and I'm able to free myself and take a step away.

"My favorite brothers," the woman says, smiling perfectly.

Her name is Bethany Warner-Jones and she is running for lieutenant governor on my brother's ticket. Young and rocketing upward like Drew, she is the perfect distraction. As she puts her hand out to my brother, I walk backwards, my eyes locked on his.

"I see your wife is handling press today," she says. "Finally came back to your senses, I see. She's a rock star."

Drew smiles. "Yeah. I'm the luckiest guy in the world."

"I have to go," I blurt out.

Bethany looks offended but I don't care. As they stand there, staring at me and shaking hands, I turn and walk away as quickly as I can.

8

When an officer took me home after I beat that stranger on the street, my father stood at the door. I walked past him into the kitchen as they spoke softly. Eventually, I heard the door close and he walked into the room. I was petrified to the point of numbness, but I remember being surprised when Drew followed behind him.

"Stand up," my father snapped.

I don't know where I found the strength, but I rose out of the chair. My legs shook, so I shifted my weight from right to left and then back. I tried to keep my eyes on him but my vision tunneled. As the blackness crept toward the center, the lines of his face faded, but his eyes flared like black fire.

"What did you do?" he said.

"I . . . I—"

My father cut off any defense I may have attempted, not with words but with his hand. He lunged at me, his fingers wrapping around my throat. He squeezed so hard that I felt like my spine might snap. Then he pushed me across the kitchen, slamming me into the far wall.

"*What did you do?*" he screamed at me, his face not an inch from mine.

For the first time, I thought he might kill me. As my lungs burned and my eyes bulged, I resigned myself, in a way. I didn't fight back. I didn't cry tears of fear or pain. But I did think about my mother, and how I might not see her again. When I did that, the sadness felt as crushing as my father's hand.

To my surprise, though, he let go of me. Coughing, my neck feeling like it had been crushed beyond repair, I fell to the kitchen floor. But I saw him turn on Drew. When he spoke, I went silent.

"What is wrong with you?" he hissed at my brother. For the first time in our lives, his tone to Drew matched the one he'd previously saved for me.

I sat up. In a way, I was perversely fascinated. I half expected my father to lunge at Drew now, grab him by the throat, too. But he didn't. In fact, he looked wary of touching my brother. But he laid into him with words, a scalpel in the deft hands of a practiced surgeon.

"I told you to fix your brother, didn't I? I told you to make sure he stops embarrassing this family. Make him less pathetic. And you couldn't do that. Just too hard for my little prima donna. Too busy with his lacrosse. You suck, by the way. Do you know that? All the other goddamn parents tell me that all the time. Every time I have to watch you ride the bench."

Drew just stood there. That smile, so like my father's, drained from his face. And I liked it. I liked not being the target. I liked the feeling that I was no longer utterly and completely alone. So much so that I failed to hear his words. To understand them. But when my father continued, everything changed. His words cut both ways, deeper than they ever had before.

"Well, I guess at least now I know. I can't trust either of you. There's just too much of your mother in both of you. Too much of her weakness.

And her stupidity. Maybe I always knew that. Understand this, both of you: If I could go back in time and do things over, neither of you would exist. I'd never make that fucking mistake twice. Believe me."

My father left us then. He walked out of the kitchen and down into the basement. I got up to my knees, looking at my brother.

"You okay?" I whispered.

"Shut the fuck up," my brother snapped, and walked away.

I WENT BACK to school and, as I sat in that art class, Steinmetz's words came back to me.

Paint whatever's in here.

I remember closing my eyes, reaching into my heart, and seeing my mother lying in her bed. I saw her sallow face, her clawing fingers. The stains on her blanket and the thickness of the air. The darkness that hung over her for almost my entire life became a living, breathing thing. And I captured it on that canvas, perfectly, in shades of green and blue and black and gray and yellow. In swirls and lines and dips and cuts. I felt something in me, traveling through me, out onto the edge of every brush I touched. My pain etched and stroked and finished until I stood spent and staring at what I had done.

"Wow," Steinmetz said.

I wouldn't speak. He wanted me to. He told me about an after-school program. A contest in the coming months. I nodded but didn't listen to a word. When the bell rang, I took the painting under my arm. Ignoring his protest, I carried it home with me that day, leaving it in the kitchen, waiting for my brother to get home from practice.

When the front door opened, my mouth went dry. I sat in the family room alone, listening to his footsteps. They stopped in the kitchen and my heart raced. I forced myself up. I moved to the doorway and saw him looking at my work.

"What the fuck?" he said.

It felt like something struck me. All that emotion rushed up, catching in my throat. I didn't know what I expected. Or even what I wanted. But when my brother looked at me, I felt so empty and alone.

"Are you stupid?" he asked.

"What?"

"Did people see it?"

"Just my art teacher."

"Great. You want Dad to see it?"

"No, I just . . ."

"You just don't think," he said.

"Sorry," I whispered.

He shook his head. "Get rid of it before Dad sees it. Understand?"

Drew walked away. His words infected me, turning the passion that birthed my art into a festering blackness at my very core. I stared at what I'd done. Those same lines and curves and swirls became cuts and gashes and gaping wounds. Every brushstroke became razor claws tearing through my chest and gouging my heart.

I started to shake. Once again, my vision tunneled, turning red at the center. My fists balled, the fingernails cutting into my palms. Then I lashed out. My first strike tearing a jagged hole through the canvas. I grabbed it, throwing it against the wall. The wood frame splintered and the remains fell to the tile floor. I stomped it, grinding it into the ground with my boot.

When it was all spent, I stared at what I had done. And I swear I heard my brother laughing at me in the other room. I stormed into the garage and buried what remained deep in one of the trash cans. I would not touch a paintbrush again for a very long time.

9

I hit the revolving door at a full run, my palms striking the glass hard enough that the receptionist lets out a chirp of surprise behind me. The door spins and I burst out onto the street. I sprint the four blocks back to the truck. I can see Lauren through the back window and I curse softly to myself. When I throw the door open, she looks at me.

"What's wrong?"

I ignore her, focusing on getting the key in and starting the engine. The tires squeal as I pull away from the curb and race down Orange. Within a minute I am on the interstate, my eyes darting from the road to the rearview mirror.

"What happened?"

"We need to get out of here," I say.

"Why?"

"The police," I answer.

She pauses, then lets out a scoff. "He won't let that happen."

I shake my head. I consider upending her ignorance, but I can't.

"He's the one making it happen," I say.

As I barrel down the highway, I try to think. Maybe I should take her to the cabin now. But I can't risk the police finding that place and what is under the tarp. Not yet.

I have options. I can amend the plan. But that thought feels painful. Life has played out like a decades-long chess match. After so many years, any attempt at a checkmate has to be perfect. And it isn't. Not any longer.

I scratch at my arm, hard. I have to stop. Nothing has changed. In a game of chess, there is always the countermove. I can't even say this is unexpected. Because I'm not sure I am being honest with myself. Did I go to the event to bide time? To convince Drew that I was just as stupid as he thought? Or did I go for another reason? To taunt him. Push him off-balance.

Sometimes, the only way to truly win is to get in your opponent's head. Drew knows this better than anyone. Except, maybe, me.

"I heard some stuff," Lauren says, and her voice grates on me before I can even comprehend the words. "That you've hurt people pretty bad, people who wanted to hurt Drew. We've all heard it. People are scared of you." She laughs nervously.

"I—"

I see the flashing light up ahead. It takes me a second to realize the cruiser is across the median, heading north, not south. It races past, the siren rattling the window.

My phone goes off. I pull it out and read the message from Drew's burner phone. The only one I'm supposed to contact him on.

Give it up bro.

Lauren leans in and reads the text before I can turn the phone away. "What does that mean . . . ? What are you doing?"

"He's just pissed at me."

"Seriously! Seriously?" She pauses, looking at me. "Oh, shit, you're not screwing this up, are you?"

I don't say anything right away. I can sense her agitation. I glance over at her and see her shoulders tightly hunched. And I see her for the first time as a human being. Not a piece in this endless game. I had thought I would tape her up once again. Bind her ankles and wrists. Gag her with duct tape. Carry her over my shoulder if I had to. Anything to keep her from ruining the plan.

Now I see a young woman with quick eyes and a practiced tongue. Along with the privilege evident in her straight back and expensive clothes, I see the tense muscles of her neck and the nervous thinness of her lips. I have the power. I can call the shots. But her humanity might as well be a mirror. In it, I see myself. And I see my brother. Two sides to the same story, one that she could never understand.

I'm about to tell her the truth, the part she doesn't know. Not all of it. Just hers. But I stop myself. I rage against her humanity. She is nothing to me. Just a pawn in the bigger game. So I stay quiet, for now.

10

My mother survived that second trip to the hospital. She came home three days after I destroyed my painting. But she was not the first woman to come through our front door. Not three hours after I jammed the remains of the tattered canvas to the bottom of the can in the garage, someone else paid our family a visit. If she knew that she was actually the spark that lit the fuse, she would never have been able to live with herself.

When the doorbell rang that night, I was in my room. I assumed it was another neighbor, there to ask after my mother and shower my father with compassion. I had no interest in watching him feed on their vapid goodwill. So I remained behind my closed door.

When the bell rang a second time, though, a warning turned inside my gut. He would never keep a visitor waiting. Curious, maybe anxious, I crept out of my room and to the top of the stairs. I saw my father standing by the door, his hand on the knob. He turned and looked at me. It was like I could feel his fingers on my throat.

I took a step back. My father opened the door.

"Can I help you?" he asked, his tone short.

"Mr. Brennan?" a woman's voice asked.

I inched out into the hallway, trying to get a better view.

"Yes," my father answered.

"My name is Marci Simmons. I work for the Division of Family Services. I wonder if I could ask you a few questions."

My father did not answer right away. When he did, his words were soft yet unreadable. "About what?"

"Your son," she said. "And your wife."

I flinched, pulling back in anticipation of his inevitable eruption. I even closed my eyes. But what happened next didn't surprise me at all.

"Come in," my father said.

His voice changed. I could tell even from up the stairs. It was subtle, and I'm sure Marci Simmons could not have picked up on it. But he became the man my neighbors knew. He was wounded, deeply, somewhere so deep that even he couldn't find it. My mouth slowly opened as I listened.

"Can we sit?" he asked.

"Of course," Marci Simmons said.

He led her into the living room. I slid down the stairs one at a time, as silently as I could.

"How is she?" I heard him ask, his words paper-thin.

"Your wife?"

"Yes. I . . . I want to go see her. It's killing me. But . . ."

He sniffled. I almost made a sound of disbelief when I heard that. Emboldened, I moved quicker, reached the bottom, and peered around the railing. I could see him in his chair, hands covering his face. His chest heaved. He was crying.

"I just can't see her like this. I've tried so hard. I've tried everything. Her disease is tearing our family apart. It's leaving me so broken. I just don't think I can fight it anymore."

Marci Simmons did not rise from her seat. She did not rush to my father and comfort him. I think, in a very real way, I loved her for that.

"There are things we could help you with. A program here in the city. I can get her in once she's out of the hospital."

"She won't go," he said, his voice cracking. "I've tried."

"I spoke to her today, Mr. Brennan. I think she's ready."

"You did? She said she would go? Oh, God, thank you. I . . ."

His head lifted as he spoke. He turned and, midsentence, he saw me. His eyes locked on mine and I thought I might get sick. I froze. His expression remained unchanged as he stared at me.

"I don't know what to say." A tear rolled down his cheek. "Only . . . thank you."

My entire body shook. I saw the tears. I heard his words. But I felt his focus on me like a pointed gun. I sensed his finger itching the trigger. I have never been so frightened in my life.

Then he turned away, back toward her. "Thank you, Ms. Simmons."

The spell broken, I tore back up the stairs and slammed my bedroom door behind me. Then I heard my dad's voice.

"Drew, someone is here. She'd like to speak to you."

LATE THAT NIGHT, a soft knock sounded against my closed door. I was awake, staring at my dark ceiling. When I heard it, I gripped my sheet in a tightly closed fist and prayed that it was a dream. Maybe I had been asleep after all.

I lay in the dark, holding my breath. I willed the silence to last forever. But then I heard it again, a little louder but still tentative. I sat up, holding my breath. And my door creaked as someone opened it.

I hoped it was my mother. I had this idea that she would come into my room and sit on the edge of my bed. She might pet my head and tell me that she loved me. That's all I really wanted. But I knew right away it wasn't her. The shadow in my doorway was taller, stronger. So much more alive.

"Liam," my brother whispered. "You awake?"

I felt fear in that moment. I don't know what I thought he'd do. But my body reacted. My back pressed against the headboard. My head swiveled, as if I searched for an exit, some way to flee.

"Liam?" he repeated.

My mouth opened, although I still couldn't say a word. His voice sounded so different. Not just soft, but tentative, like the knock. In a way, it reminded me of our mother's. Which was weird.

After that thought, I finally answered. "Yeah."

"Can I come in?"

My eyes narrowed but it was too dark for him to see that. "Sure."

He walked across my room and sat on the edge of the bed. I fought the urge to slither away from him. He wasn't too close, and he never touched me, but it was like there was a current of electricity between us, one that only I could feel.

"I . . . I'm sorry," Drew said, his voice cracking.

I couldn't believe it. I heard an emotion in him that I'd never dreamed could exist. And it was directed at me. I fought the urge to reach out, to hug my brother.

"What?" I asked instead.

"I just . . . He makes me do it, Liam. He . . . there's something about how he talks to me. I don't want to, but he makes me. I like you. I really do." Even in the darkness, I saw his head tilt a little. I felt him considering me like he might a dumb animal. Or a fellow character in some overwrought drama.

"I didn't want to hurt you," he continued. "I never want to do that. I just don't know what to do." He paused, like he needed to get ahold of himself. "When that lady came today, and I talked to her, I wanted to tell her. Everything. All the stuff he does to us. To Mom. But I couldn't. I tried, Liam. I swear I tried."

I didn't know what to do. Or what to feel. The urge to comfort him grew stronger and stronger with each word. At the same time, some instinct deep in my gut held that in check. I felt frozen between these two opposing forces, so I stayed as still as I could.

"It's okay," I said, but the words sounded empty to me.

"No, it's not. It's going to be better. You'll see. I'm not going to let him do it anymore. I love you, man. I do. But he told me I had to toughen you up. That's why I treat you like I do. But I'll do better. I'll be stronger. I promise. I'm going to be stronger for you." He laughed. "For my little brother."

I couldn't speak. There wasn't a single word I could come up with. It was like I found myself suddenly transported back to that moment so long ago, a young Drew on his haunches, my shoelaces in his hands. Every muscle in my body seemed to tighten at once. A searing cramp started in my calves and ran up my legs, into my back. But I didn't move. I didn't make a sound.

In the dark, I never saw his hand. But I felt it touch the top of my head. Rub through my messy hair.

"I promise," he whispered one last time. "But you have to do something for me first. When you talk to that lady . . ." His hand grew heavy on the top of my head. "Don't tell her *anything.*"

Then Drew stood up. He walked out of my room and silently shut my door. As soon as he was gone, I started to shake. I couldn't stop. Then the tears came. My chest rattled and I couldn't breathe. All I could do was sob, alone and in the dark. But I couldn't understand why.

11

I see more flashing lights. This time, they are behind us. Still far away. But I know they will catch up. My foot presses the gas pedal all the way down to the floor and my truck barely speeds up.

"The police are in his pocket," I say.

Out of the corner of my eye, I see her turn and look at me. Her head tilts.

"What are you talking about?"

"The only way to deal with them is to go through him first. Ever since he worked at the Department of Public Safety. You know that."

"So what?"

We both hear the sirens. She spins around in her seat, looking out the back window.

"What the fuck?"

I say nothing. She turns on me.

"Why are the police chasing us? Jesus, you're—"

"I messed up," I say. "That's what Drew thinks."

"Shitshitshit," she says. "God damn."

I focus on driving as she rattles beside me.

"We should just pull over. We'll say it's all a misunderstanding. It'll be cool. Drew will—"

"He'll do what's best for him. And for the campaign. You, of all people, can picture the story. His brother and his press secretary ditching a car, speeding down the highway together. Maybe we don't go to jail. But you can kiss your job good-bye."

She spits out a laugh. "That's going to happen no matter what."

I turn and look at her. "Not if we finish what we started. Not if we make him *happy*."

The word cuts through her like a razor blade. Her eyes widen first, but then the muscles of her face loosen.

"Yeah," she says. "You're right."

My truck can't outrun the police. There's no way. But I need to stay ahead of them, just long enough. The exit I need is only a few miles up ahead. I can see the large green sign. I drift into the right lane, looking out the rearview mirror. The cruiser behind me stays in the left.

I dare a glance at Lauren. She is staring straight ahead, her jaw set. I think she understands. I hope she'll listen to my logic for just a little longer. But I'm not so sure.

I merge onto Route 141. The cop is still in the left lane. Passing the exit without noticing us. My chest loosens as I realize I have a little more time.

"Look, it's cool. We'll go back to the cabin and grab your bag. Then I'll drive to the trailer. I can call Drew. Let him know that we'll be there. He'll be fine. He's just—"

"Fuck you!" she screams. I hear the return of her panic. "Let me out."

Her sudden aggression surprises me. In it, I see through the veneer, down to her pain. And her fear. She's just figuring it out. She's learned a small truth about my brother's nature. My family's. I feel for her, truly, but she's not going anywhere. I can't let her go to the police.

She thinks she can play the game but she doesn't even know the rules or the stakes.

She keeps talking but I zone out, her words fading behind the thoughts racing through my head. I honestly did not think my brother would escalate so fast. This was his plan, and by getting the police involved at this point, he's basically given up on it. Maybe he thinks I won't tell Lauren what he wanted me to do to her. And why. Maybe, even if this turns south and she somehow goes back to him, he thinks it won't matter if I did. That he can fix it with her, like he does with everyone else.

"I won't tell them it was you," she says, the words tripping over each other to escape her lips. "And I'm done with Drew, if you're worried about that. I won't go anywhere near him."

"You think so," I say, half listening and half planning my next move. It's just a matter of changing the order around. Maybe having the police on my back isn't an awful thing at this point. It had to happen eventually. I had already accounted for that.

"I promise. I—"

"Shut up."

I interrupt her but don't scream. In fact, I'm not even mad. Just a little annoyed. And it's hard to have someone talking so much when I'm trying to think. But I have it covered. I know what to do.

She's crying again. Maybe I was harsher than I thought. I don't know. But I approach the intersection with Faulkland Road. To reach the cabin, I would continue north. But I decide to take the left instead. Toward more familiar ground.

I can feel her tense up beside me.

"Why'd you turn? Jesus, where are you going?!"

Then, suddenly, Lauren grabs the door handle. Before I can react, she's pulled the latch. As we race down the road, her door swings open. She twists her body, trying to jump. Her seat belt catches, pinning her, at least for a second.

"Let me out!"

With one hand gripping the wheel, I reach out for her, grabbing her by the shoulder of her jacket. The nylon fabric slips between my fingers. So I dig, clawing at her, trying to get a grip.

The seat belt hits my arm as it unclasps and swings home. Her weight shifts, moving close to the door, which swings shut but doesn't latch. She hits it with her shoulder and it opens again. She teeters on the edge. And my grip slips.

I feel strangely calm. My instinct is to stop her from jumping out of a moving car. At this velocity, she'd get pretty messed up if she did. At the same time, I think about how I could let her go. I could just watch her tumble to the pavement. Watch the impact tear away her expensive jacket. Peel back her skin. Pulverize the bones of her forearm as she tries to brace against the impact.

I definitely have plans for Lauren. She has a part to play. But as I realize now, no strategy is foolproof. There will always be counters. There will always be a need for adjustments. If I let Lauren go, if I let her fall to the street, I would have to adjust. That's all.

But, again, I think of her. What would she think if she sat in the car with us? If I let this happen, how would she look at me? A part of me wishes I could let Lauren fall and not care about it. Drew could. If he sat where I did, he'd probably push her and laugh his ass off. He certainly wouldn't give a care about what she thought. In fact, that very idea makes me laugh out loud.

Lauren is almost out of the car. My laughter just seems to make her try harder. I see the entrance to a residential neighborhood to my right. There is a car waiting to pull out after I pass. It's near the center of the road, which doesn't give me a lot of space to make the turn at this speed. But I think about that old ride at the church carnival when I was a kid. The one called the Scat. We stood against the wall and centrifugal force pressed us to it as the ride spun in a circle. And, still holding on to her,

I flip my hand on the wheel and turn it as hard as I can. The car lurches to the right. Lauren's body, wanting to continue forward, is thrown back into the car as I am pressed against my closed door.

I feel the car tilting, like it might go up on two wheels. Instead, the back tires slip. The car fishtails, just a little. But it is enough for the back end to slam into the stopped car at the intersection. The impact whips my head to the side and I hit the window. It cracks. Lauren, unbuckled, seems to tumble, most of her weight striking my side. Her thigh, though, slams into the dash. And I think her head hits the steering wheel. It happens so fast, I can't be sure. But when the truck stops moving, I hear her groan. And I see blood dripping out of her open mouth.

"Shit," I say.

I can feel her shaking beside me. The truck's engine has stalled. With a quick look out the window, I see the driver of the car I hit crawling out the passenger door, stumbling out onto the grass.

I turn the key, and it won't start. Lauren moves. Blood, her blood, leaves a stain on my pants. She groans, or says something I don't understand. I turn the key again. The engine rumbles. When I get the truck moving, I hear the side panel scrape against the back tires. But we move. I drive a few yards into the neighborhood and make a three-point turn. When I am facing the other car, I see the woman sitting on the ground. Her face is bloody and she looks like she might be in shock.

I think I hear Lauren say, "Help her." But that's probably in my head. I doubt she's thinking about anyone but herself. Then, as I reach the intersection, I hear the sirens. Those are not just in my head. Those are real.

She hears it, too. Lauren's head whips around and she looks out the back window.

"They're coming," she says.

12

I hit the brakes and turn the wheel, hard. The truck fishtails again, and I hear a horn blare behind me, but I don't care. The front tires hit the grassy median I just passed. The cab lurches from the impact and the tires rise into the air. Then the back tires hit and the front slams back down. I lose control for an instant. The truck veers to the left. But I correct just enough. The tires catch and the frame screams as my pickup rumbles down the road.

The light is red up ahead. I don't wait for it to turn. Slowing down just enough, I inch into the intersection. More horns blare but I cut into traffic and speed up.

"Do you see it?" I ask, weaving around a slow-moving Chrysler.

She won't answer me. I can't say I mind, though. This silence is welcome after all her talking. I count on her shock from the accident to keep her from trying to jump out again, at least for a time.

I slam the brakes again and veer across oncoming traffic, bumping over another curb and into a shopping center parking lot. We skid as I try to slow down. I head toward the fire lane that runs behind the buildings.

"I see it," she whispers.

I check the mirror and she's right. Flashing lights appear down the street.

"Shit."

I make it around the back of the shops just as the cruiser passes the stoplight I ran. I speed up, passing loading docks and dumpsters. Then I see an open bay up ahead. I don't slow down to see what's inside. Instead, I yank the wheel to the right. We fishtail again and dart into the garage. I see car stereo equipment and a sign for an electronics shop on the wall as we jerk to a stop.

"Jesus," Lauren says.

I ignore her. Throwing open my door, I jump out of the truck and sprint to the garage door. It takes me a second to find the manual release. I yank the cord and jump up to grab the edge. The wheels cry out as I pull it down. It slams to the concrete, the panels rattling like a peel of thunder.

"Hey!" someone yells behind me.

I turn to see a young guy, maybe twenty. He's wearing black pants and a black collared shirt with a logo that matches the sign on the wall—*Electric Shack.* He has sparse facial hair and gauges in his ears.

"Get out," he says, taking a step toward me.

For a second, I find it funny. The guy's half my size. I could barely fit my arms into his skinny jeans. I could handle him. It would take a minute. And make noise. Loud enough for anyone inside the store to hear. So I pull the pistol from behind my back instead. I take a step toward him, the barrel pointing in the direction of his forehead. I put a finger to my lips.

"Shhhh."

The kid looks like he's about to run. He could probably make it if he did. Even if I wanted to shoot him, I couldn't with the police right behind me.

"You go back inside," I say. "You'll have to deal with my friends who are robbing the place. And they're some dangerous guys."

The kid freezes. He looks utterly confused. As what I said slowly dawns on him, he checks the door leading back into the store. Then looks at me.

"Come here, but stay quiet. I don't want to hurt you. We just want to steal shit and get out. Easy as that."

I know the stereo equipment filling the garage and the store means nothing to this kid. I doubt the job does. So I lower the gun, tucking it back into my waistband. Smiling, I wave the kid over.

He's still not fully convinced, but then he takes the first step in my direction. That's when I know I have him. The kid puts his hands up like he's in some kind of movie.

"It's cool," he says.

Then a flash of blue light shines across the far wall. It turns red. The kid sees it. I see his thoughts in the sudden sharpness of his eyes.

"No," I hiss, pulling the gun out again.

I move this time, taking long strides toward him. His eyes widen. He turns toward the door, but I catch the back of his shirt. I yank him back and he loses his balance. As he falls to the ground, I go down with him. My knee strikes him square in the chest and I lean down, my face close to his. I don't say anything. I lower the gun until the tip presses into the crinkle of skin between his eyes.

The lights grow brighter as the cruiser nears. I press down on the kid, hard. Then the passenger-side door opens. Lauren steps out of the truck. She stands, looking from me to the bay door and back, the look in her eyes matching the kid's almost exactly.

"No," I say again.

And she takes a step toward the garage door.

13

———

Lauren Branch takes a second step away from me, toward the closed garage door. The kid under me makes a noise and I realize the gun is still digging into his face. Her eyes meet mine. We stare at each other as the cruiser moves slowly closer outside.

When I first thought to do this, when I laid out those first few steps of the plan, I never imagined a simple truth that I have learned since: I suck at controlling people. For a second, I just look at Lauren. I imagine her throwing open the bay door, flagging down the police. It would be over then. In fact, I would have made my brother's job easy. He'd be thrilled to learn that the police found me in some stupid electronics store, threatening a pimply teenager with a pistol. Lauren would play the victim. Drew would play the distraught brother and substitute father figure for his screwup sibling. And maybe he'd end up winning his election. He'd get everything he ever wanted. And I'd go away, forever.

I can't control her. I know that. My brother probably could. He'd find a way to convince her to turn away from the door, get back in the truck, all the while making her think it was her idea in the first place.

But that's not me. He's always been the brain. I've always been the muscle. Whether I wanted to be or not. All I've ever had is violence.

So I keep it simple.

"You take another step and I'll kill this kid," I say.

Lauren freezes. She turns and looks at me, her eyes suddenly focused by fear. She searches for the bluff in my words. But I'll do it if I have to. That's what she sees instead. And that's why she doesn't go to the police.

I OPEN THE bay door as slowly as I can, leaning out to see if the police are gone. The fire lane is clear, so I throw it the rest of the way up and head to the truck. We don't have much time. Someone from inside the store could come out at any moment.

When I turn, I see the kid. He's still on the floor by the back of the garage.

"We weren't here," I say to him.

He might run inside, tell his boss. Or he might call the police. He might not, though. I think it's more likely he'll just disappear. Never show up again. But honestly, I just don't care. We'll be gone. And the police will find me eventually. So I back the truck out of the bay and we drive away.

The neighborhood isn't far. I pull out of the parking lot and don't see any police yet. So I speed up. But as I do, the back wheel drags against the dented panel. I figure it might blow at any second.

Lauren's hand covers her mouth. She mumbles something. I glance over and it looks like the bleeding has stopped. But when her hand moves, I see her lip has already started to swell.

"Buckle your belt," I say.

"You're crazy!" she says.

I don't answer. Instead, I look out the windshield and I'm a little kid again. Instead of my truck, I sit in a dingy yellow school bus that smells like sour milk. Instead of Lauren beside me, it is my brother, but a kid again, staring out the window just as she does. Pretending I don't exist, just like she does.

Up ahead, I see the sign. It reads *Woodside Acres* in a flowing but faded script. It is a sign that is as much a part of my childhood as all the memories that come crashing back at the sight of it. We are home again, Drew and I. Like our stories are on a timeless loop.

I take the turn into my neighborhood, hard. I hear the quarter panel grind against the back tire but it doesn't blow. So I floor the gas pedal. The speedometer hits forty as I race past two-story colonials with aging pastel siding and mature trees. I see two kids on bikes stopped at the corner. As I move closer, I swear one of them is Carter. That he's returned to haunt me. At the same time, I smell it, I swear. It comes out of nowhere. Flowers and a slow death. I wipe at my nose but it doesn't help. The aroma is inside me. Filling me to the point that I might get sick.

I turn onto Elder Street. Pass the Clarksons' old house. Drew played lacrosse with their son Eric. Maybe his parents still live there. I have no idea. Eric's BMW isn't there, though. But that was twenty years ago. That car has to be long gone, but I look for it regardless.

Another turn and I pass Carter's house. I feel like I am standing on that doorstep, looking up at his mother, trying to find the words to apologize for lashing out with that branch, not caring if my words soothed my friend, only worried that they be enough to assuage my father.

I hear the siren. It's close but the police cruiser isn't in view yet. I turn again and I see my old house. It slams into my chest. Taking my breath away. Lauren disappears. The car vanishes from underneath me. And I melt down, through the years, my age stripping away like horribly burned skin.

I am young again. Alone. Praying that my mother will come back to me. Even if the smell follows her home.

14

Mom did come home from the hospital, but she didn't stay long. Instead, she walked up the stairs and came back with a packed bag. My father hovered at her side as she kissed my forehead.

"I love you, Liam," she said with a weak smile. "I'll be home real soon. And everything will be okay. I promise."

I hugged her, burying my face as much as I could in her sharp shoulder. I closed my eyes but could feel my father's attention on me. When I cracked one eye open, though, he had turned away, looking toward the front door.

"I love you, Mom," I whispered.

She pulled away. I noticed the tears in her eyes before she turned. I remember thinking it was about Drew. He wasn't there to say good-bye to her. I thought that must have upset her. I wanted to grab ahold of her, pull her back. I knew she needed to go to the rehab Marci Simmons had arranged. And even at my age, I felt this sliver of hope that this might actually change things.

My father took Mom's arm. I stared, the contact between them drawing me in like some powerful magnet. I couldn't look away until the door shut behind them. It wasn't until after that I realized it was the first time I had seen him touch my mother since that day with the neighbor in the front yard.

TO MY SURPRISE, a week later Marci Simmons visited again. This time, though, she was not there to speak to my father. After he invited her in, I heard my name. I was upstairs again, trying to listen, but their voices were hushed for some time. Then my father's rose, vibrating inside my chest.

"Liam!"

I stumbled rising to my feet, and then rushed down the stairs.

"Yeah," I said when I reached the bottom.

"Ms. Simmons would like to speak to you."

I looked at my father first, trying to get some sense of what he wanted me to do. It felt like a trap, even then. I swallowed, turning to Marci Simmons, and realized she was watching him.

I felt like I had fallen into someone else's dance. As Marci watched my father, he refused to look at her. His cheeks reddened. I felt this urge, a desperate need to fix it, to make it go away.

"Okay," I blurted out.

Her eyes moved to me then, and I think I saw her for the first time, really. I took in her thick wool sweater with sleeves that hung down to the first knuckles of her hands. Her hair flowed down her back and around her shoulders in styled waves of silver and brown. It was striking, so different from all the mothers I knew, like she wore her age as a badge of courage. Reading glasses hung from a gold chain around her neck and she carried a canvas bag with an embroidered design that looked straight out of India.

She's not a mom.

The thought sprang into my mind like a warning siren. I didn't judge the woman. And I didn't really mean she wasn't a mom. I just realized immediately, somehow, that she was not a mom in our circle. She was new and different, but not in a good way. The air in the house crackled with the potential energy of chaos. And I felt this woman in her natural colors and bohemian hair might be the lightning rod.

The feeling grew stronger when my father led Marci into his study. He stopped at the doorway. To my surprise, she passed him and took the same chair she had the last time. I stopped, still so utterly unsure of how to proceed, like I stood on the edge of a minefield, one that I really had no desire to cross.

"Sit down, Liam," my father said, pointing at his chair.

I hesitated still, but the energy radiating off him finally pushed me into the room. Without another word, he stepped out and shut the door behind him. I stared after his exit, almost afraid to look at the stranger sitting across from me.

"Hi, Liam. My name is Marci. Can we talk for a little while?"

I nodded, uncomfortable with the way she spoke to me, like she thought I was ten years old, not in high school. Worse, there was something else, a kind of pity, or charity. Part of me wanted to reach out for that, take it in, but it also disgusted me.

"So, Liam, how are you?"

"Good."

"My name is Marci Simmons. I'm a psychologist at the hospital your mother visited recently. I used to work with the police before that." She smiled. "And a long time ago, I was a counselor at an elementary school. So, what grade are you in?"

"Ninth."

"Do you like school?"

"Sometimes."

She laughed. The sound, soft and real, brought with it a wave of relaxation. I looked at her. For some reason, she put her glasses on then. The lenses magnified her eyes. I remember thinking how different they looked from Drew's, of all people. His were always sharp, intense, like he had X-ray vision. This woman looked at me, not through me. She saw all of me, but not more than I wanted to show. Somehow I trusted her, and as the conversation continued, my answers grew longer and longer.

"How is everything at home?" she asked.

I almost laughed. What could I say to that? Thankfully, she realized the scope of that question did not fit the moment. She smiled.

"Stupid question, right? I know about your mother. I know she's sick. And I know she just left to get the help she needs. Do you know what's wrong with her?"

I nodded. "She's an alcoholic."

"Yes, she is. And you know that if she doesn't get the help she needs, she might die, right?"

I was surprised by her question, yet I did know that. And, in a way, it had seemed to me that no one else did.

"I just want her to get better," I said.

But I didn't really know what that meant. She had never been *better*. Not for a long time.

"The place she is going to is great. But it isn't enough. When she comes home, she'll need support. That's why I'm here today, Liam. That's why I wanted to talk to you. The night your mother was taken into the hospital, you were in a fight. A thirty-two-year-old man said that you attacked him when he tried to help you. When the police talked to him, told him about your mother, he chose not to press charges, but that's not normal behavior for a fourteen-year-old. You understand that, right?"

I nodded.

"I understand that you were upset about your mother, but I wonder if it was something bigger than that. I talked to your brother last time I was here. He's very impressive. President of his class. Varsity lacrosse player. He told me that everything was okay, but that your mother's illness has taken a toll on everyone. Mostly your father."

She paused, looking directly into my eyes. I felt an itch flare up from the inside out. I looked to the door, like if I could see through the wood and brass I would find him crouched on the other side listening to my every word.

I wanted to scream. To cry. I wanted to trust this woman with the truth. But to be honest, I didn't even know what the truth was. I felt like every step of my life up until then had been on a world with absolutely no emotional gravity. I swayed left and right and up and down, some days thinking I understood, some nights going to sleep with my father's burning eyes on my mind. Maybe I didn't know any better. Maybe nothing was as it seemed. I just couldn't be sure. Not then.

So, instead, I said nothing. I sat there watching her. She fidgeted before I did.

"Liam, are you okay?"

"Sure," I said.

"No, I mean it. I really want to know if you're *okay*."

I blinked. But I didn't respond right away. I had no idea what to say. Not because I was scared or nervous. Instead, reality seemed to tease me, staying just out of sight.

She leaned closer. "How is your relationship with your father? Do you get along? Is he present?"

I laughed. It burst out quicker than I could close my mouth.

"What's funny, Liam?"

"Nothing," I said, looking at the floor. "I didn't mean it."

Her eyes widened. Marci's mouth remained slightly open as she thought about what to say next.

"How about your brother?"

"We get along fine," I said.

"No," she said, getting even closer to me. "Does he get along with your father? Are they close?"

I tried to remain completely still when she asked that. I was so afraid that if I moved, even just a little, she'd see the truth of it. She'd know what was going on in my house. Yet, as I struggled, I let myself wonder, What if she knew? Would she help me? Could things be different?

I looked into this stranger's eyes and I saw something in that moment. I don't know exactly what it was, but it made me think of my mother. Her disease. And her smile. Her fingernails and that sour smell. I think, for the briefest of moments, I trusted Marci Simmons. I think my mouth even opened and the words formed deep in my throat. But she spoke first.

"Does he touch you, Liam? Your father? In ways that he shouldn't. Ways that make you uncomfortable."

The spell shattered. My eyes focused and I saw her truth. She didn't understand my life. Instead, she saw it like the movies she watches at night while sitting on her comfortable couch, maybe with a big lazy cat on her lap. How could she be so wrong? As obtuse as my father was subtle. I thought she might understand. That she might be able to help.

"Liam?"

Eventually, hope can be more painful than despair. I thought about Drew's strange apology and I let it grow and bloom inside my heart. Maybe I wasn't alone. I thought about my mom. She was going to treatment. Maybe it would work. Maybe she would come home to me and things would be better. Like in a story. The smell would be gone forever. And my father would just give up. He'd slip away one night and never come back. Leaving the three of us alone, together.

Hope is a dangerous thing sometimes. It can be the mask that hides the truth. The pause that lets help slip through your fingers. My father never abused me, not like she thought. But maybe, if he had, maybe if it had been as clear and horrible as that, I would have spoken up. I would have told her the truth. Or what I thought was the truth. Instead, thinking of Drew and my mom, of the possibilities, I shut down.

"Of course not. Everything is okay. We're just worried about Mom."

Out of the corner of my eye, I saw her shake her head. She stood, her arm reaching out to me.

"Here's my card, Liam. Keep it. And call me if you ever need to talk. Or . . . if you need help. Okay?"

I nodded. Marci Simmons left shortly after that. Once the front door closed behind her, my father appeared, and I can never forget that moment. He nodded, a small thing, barely noticeable. But in it I saw approval. Like I had finally done the right thing for a change. Despite it all, that small, possible figment filled me with an almost painful flare of pride. And an even more fiery need to experience it again.

Instead, my father walked out of the room. And I didn't see him again for four days.

15

My past is an abusive relationship, one that didn't fit into some textbook diagnosis. I know what it does to me. The pain it causes. To someone else, it would seem so easy. Move on. Build a new life atop the ashes and never look back. Even I know that is the best thing I could hope for. That knowledge, however, is no better than a dream. No better than a wish. Because I keep going back. Thinking the impossible. That it will be different this time. It will be better.

Though my truck doesn't slow, time does. I am back in my father's study. Marci Simmons's kind face watches me. Her eyes pull at the truth. They hint at some miracle, if only I speak. If only I trust.

Would I have told her? If I knew then how it would all turn out? I don't know. But I don't think so. But why? I wonder. I feared what he would do, certainly. That wasn't it, though. The real reason feels like a stone forcing its way up my throat. It was her. I just wanted my mom to come home. And I wanted it to be different. I prayed for it, in my own way. And I couldn't do anything to risk that chance, no matter how unlikely it may seem.

"What are you doing?" Lauren says, her voice strangely emotionless.

My foot presses the pedal down. The truck lurches forward. I hit the next turn, leaving my childhood home behind. I hear the siren, maybe sirens now. They sound close. But it doesn't matter. I'm here. I've led them here. I picture the police reporting back to my brother. Telling him where I brought them. Where I gave them the slip. I can almost see his eyes narrowing. His thin lips going flat and hard as the first hints take hold. He can be the one who has to remember. The one living in the past for a change. Because that's where I need him to be. I did what I had to do. And now I can go.

We pass the Richardsons'. Then the Chungs'. Between the next two houses, I jump the curb, careening into their side yards. Lauren's hands slam into the roof of the truck. She screams, curses, as we are thrown up and down. The truck's tires kick up grass and mud as I race toward a line of oak trees.

"Oh, God!" Lauren moans, covering her eyes, expecting a fiery end.

Then I am passing between two thick trunks. The ground hardens, smooths, and I slow down, finding the two ruts of an old emergency access road, one that I used to ride my bike on as a child. It leads through a thin slice of woods before joining a paved one-lane road. The truck lurches one last time as I pop up onto the asphalt. After that, it's easy. I just follow the lane back behind my neighborhood until it comes out of the trees and runs parallel to the entrance. From there, I merge onto the highway and leave the police behind.

FINALLY, LAUREN HAS nothing to say. She stares out the window as I head north, away from the cabin again. When I turn on the radio, I have to find the local news station. I probably should have preset it before all this, but I didn't think of that. Once I find it, it doesn't take long for the reporter to mention Lauren's name.

*This morning a young staffer working for Andrew Brennan's gu-
bernatorial campaign went missing after leaving the YMCA on
Pennsylvania Avenue. Her car was later found a few blocks away,
allegedly abandoned by the prime suspect in the case. Police are
asking everyone to be on the lookout for a white late-model Ford
pickup with damage on the driver's side. It was last seen in the
Pike Creek area, near Woodside Acres, Brennan's childhood neighborhood. The authorities ask that you contact them immediately if
you see the truck. But do not try to—*

I cut it off. I feel Lauren's eyes on me.

"You're done," she says.

I look at her. At this point, I don't even want to slow down because
I think she might try to jump from the truck again. A part of me just
wants to tell her the truth. Maybe that would convince her to stop
trying to escape. But maybe it wouldn't. She knows Drew. She knows
him *well*. His claws are probably in deep. I could tell her the truth and
she'd still take his side. I have no doubt of that.

At the same time, I need her ignorance. It is my final weapon. The
last step in the plan. I just need to get there without letting the police
catch up with us. And there's no way I'm going to be able to do that
in my truck. Not anymore. So I pull out my phone and send a text.

Is the car in place?

Once again, Lauren looks over my shoulder.

"Who's that to?" she asks.

I look at the screen. The text is to a cell that is not in my contacts,
so no name appears. I wonder, for just a second, if she might recognize the number. But that probably doesn't matter, anyway.

"A friend," I say.

Her eyes narrow. "Drew?"

I shake my head but don't say no. She fidgets beside me, muttering. A second later the response comes in.

Yes, but it's early. Everything ok?

Change in plans, I reply.

Do u need me?

Not yet.

"Where are we going?" Lauren asks.

"I'm getting rid of the truck," I say.

"Then we're going to walk away, huh? That sounds like a great idea."

I shake my head. Although her lip is huge now, her sense of superiority has returned. And I wish it hadn't. With my teeth grinding together, I just focus on my destination.

"Drew told me that you mess everything up."

"What, when you were sleeping with him?" I say.

She scoffs. "So what? Why do you care?"

"Patsy doesn't deserve this."

"Oh . . ." She laughs. "He told me that, too. I didn't really believe it, though. I mean, how typical. Being in love with your sister-in-law. But now that I know you better, I can see it. Kind of fits you."

I just need to get to the office and leave the truck. It's not far now. But she won't shut up.

"He said Patsy can't stand you. She thinks you're worse than I do. I'm not surprised, though. She's pretty stuck-up. She thinks because her daddy was someone, she is, too. But she's never done a goddamn thing."

"She's done more than you have."

Lauren pauses. I feel her getting closer to me.

"You really hate Drew, don't you? I get it. He can be pretty awful. I've seen it. I have." Her hand comes to rest on the console, inches from my thigh. "I hate him, actually. I was just afraid to tell you that. I was using him. Because all those fat old politicians are like an all boys' club. I didn't have a choice. It was the only way in. But I'm there now. They know my work. They know how important it is. I could get a job with any one of them. Bethany calls me all the time.

"Look, maybe we're on the same team. What if we go to the police and I tell them that he's been hurting me. And that I came to you for help. Look . . ."

I turn. She pulls up her sleeve and I can see the bruises on her arm. They look like the dark outline of my brother's hand. Or mine.

"I did that to you," I say quietly.

"So what?" She laughs. "They won't know any difference. This could be good. I'll call Bethany. Get her ready. She can step in. Take over the campaign. Do it for the ladies. Right?"

I don't say anything. I see the line of squat concrete office buildings up ahead. When I turn into the lot, I roll slowly past a white sign with thick brown lettering. It reads:

SIMMONS PSYCHOLOGY SERVICES

When I see it, I feel strange, like I'm suddenly thrust backwards in time again. Like I am a little kid, barely able to see the sign over the dash of my truck. I slow, pulling lengthwise into a line of open spaces across from the building. There is another sign by the office entrance. I see three plaques with names. The top one is for Marci Simmons, PhD. I picture her thick wool sweater and her long skirt. I see her eyes, large and soft, the way they somehow attracted words like a magnet attracts iron.

As I sit there, staring and fighting the memories that flood back to the surface again, the door to the office opens. The second stretches out to a lifetime of torture until I see a woman, not Marci Simmons, and a teenage boy exit onto the sidewalk. Her eyes are swollen and red. The boy looks like he might have just been run over by a large truck full of raw emotion. They walk toward a black Volvo without saying a word.

The boy is what gets me. He is probably thirteen or fourteen. His clothes look well cared for and expensive. His hair is blond, not dark like mine. But in his eyes, I see it. I see myself.

I am mesmerized. I think about my mother, my father . . . Drew. The years of my childhood. Watching everything decay and die while I knelt on the once pricey carpets watching reruns of *Taxi* and *M*A*S*H*.

This kid knows. He's seen it. I swear he turns and our eyes meet, and I am sitting there looking at my younger self. I try to remember a day back then. Maybe I was here. Maybe I saw Marci. And maybe a man in a beat-up white pickup watched me from behind the glass of his windshield. Maybe our eyes met and I knew, even then, where it would all end up, the full circle that would spiral ever downward. Am I him or is he me? Time is an endless loop, eating its own tail, and we are both stuck in this moment.

16

My mother had still not returned home from rehab. I stood in the kitchen, staring at the open refrigerator. It was virtually empty but for a new case of Drew's Muscle Milk protein shakes. I thought about ripping open the box and taking one, but I knew he'd kill me, eventually. Not that I expected him to come home. At school, I heard he was seeing some girl. He'd been staying nights there, a lot. For a couple of weeks.

During that time, I had developed an uneasy relationship with loneliness. I went days by myself in that house, punctuated by hours behind the closed door of my room, hoping the soft voices I heard would not approach.

When I closed the refrigerator, I started talking to myself, something of a new habit.

"Today's Tuesday. Even if he's coming home, it won't be until after lacrosse. Maybe it won't be late. It hasn't been as bad, lately . . . when he's home. Not that he's around much."

My conversation abruptly ended when I heard the front door open. For a second, I thought it was Drew. And I think I was happy about that. I even started to move toward the foyer. But then my father appeared. When he looked at me, I lowered my eyes.

"Your mother is home," he said.

That moment was so weird. I should have heard his words and understood them immediately. Mom had been gone for over a month. I needed her home. But for some reason I remember being lost in the sound of his voice, like I hadn't heard it in years. I wanted more but he just passed through the room on his way to the basement.

"Liam?"

Her call floated into the house and my heart fluttered. I moved so slowly across the tile, afraid that it was all a dream. That I was still alone. Then I saw her, and the truth was I barely recognized my mother. She stood in the doorway, her back straight, her eyes clear and bright, and her hair perfectly done in shining black waves that fell around her shoulders.

"Baby," she said.

I didn't run to her. I wasn't a little child anymore. But that urge was difficult to fight. Instead, I moved carefully, as if at any minute some bend of light would reveal her as a cruel mirage.

I stopped a few feet from her. My mother's smile broadened. She put her arms out and I let her hug me. I remained stiff, however, and she sighed.

"It's going to be different, baby," she whispered near my ear. "I promise. I'm good. Really good. And your father's changed. You'll see."

"Okay," I said.

The truth is, I wanted more than anything to believe her.

THE NEXT DAY, I came home from school to find the refrigerator filled with food. Not just condiments and old milk. We had fresh fruit and vegetables. Meat. Bread from the bakery downtown. I didn't know what to eat first.

"Liam?" she called from upstairs.

I froze, my chest tightening and the hairs on my arms standing on edge. I waited, expecting her call to come again. Picturing myself slinking up the stairs to her bedroom door. Finding her in bed, that smell filling my nose, and her new red nail polish chipped and flaking like dried blood.

As I stood there, holding my breath, I heard footsteps. I let the air out when I realized they were too light to be my father's or Drew's. When my mom walked into the kitchen, all my fears vanished. She was dressed. She stood up and walked without the hint of a sway. And when she spoke, I heard no slur to her words.

"How was school today?" she asked.

"Good," I said.

"Anything new?"

I blinked. For some reason, I thought about my painting, the one I destroyed when she was still in the hospital. Part of me wished she could see it. But then I thought about the lines of that work, the way she appeared on the canvas, like the haunting instant between life and death, and I felt embarrassed by what I had done. This woman looked nothing like that. She looked alive. And healthy. Like every-one else's mom. Better, even.

With all that on my mind, I just shook my head.

"Let me make you something to eat," she said, so happy. "How about . . . ?"

She paused, looking confused for an instant. At first, I got worried again. But then I realized she just had no idea what to fix. She didn't know what I liked, or what I didn't. I was her son, and yet she knew almost nothing about me. The realization was crushing.

"I'm not hungry," I said.

"Oh," my mom said, disappointed. "Okay. Sit down with me."

She sat at the kitchen table and patted the seat beside her. I took it, looking away at the window by the sink. I could feel her fidgeting.

"Liam, do you trust me?" she asked.

"Sure," I said.

"No, really."

"Yeah."

She nodded. "I think I am going to get a job. I need to do something for myself."

"Did you ever work?" I asked.

"Of course," she said, laughing. "I was a middle school teacher when I met your father. We met at the school, actually. He ran a robotics seminar."

She paused. I waited, desperately needing more. It was like the smallest corner of some veil that hung between me and my reality had been suddenly peeled up. I got just a peek of the truth. At the same time, though, I didn't want to think about my father. I didn't want to hear about it. The hatred that grew inside me kept my mouth shut. It kept me from asking my mother more questions.

Our stillness hung between us. It made me nervous. So when I finally spoke, my words meant nothing.

"You should get a job . . . if you want."

"I'd have to ask your father," she said.

The silence that followed felt even heavier. Even more dangerous. That time, she broke it, though.

"Drew loves you," she said. "You know that, right?"

I laughed nervously.

"Seriously," she said. "I know it might not seem like that all the time. But he does. He just thinks about himself too much sometimes. He'll grow out of that. You'll see."

I nodded.

"You two need each other. You need to be close. Family's the only thing you can count on in life. The only people you can really trust." She fidgeted again. I looked at her and saw the tears in my mother's eyes. "I'm so sorry. So sorry."

Sitting right beside me, my mother sobbed. She kept apologizing and apologizing. It made me vibrate, but I finally turned in my chair and put my arms around her.

"It's okay," I said, over and over again.

Her breath caught. "Oh, Liam."

"Mom, it's okay. Everything is going to be okay."

"It is," she said, her crying suddenly sounding like a laugh. "I promise, it is."

As I held her, I heard the garage door open. I heard my father's car pulling in. It was a little after 3:00 P.M., way before he would ever get home. Immediately, I let go of my mother and stood up. She watched me with sadness in her eyes. But before she could say anything, the door to the garage opened. My father walked into the kitchen.

"We have to go," he said. "You have a meeting."

The worry left my mother's face. She smiled so broadly that I thought her face might split right in half.

"I do," she said. "Thanks for coming home."

He glanced at me before answering. "Sure. I told you I would."

"Well, thank you."

My mom rose from the table and gave me a hug. When she pulled back, I saw the look in her eyes. It seemed to tell me that she was right. That things would be different. And this small act of my father keeping his word proved it. Despite myself, I nodded. No matter what, hope and childhood are never too far apart.

17

I wait for the mother and her son to drive away before I can move. Slowly, I take my wallet out. I pull out a tattered old business card, one I have carried for so many years. Her name, Marci Simmons, has faded but can still be read. I place it on the dashboard, carefully, before turning to Lauren. I pull the gun out from behind my back as I speak to her.

"I'm going to get out first. If you do anything stupid, I'll kill you. Don't think I won't."

"Jesus, Liam," she says, looking at me like I'm a child. "Aren't you listening to me?"

"Just do what I tell you to do and everything will be fine."

I get out of the truck and drop the key onto the pavement. Then I walk around and open her door. She gets right out, like she's on my team.

"Where are we going?"

I nod toward a worn path that crosses to the parking lot of the next office complex. We cross it and I head to the farthest building and lead her around the corner. A silver Mazda is parked all by itself in the last spot.

"Get in," I tell her.

She looks at me, her eyes clear and raised. All the fear and uncertainty I saw during the chase with the police seems to have vanished. It unnerves me. So once she is in the seat, I hurry around and get into the driver's side. The keys are under the visor, just as I knew they would be.

"You have this all figured out, don't you?" she asks.

I ignore her, backing out of the spot. It's time to return to the cabin. To face our demons.

"Seriously?"

I catch movement out of the corner of my eye. Then hear paper crinkling. I turn and see she is holding a rental agreement. Slamming on the brakes, I rip it from her hands.

"You rented the car in your name? Are you kidding?"

"No," I say, the word sounding lame even to me.

"I saw it on the agreement."

"You did not."

"I saw 'Brennan.'" She laughs. "And I doubt Drew would rent the car for you."

I just look at her. For a second, I see the uncertainty. She's wondering if Drew would. If there is more to all of this. Finally, she might be starting to get it. I jam the agreement into my front pocket and drive. But I know she's not done. She has more talking to do.

"Why go see him? Why take that chance?"

Back to Drew. Like she can get into my head. She doesn't understand the game. I wanted him to see me. It was my idea. I was in charge. I wanted him to wonder how I had the guts to show up after all of that. And I knew he couldn't do anything. Not without knowing he could get his hands on Lauren before anyone else.

But then Bob showed up and mentioned the girl in my truck. That was enough of a clue. Drew knows something is up. He thinks I've gone rogue. Although him finding that out has always been a part of the plan, it's too early. Drew has decided he can cut bait. He pushed all in, getting the police on our tail. I'm surprised he released the description of my truck. I hadn't expected that, not yet. That decision hinted at things being off-balance. The thought gave me just a sliver of hope.

For the moment at least, I am still one step ahead of him. That has to be enough. But it doesn't help her. Lauren can't understand what's happening. Why her charms aren't working on me. She can't know how deep this runs. But there's not much I can do about that.

"Talk to me!" she suddenly screams.

I startle. When she punches my shoulder, I can barely believe it. She does it again, though.

"*Talk to me!*"

I don't acknowledge her. Instead, I merge back onto the highway leading to the apartment complex. When I speak, my answer is simple and clear.

"No."

18

L iam," my mother called from downstairs.

I startled, my pencil skidding across the page as a picture flashed behind my closed eyes, my mother lying on the kitchen floor with blood pooling around her head. It had been over a month since she had gotten home from rehab, but the sense that the other shoe was about to drop never truly left me.

"Yeah?" I called back from my bed.

Without realizing it, I had started to draw. I still wouldn't paint, not since the night I brought the picture of my mother home. Not even in art class. But my constant doodling had expanded, taking over entire notebooks.

"Come down," she answered.

I heard something playful in her tone. I think I even smiled as I moved off my bed and headed toward the hall. As I stepped out, I almost walked into my brother.

"What does she want?" he asked.

"What?"

"Mom," he said.

I looked at him. It is hard to explain those days. Mostly, he just wasn't around, spending the majority of his time at his girlfriend's house. She didn't go to our school, so I hadn't met her yet. I remember being fascinated by the entire thing. In fact, I had wanted more than anything to talk to him about it, see what it was like to have a serious girlfriend, but I never had the chance. He seemed to be avoiding me.

For his part, he had avoided Mom in the same way. And she him. They spoke. We'd had two sit-down dinners, which were totally awkward. Even Dad joined us for those. Drew had answered questions about school and lacrosse. But after, he slipped away and the house returned to an expectant silence.

"I don't know," I answered.

He shook his head and walked into his room. I watched him go, that feeling of unease crawling up my back.

"Baby," my mother called.

I cringed. As her eyes grew clearer and clearer, my mother had started calling me that more and more. It made me uncomfortable when no one else was around. With Drew just down the hall, the sound made me want to jump off a building. Instead, I hurried down the stairs and found her by the door to the garage. She had a jacket on and I saw car keys dangling from her long finger. I stopped, staring at her.

"Are you going out?" I asked.

"So are you," she said with a smile.

"Uh, is it okay if you drive?"

She laughed. "As long as your father doesn't find out."

She reached a hand out to me. Her shining red nail polish beckoned me forward. Her skin felt cool and dry. And she smelled of flowers, and only flowers.

———

"MOM?"

We sat outside the giant pet store by the mall. She turned the engine off and opened the door. When she spoke, there was a lilt to her voice I had never heard before.

"I want to show you something," she said.

I followed her into the store. We had never had a pet, so the smell felt like a slap to the face. I covered my nose, which made her laugh. And she hurried down an aisle filled with dog chew toys.

"I thought about a puppy," she said over her shoulder.

"What?"

"A puppy," she said.

"What are you talking about?"

She took a sharp turn, heading toward the back corner of the store. I saw the cats before she reached them. Stacks of three cages lined a portion of the wall, rising almost halfway to the ceiling. A single adult cat, orange and white, slept in one. Three kittens played in another. My mother reached them and stopped. She swayed a little as she watched. I stepped up beside her.

"But a dog is too much, right?" She turned and smiled at me. "So pick one. Whichever you want."

I stood there, unsure what to do. Part of it was that I was a teenage boy in a pet store with my mother looking at cats. I fidgeted, looking around to make sure I didn't recognize anyone else. The bigger question racing through my mind, though, was whether my mother was okay. She looked clearheaded. *Sober* would probably be the correct word, but even then I didn't think of it that way. I had absolutely no idea why she wanted us to get a cat.

"I don't know," I mumbled.

"Come on," she said, grabbing my sleeve. "Pick one."

I took a step closer to the cages. I felt so weird, kind of like I had a fever, chills when I wasn't even cold. And sweaty in a strange way.

"Are you . . . ?"

I couldn't figure out what to ask. She laughed and pointed to one of the smaller kittens, a brown-and-white tabby. It sat in a small litter box while two larger kittens wrestled in the middle of the cage.

"Oh, look at that one."

She moved closer to the cage, sticking a finger through the bars. The kitten stared at her but didn't move.

"He wants to come home with us, doesn't he?" Her pitch rose. "Hi, baby."

A woman in a green smock joined us. She started talking to my mother and all of a sudden we were buying that cat. Once my mother filled out about a hundred forms, she breezed through the store aisles, the smocked woman in tow, picking out a litter box, toys, even a cat tree. By the time she was done, someone had to help me carry it all to the car. With my arms full, I turned once to look at Mom. She held the small cardboard box with our new kitten up to her eyes as she whispered.

"You're going to love your new home. It's going to be great."

DREW WASN'T HOME when we got back. I have to admit that while at the store, I thought the entire cat thing was crazy, but when we got it out of the box and it started running around the house like mad, I got into it. We spent that day together, Mom and I, setting up all the cat's new stuff and playing with it. We laughed and goofed around. I felt young, and happier than I could remember.

"Do you remember that day with the caterpillar?" I blurted out.

My mother's eyes met mine. She scratched the kitten's chin as her eyes narrowed.

"Caterpillar?" she asked.

"Nothing," I said.

She just smiled. "Do you want to make some cookies?"

"Cookies?"

"Sure," she said, springing up so fast that the kitten launched off her lap. "Come on."

I followed her into the kitchen. She swung open cabinets, pulling down bowls and her old stand mixer, which I hadn't seen in years. Then she moved to the pantry. I stood by the kitchen table, already pretty sure that we didn't have any of the ingredients we needed. I didn't want to tell her that, though. I sensed something in her jerky movements and in her decision to suddenly adopt a cat. Sort of like that day when my parents had been outside talking to the neighbor. Like a fuse had already been lit.

When she finally backed out of the pantry and looked at me, I saw her disappointment. I thought she'd just give up. Instead, her long fingers touched the side of her face. Then she smiled.

"Smoothies," she said, beaming.

My mother laughed as she dug through the groceries she had bought the day before, tossing a half-empty container of fresh fruit and a jar of peanut butter on the counter. To my surprise, she found the blender, taking a minute to scrub the years of dust off the clear plastic. As I watched her work, I felt strange—shaky, I guess. Like I'd eaten too much sugar already. But after a second, I got caught up in her energy. As we worked together, our movements in the kitchen took on a choreography, like we danced to some silent music only we could hear.

Our fun hit a crescendo as the blender blades roared, pulverizing ice cubes and fruit, mixing it with milk and sugar. When it was done, the silence seemed to take us. Without a word, she poured two glasses and we carried them to the table. We sat and she leaned forward, asking me questions about my life.

"Do you have a girlfriend?"

"Mom, really?"

"Seriously. You're so handsome."

She asked me about grades, too. And sports. Her questions flirted with home life, but she'd stutter-step, diverting to safer topics. Until she said something about Drew that I would never forget.

"Your brother's gone," she said, looking over my head.

"What?"

Her head did a very quick shake. "He's not home."

I knew that was a recovery. I knew she meant something else. Although I wanted to let it go, to let the evening spread out until it became some new version of my life, I couldn't help myself.

"You said he was gone. What do you mean?"

"Nothing, baby," she said.

"No, seriously. Are you talking about him and Dad? About how they act together?"

"Liam, no," she said. "I just meant he wasn't home."

"He hates me," I said.

"No, he doesn't. Why would you say that?"

"He told me he does," I said.

"No, he—"

"He told me that you were dead. He made me believe that."

Her irises seemed to waver. One hand touched her forehead. "What are you talking about?"

"He told me I killed you. That I embarrass you. That I'm the reason Dad treats you like he does."

"Stop!" she snapped.

It was the first and only time my mother ever raised her voice. It cut right through my thoughts. My admonitions. Right through my heart. I blinked, and I saw my mother in a new light. I saw her fear. Her avoidance. Her need.

"I'm sorry," I whispered.

She stood up and came to me, taking my head in her arms. She hugged me to her chest. She was warm and real. I never wanted to let go.

"It'll be different," she whispered.

But she was wrong.

19

Later that evening, when we heard my father's car turning into the garage, I think we both stiffened. My mother sat on the floor in the family room, the kitten on her lap fast asleep. I looked at her and she just smiled. But as we listened to the garage door going up, I saw her picking at her nail polish.

Neither of us spoke again until the door opened and my father walked into the house. He seemed to sense something before he saw our new pet. He stopped, glancing at me first. I recognized that look, like I'd done something stupid. But then he saw the kitten. After that, all expression left his face. He appeared neither angry nor upset. He just stared at it for a second.

My mother managed a smile, which made me feel a little better.

"What do you think?" she asked.

He nodded. "Don't forget you have an early meeting tomorrow. I'll pick you up at two."

Dad walked away, back to his basement, leaving us alone with the cat.

———————

I WOKE UP the next morning with the kitten sleeping on my neck. I almost swatted at it before I realized it was him. Gently, I petted it just below his head. He arched and the rumble of his purr vibrated against my vocal cords.

When I finally got up, he followed me around for the rest of the morning. Drew didn't pay the cat any mind. When our ride showed up, I had to be careful to keep him from bolting out into the yard.

"Dad's pissed," Drew said as we walked up to his friend's Honda.

"About what? The cat?"

"What do you think?"

That was the extent of our conversation. He got into the front seat and they ignored me the rest of the way. I sat in the back looking out the window and fighting the growing dread that I felt. It lasted the entire ride and most of the day, returning twofold as I got off the bus that afternoon. I walked up to the door as slowly as I could, somehow knowing something was wrong.

My unease peaked as my fingers touched the cool brass door handle. I turned it, expecting some horrible, ghastly scene to slam through the crack in the door. Instead, the house was deadly silent. I stepped in, and for a second, thought I'd been wrong all day. Then my eyes went to where the cat tree had been when I left for school, by the bay window that looked out to the front yard. It was gone.

I moved through the empty house, noting every absence. No food. No litter box. Even the tiny colorful toys that had littered the floor were gone. There was no sign of the kitten, either, no matter how hard I searched. For a time, I just stood in the family room, debating with myself. In a very surreal way, it was like the day before had never happened.

Minutes passed. I haunted my own house, frightened to make

even the slightest sound, like each step I took might trigger the chaos that I knew would follow. I moved from the kitchen to my bedroom and then back down to the foyer. I even tiptoed down to the basement, half expecting my father to be sitting in his workshop, tinkering with some model like he always was.

Hours passed. I picked at some food while sitting at the kitchen table. I turned on the television and watched a rerun of *M*A*S*H* with the volume barely audible. The light grayed as the sun set behind the line of trees across the street. Gloom spread from room to room until I sat in darkness, the only light coming from the television as it quietly droned.

I certainly did not want my father to come home. I dreaded that moment. As for Drew, it was more complicated. He wouldn't care about that cat. Nor would he care much about the bigger nightmare that had crept to life inside my mind, the one growing with each passing minute. What I really prayed for was to see my mother walk through the door, returning from her 2:00 P.M. meeting. Smiling as if nothing had happened. Even if it meant losing that near perfect day before. I would have given it up just to see her.

At 8:00 P.M., I went up to her room. It was empty, but the bed was made. I took air in through my nose, fully expecting that sour smell to fill my head and break my heart. Instead, I smelled her perfume and nothing more.

Back downstairs, I thought about calling my father's office, but didn't. I even thought about trying to figure out where my mother's "meetings" were held. I thought that maybe I could call there. But I had no idea. So I paced, and waited, my nerves fraying with every passing second.

At 9:17 P.M., the front door swung open. I was in my room by then. I bolted out into the hallway in time to see Drew mounting the first step.

"What?" he said.

"Mom's not home," I said, my voice hoarse.

"Dad?"

I shook my head.

"Then so what. They're obviously somewhere together. Didn't she have a meeting today?"

"At two."

He shrugged. "Go to bed, Liam. And don't make a fucking big deal when they get home."

He brushed past me. I turned, watching him, filled with confusion and an ominous sadness.

AT 11:24 P.M., as I lay in the darkness with my eyes wide, the door opened again. Drew's warning filled my thoughts. I slipped from bed but didn't rush out of my room. Instead, I moved quietly to the door and opened it just a crack.

I saw her coming up the stairs. Somehow, even in the darkness, I could make out the look in her eyes. It was distant and lost, like she stood on a cliff one second before making the decision to jump. It scared me so much that I just remained kneeling on my floor, peering out as she shuffled by. I heard her muttering something to herself as she passed, but I couldn't make it out. The sound of her voice, though, shattered the moment. I threw my door open.

"Mom?" I said tentatively.

She turned. That look froze me once again. Even when her thin lips rose in a pantomimed smile.

"Hi, baby," she said, thinly.

"Where were you?"

Her head tilted. "I . . . He never picked me up."

"Dad?"

Her head shook. "Good night, baby."

That's when the smell hit me. It was faint, maybe even a trick of my mind. But it was as sour as my worst thoughts. I turned, walking back into my bedroom, and I realized she'd never said anything about the cat being gone.

20

———

You're driving in circles, Liam."

God, I just wish she would shut up. No matter what I do, she just keeps going. Keeps digging. Keeps using her words like a scalpel—careful, efficient cuts. I see why she is so good at her job. Why Drew uses her. She is the kind of weapon he loves. Subtle and deadly. Unlike me.

"Why don't you just run away? Let me out and just go. I won't tell them anything."

Her words slip into me. They gnaw at my resolve. Not just these, but everything she's piled atop me since I took the tape off. I know what she's doing. I can see right through it. She is spinning my reality into her story. But there is an allure to it, a kind of dangerous beauty. Like honey dripping from a bee's nest. No matter how much it's going to hurt, I want to grab hold of her tale. Taste its sweetness. And let it be real, for just a second. Let my life be something that it never was.

"Are you okay?" she asks softly.

Could she mean it? Could she care? I hold my breath, trying to shut her out. Keep myself focused.

"I get it, Liam. All this back-and-forth. You're just scared. But it'll be okay. I've got your back. It'll be okay."

Her hand reaches out. She touches my forearm. My tattoo. Every nerve in my body fires. My eyes shoot down.

"Don't touch me!"

Her eyes widen. And she recoils. Driving down the road, I turn on her, my words pouring over her like fire.

"He told me what he does to you."

She stiffens. "What?"

"He brags about it to me. Maybe to other people, too."

"What are you talking about?"

"I think you know what I'm talking about," I say. "There's a fine line between hurt and pain, right? Fun and danger? Excitement and fear?"

She looks at me, incredulous. "Really? This is where you're—"

"Love and shame," I finish.

She has no answer to that. I don't know the truth. He never told me anything. But I can guess. I can always guess.

"Patsy knows, too, Lauren," I say, staring at the road ahead.

Her response is silence, so much so that I can hear her breathing just audible over the sound of the car's tires on the pavement. This news shouldn't surprise her. In his arrogance, my brother did nothing to hide the affair. But from her response, I know already that it is enough. That no matter how much she knows it is the truth, that it was always going to be the truth, my brother's web has her snared. His words hold her down as much as the strength in his hard, crushing hands. His promises lay heavier on her chest. His lies surround her as visibly as the heat rising from my anger.

"And you let him do that to you," I add.

I see the nod. It is a wisp, but I see it whether she wants me to or not. And I guess that's enough. My brother has her as deeply as he's had me for so many years. I never expected anything else. At some point, she will betray me. Strange how little that seems to matter now.

21

I pull around to the back end of the apartment complex and park the Mazda beside the entrance to the access road. Coming back to this place is like stepping into my own grave. One I have spent months digging. It turns my stomach. But it's time.

With a quick look around, I get out of the car and unhook the chain that spans the trail. When I get back into the car, Lauren doesn't move. She hasn't since I laid into her. She just stares out the window again.

I don't bother putting the chain up. We won't be here long. At the top of the rise, I crack my window. I let the sound of the birds fill the car, countering her discomfort. It calms me, a little. By the time we reach the cabin, I'm refocused. I will do what I have to do. It will hurt. But I can't care about that. Not anymore.

When I park the car, she inches away from me, leaning on her closed door. I get out and head to her side. Before I reach the door, though, my phone rings. The call is from Drew's burner.

"You stay here," I say, though I'm not sure she can hear me through the closed window. Then I answer the phone. "Hello."

"We found your truck," Drew says, his voice flat and hard.

The adrenaline forces me to move. With my eyes on Lauren, I back toward the water's edge. I can hear the soft lapping of the current against the bank. It calls to me like a forbidden whisper.

"I thought you would," I say.

"You really think that lady, that shrink, is going to help you? You're such a child, Liam."

"Did you call your buddies at the station? Did you tell them it was me?"

He laughs. "Look, I don't have time for this. I have to be at a meeting at Buena Vista in fifteen minutes. Then I have dinner with Frank. I'm going to give you one chance. Get her to the trailer, now. Forget the hotel. And the rest of the plan. Just finish it. Do what you have to do. And get rid of her. Understand?"

I don't say anything. When I look back at the car, I see Lauren. She stares at me through the window. He's changing the plan. No more hotel. No more of his "fun." This means something. He never changes. He never gives up even a hint of control.

"Liam," he says, interrupting my thoughts. "Don't make me say it."

"Say what?" I snap, my voice rising.

"Say what I'll have to do if you screw me. One word and you're spending the rest of your life in prison. Does that sound good?"

I reach the lake. The sun shines off the water, white ripples rolling along the surface. I wish I could just walk out into it, let it carry me to the bottom. I wish the water would fill my lungs until I settle forever in the silt.

"Do it!" I snap back.

The line is silent. I grip my phone so tightly that I might shatter the glass and plastic. The birds continue to sing over my head, but they sound wrong now, harsh and grating. God, I hate him so much.

"Dad was right about you," he says finally. "No matter what, though, I couldn't fix it. I couldn't toughen you up. I tried. I really did."

"Why, Drew?"

"Because you were always crying about Mom. And you embarrassed him. You were always doing stupid stuff. Like that day when Mom was in the hospital and you beat that dude up. The one who was just trying to help you. Just dumb."

"Do you hate me?" I ask.

"Does it matter?"

"It does to me," I say. "Just say it outright. Just say it."

"You're so dramatic," he says.

"Why, Drew? Why do you hate me? Because I tripped you when you were ten? Is that it?"

Drew can't stop laughing. "You are such a baby, Liam. Dad was right. He came into my room that night you kicked the shit out of his model. He told me that you were my responsibility. That I had to do something about you. Or it would go bad for me."

"I don't care, Drew."

"You do," he says. "You always care. You cry and whine and crawl through life like some slug. You're pathetic. You always have been." His laughter cuts more than any words he might throw at me. "I know you're trying to screw me over. If you were even a little bit smarter, I might be worried about that. But I'm not. You know why? Because you'll mess it up. You always do."

As always, he does enough. His taunts set me afire. My vision tunnels and a feral sound rises up my throat. It turns into a scream as my arm cocks back and whips forward. The phone leaves my fingers, sailing through the air, over the water. I swear I can hear his laughter before it plunges through the sunlight and sinks to darkness.

22

After my father left Mom at her meeting, he disappeared again for days. As if emboldened by his absence, that sour smell seemed to subtly grow like an invisible yet deadly mold. It started as a hint, buried under my mother's perfume as she moved past me in the kitchen. Then I'd notice it in the hallway by her bedroom. By the next day, it had wafted down the stairs, hanging damp and thick in the foyer, rushing out to greet me every day when I came home from school.

Drew was there during that time, but he refused to speak to me. When I brought up either Mom or Dad, he simply walked away. I actually missed him telling me I was stupid or calling me a loser. Even that would have been better than shuffling through those days so full of dread that I could taste it against the back of my throat.

By the fifth day, Mom stopped leaving her room. I checked on her that evening and she was sitting up and reading a book. I have no idea where it came from. She smiled at me and patted the mattress. I walked over but didn't sit down. I couldn't. I felt like if I stopped moving for too long, the specter that haunted our house would wrap its bony fingers around my throat and laugh as it crushed my life away.

"Liam, did you feed the kitten?" she asked.

I remember feeling so cold when she said that. I blinked, unsure not only of what to say, but of what was real.

"It's gone, Mom," I whispered.

"What?"

"The cat isn't here anymore," I said.

She waved me off with her thin fingers.

"Don't be silly," she said. "Sit with me."

"Is Dad coming home?" I asked, unmoving.

"Of course. He might be late tonight, though. Work's very busy."

Slowly, I backed away from her. The smell turned my stomach. I felt dizzy and overwhelmingly nauseous. I watched my mother, praying that she didn't call me back. But dreaming that she would, and that everything would return to that oasis we lived in when she first returned from rehab.

When I reached the doorway I turned, rushing to the bathroom. I doubled over, my stomach seizing, but nothing happened. Covered in a cold sweat, I stood back up and walked out into the hallway. Drew was standing in his room. He watched me, not talking. I expected his eviscerating smile. Instead, his face remained emotionless until he shut his door between us.

ON DAY EIGHT, my father returned. Mom hadn't left her room. Nor had she eaten, even though I had taken to bringing what food I could find up to her room. I stood and watched him enter the house. For the first time, a primal anger rose inside me. I pictured rushing him, wrapping my fingers around his neck, an enactment of the dread I'd been surviving for days.

But he surprised me. I had expected him to ignore me and Mom, maybe even Drew, and disappear into his basement. Instead, he came up to me, his eyes sharp.

"Where's your mother?"

"In her room," I said.

He hurried past me. I stood frozen, listening to him rush up the stairs. My mother's door opened. Time passed, minutes, but I don't know how many. I just stood there, like things could end up differently. When he appeared, storming down the stairs, I knew.

"Call 9-1-1," he snapped. "Tell them we need an ambulance."

I didn't move fast enough. The entire thing felt so surreal, like it wasn't really happening. Then Drew joined us. My father turned to him. I expected his anger to erupt again, but it didn't.

"Come with me," my father said. "We need to help her."

He and Drew ran out of the room. My father called back to me. "Call 9-1-1."

23

*M*y phone.

I see it flying through the air. Plunging into the dark water. Sending a growing ripple back to me. I might as well hear the muffled sound of it landing atop the rusted metal roof of some abandoned SUV. Maybe the force is enough to break through, finish the erosion that the water started decades before. It could keep falling, bouncing against what remains of a seat, through a hole in the floorboard, finally reaching the cloying earth below. Where it can sink into the ground like a corpse, never to rise again.

I laugh. That's just not true. Maybe, for some, the dead stay dead. For me, that's never been the case. At the same time, hatred rides the current back to me. As do rage and fear and loneliness. It is as if all of my pain, every last shard, is dredged up from the cold, lifeless bottom. The air around me thickens with the flooding tide, threatening to choke away my life on the spot.

I spin, my skin afire. My eyes burning. My hands balling into tight fists. The passenger-side door of the Mazda swings open. I see her pale face. Her eyes as wide as mine, yet filled with fear, not rage.

Lauren stumbles, holding on to the doorframe, her feet slipping on the dirt. I lunge after her, a sound rising in my throat, grating past my teeth. It is raw and inhuman. She whimpers when she hears it.

Lauren finds her footing. She runs, sprinting away from me. With each breath, she makes a noise, too. So different from mine. But it feeds me. Like a drug. I need it. I devour it.

She rounds the car and heads back the way we came. I close the distance between us. A smile pulls at the muscles of my face, causes my teeth to click together. I thrust my arm out. Pushing her between the shoulder blades. Her feet lift off the ground and she falls. She uses her hands to brace for the impact. I see her wrist twist unnaturally to the side. She screams.

Without a word, I grab her jacket. As she cries, I lift her and drag her back toward the cabin.

24

My fingers tightened around my mother's cordless phone. I stood frozen in the kitchen, unable to put it down. Somehow, I knew it was different that time. But there was nothing I could do about it.

The sirens grew louder. Flashing lights shined through the windows at the front of the house once again. Inside, there was nothing but silence. No one moved, it seemed. I don't even think I was breathing.

Then I heard footsteps upstairs. They seemed to shake the house as someone came down the steps. Drew's voice rang out, startling me.

"They're here," he called out.

"What?" I asked.

But he didn't answer me. Instead, he ran back up to the bedrooms. Slowly, I walked out into the foyer. Glancing at the stairs, I moved instead to the window, parting the curtain. The ambulance turned onto our street.

"Move," my father said behind me.

I never heard him come down. When I turned, he looked past me, out the window. I backed away and he ran a hand through his slick hair, something I had never seen him do before. Giving it a strange little tussle. Long clumpy strands fell before one eye.

Drew came next. He stood behind my father, reminding me of some loyal dog awaiting command.

"Go out and meet them," my father said.

Drew never said a word. He just ran out of the house. My father watched from the window. I turned away from him and that's when I felt the strange pull from upstairs. It drew me closer, inch by inch. At the bottom of the steps, I turned, expecting my father to berate me for being in the way. But he didn't, so I continued up, shuffling down the hallway, closer and closer to my mother's room.

The smell had changed. At first, it reminded me of the woods out back. When the leaves have fallen and it rained. Sweet and putrid, as the old decays under the new. The sour smell was still there, under this new layer. The two became a physical barrier, stopping me a few feet from the doorway.

I heard my father's voice. At first, I wasn't sure it was him. It sounded foreign, unnatural.

"She's upstairs," he said.

I'd heard that tone before. When Marci Simmons first visited. It was subservient, passive, like some mockery of caring. It unnerved me more than the smell. Pushing past the barrier, I moved forward, more to be away from him, this new him, than to see her.

"She was going to meetings. She seemed better," my father said, his voice cracking. "I didn't know what to do. Please help her."

I reached the doorway. Footsteps rushed through the front door. My fingers wrapped around the cold door handle as the paramedics reached the bottom of the stairs. I turned it. The door swung open. The foul air struck me across the face. Behind me, my father continued to talk. Continued to snivel and whine like some terrible parody of a real human being.

My mother's lamp was on. The light shined across her face at an artistic angle, deepening the contours of one eye and sharpening the bone of her cheek. Her mouth seemed set in a soft, embarrassed smile. I took a step closer, wanting to brush a wisp of dark hair off the impossibly pale skin of her forehead.

"The room at the end of the hall," someone said behind me, maybe Drew.

I moved quickly, going to her, sitting on the side of the bed like she had asked. It was cold, and a darkness seemed to surround me, like the rest of the room simply ceased to exist. As my hand reached for her, I took in all the colors that painted my mother's death. Her iridescent skin. The sharp contrast of the shadows. Red fingernails at the end of limp, skeletal fingers. A blue blanket I had never seen before covering her up to her exposed collarbone. The twinkling reflection of light across the surface of a clear glass bottle, upended beside a damp circle on the textured carpet.

"Son."

I reached for her. Her forehead felt like a stone polished for centuries by icy water. My tears transformed the painting of her death, clouding the edges as if an impressionist painted over reality in soft circles of life and emptiness.

"Son."

With all my heart I prayed that it was my father who had used that word. I imagined him standing in the room, his arms open to me, his eyes sharing my grief. But when I turned, a stranger in a dark uniform stood beside me.

"We need you to move," the man said.

I did. I ran from the room. I ran from my father, my brother, and what I felt they had done to my mother. I ran, vowing never to come back. Never to subject myself to them. I ran to be free, but real life doesn't exactly work like that.

25

Her feet kick at the dirt. Mud splatters her shins and the bottoms of her exercise pants. I don't let Lauren get her feet under her. Instead, I pull her up the ragged steps and onto the porch of the cabin. At the door, I let her fall to the planked floor.

"You move and I'll fucking kill you," I say.

With an eye on her, I unfasten the padlock and push the door open. The smell rolls out over me, earthy and thick. There is a cloying hint of death that sticks to the skin of my face and burns my eyes. I don't know if it was there earlier, or any other time I entered the cabin. It might be in my head, in fact. But it makes me angry.

"Get up," I say, standing over her.

She freezes, so I grab her by the arm. Right where she showed me her bruises. She flinches but I pull her up and push her into the cabin. Lauren stutter-steps, but I push her again, toward the tarp.

"I'm sorry," she cries.

I grab her by the back of her jacket, pulling her now. I bring her down, forcibly, closer. My hand rises, getting a fistful of her shining black hair. It is soft and perfect against my fingertips, which just makes me clench tighter. She whimpers as I reach down and slip my other hand under the tarp.

I push her head down. Closer, closer. The tarp comes up. The first bone appears from under the plastic. It is more black than ivory. A femur. Even she must know it is human by the size. I stare at it for a second. It bores into me. Right to my soul. But I don't have time for that.

The tarp folds over. And the remains sit on the floor in a haphazard pile. Atop the ribs and the bones of an arm, the top half of a skull stares darkly back at us, like oblivion rests just inside those empty sockets. The detached jawbone hangs at a jaunty angle. Like it's laughing at us. At me.

My fingers somehow tighten, nearly pulling the hair from her scalp. I force her lower. Closer.

"Look at it!"

She fights, trying to turn her head. Her eyes are closed. She keeps making that sound. Where it drove me insane earlier, now it just grates. Making me even angrier. I push harder. Her nose is an inch away from the skull.

"*Look at it!*" I scream.

PART THREE

HER PLAN

1

*L*ook at it!”

Lauren's eyes shoot open. A fiery red flush sweeps across her cheeks. She's shaking now. Crying and choking. She stammers and sputters. Her eyes close again.

“*Look!*”

Something snaps inside me. It is as if I have spent my entire life building millions of fragile walls. The sound of her fear. The whimpers of pain. The feeling of struggle against the muscles of my forearm, it all crashes over me, over the walls, right to my core. And that core is nothing more than a damaged child. As such, I lash out. I don't want to. Nor should I. But I'm not calling the shots. My past is.

I shake her and scream. She cries out, louder. I push her. Her skin touches the bones. I feel her revulsion against the back of my hand. Her eyes close. I let them stay that way.

Maybe I hold her there too long. Longer than I need to. Maybe I want her to know. To understand. To experience just a hint of our life.

Or maybe I'm lost. I'm not as strong as I think I am. Maybe the flood of emotion is too much. I am caught up in it. Swept away by the current. Barely breathing as it takes me farther and faster until the cold, dark end.

My fingers untangle from her hair. I lean back on my haunches, my hand moving away from her head. She backs away from the bones, slowly, tentatively. Her head turns but she doesn't stand. Instead, she kneels on the floor, listless, lifeless. All her silken words are gone now. She is a victim now. Just like all of us.

2

If I had been stronger back then, when I was young, things might have been different. I might have stood up to my father the day she died. I could have lashed into him, blamed him for, at the very least, ignoring my mother's disease. Letting her die. Yet, even then, from the moment I saw her pale, lifeless face, I decided it was far worse than that. I decided he had killed her.

I wasn't strong, though. Instead, I returned to my home like a ghost. I haunted the drama unfolding in the house, the frantic work of the paramedics, my father's sudden outpouring of caring words. I drifted among the living, feeling closer to her than to them. Eventually, I slipped away, past the rattle of the heavy stretcher as it rolled out the front door, up to my bedroom. I stepped in and closed the door. But I didn't move. I simply stood alone in the dark.

The hive of activity that had descended upon my father's return home never seemed to end. The ambulance left and the neighbors arrived. My father spoke gravely to people over the phone, accepting their condolences with the words of a heavy heart. My brother played the strong son, always at his side, lowering his head as people spoke fondly about a woman they could not have known.

I emerged only out of necessity. My hood drawn around my burning cheeks, I walked the hall like it was another dimension. I could see and hear this world, but it passed me as if I was nothing more than air. I didn't eat. I don't think I drank. Instead, I sat on the edge of my bed listening to the cadence of heavy conversations through the thin walls of my room.

Sometime past midnight, the house quieted. I waited, for how long I am not certain. Eventually, I rose and slipped downstairs. Cold, fresh air blew against my face as I stepped into the foyer. In the front room, the curtains billowed out.

Even today, as things seem to barrel toward a full circle, I relive this exact moment. I stood, my bare feet on the frigid tile. My eyes closed, I tilted my head back. I took that cold air in through wide nostrils. Up until that moment, I had wanted my old mother back. That sweet, beautiful woman who held a gypsy moth on the end of her finger. Yet, as I smelled the sterile emptiness that would swallow my life, I found myself aching for my mother's sour scent instead.

THE NEXT NIGHT, a man in a black suit visited. He and my father sat at the kitchen discussing the funeral arrangements.

"She would like that," my father said, and my blood boiled.

I took a step back, away from the corner from which I had been eavesdropping. A hand landed on my shoulder and I jumped.

"Where have you been?"

I spun around to find Drew. He was dressed in real clothes, not his typical lacrosse shorts and sweatshirt. I felt oddly little, even though I could almost look him in the eye by then.

"What?"

"Dad's been looking for you."

"Me?"

The look of disgust on my brother's face as he pushed past me might have crushed me if I hadn't felt so off-balance. I remember trying to make sense of what he said, asking myself if my father had been looking for me. Could that be possible?

I stood there, frozen, as my brother entered the kitchen. My father introduced him. The man in the suit, like everyone else, offered his condolences. I took a step toward them, feeling the need to join this, to be a part of my family. But I couldn't. No one wanted me in there. No one cared whether I lived or died.

So, instead, I slipped back up to my bed and waited. For what, I had no idea. Not yet.

3

Lauren and I hover near each other like betrayed lovers. As if our intimacy, turned dark and dangerous, is now over. And neither of us knows what to think. How to feel. I look away, at the crumbling walls of this long-forgotten building. She stares at the floor, anything not to see what I have done.

Like so many times before, when I feel the adrenaline seeping from my body, I try to find the innocence. I reach out for those moments of childhood that invoke the nostalgia I hear others speak of. I try to re-create some cliché of a relationship between me and my big brother. We'd run through the neighborhood, laughing and wrestling in the clover. We'd sit in the darkness watching a movie on the television, one that our father never would have allowed us to see. We'd whisper and conspire while playing cards for hours.

Those things aren't real. They didn't happen. I think they didn't. But when I press, when I try to be sure, the images slip away like sand through my fingers. The memories behind me fade away. I try to focus on Drew's face. He is on one knee before me, my shoelaces wrapped around his fingers. I look up at him and I feel something so real, so primal. Maybe it is something, as the older brother, he has never felt. He is just a boy, yet my eyes see him so differently. I see a force, something almost inhuman. I watch his every move and my fingers mimic without my knowing. I see the size of his hand compared to mine. I see his straight back and his thin smile. He speaks, telling me a story about a rabbit and a hole, and each word changes me, but not in any way he can know. I let his voice wrap around me and all I can do is wish that one day I can be as strong, as smart, as brave, as cool.

I have heard people say that they do not want to be a role model. That they never asked for someone to look up to them in awe. In those words, I have heard the fear of responsibility, the rawness of guilt. Maybe no one wants their every action scrutinized. No one wants to feel like they have to be perfect for someone else's benefit. Their hesitancy means nothing, though. For they have no more choice in the matter than those looking up to them in the first place. No one chooses to be a role model. And no one chooses who their role model may be. Instead, people pass through our lives. Some like weather, changing things, sometimes turning things upside down, yet leaving nothing permanent behind, like they never existed. Others pass through like time, leaving nothing behind unchanged. For those, their presence, their influence, simply grows, merging with our souls, making us who we are, like words make up the past.

Why couldn't it end there? Why couldn't I just freeze time? I could sit on the forest floor, looking up at my big brother, worshipping him like an idol. His strength could mold me into the man I should have been. His caring could have guided me as a husband. His patience as a father. If only it had ended in that moment. If only one of us had died right then and there. Then, maybe, things would be different. Maybe not perfect, but better.

4

———

Virginia Brennan is the love of my life. She was my high school sweetheart. The mother of my two boys. Together we built a home. And promised to share it forever.

"She was kind and thoughtful. Smart and compassionate. She loved to read under the covers on winter mornings. Some of you might know that she played piano like an angel. And she was the best teacher I have ever known.

"But there were sides to my wife that very few people knew. She flared with a wild joy, like a summer carnival. Like a burning flame. But like both, time would pass and the light would flare out. And the darkness would fall over her. Over all of us.

"Virginia was stolen from us. She was pulled away bit by bit. The demons that haunted her never truly let go. They dug their claws in deeply. Even in the end, when a glimmer of hope returned, they stormed back, laughing and screaming and tearing. They stole her from us.

"Alcohol. Maybe I shouldn't name the beast here, in this church, in front of so many people. Maybe, instead, it should remain in the shadows, sheltered safely behind shame and pain. But I can't do that. I can't let it have that final victory. It took our Virginia away. And I pray that she be its last and final victim."

I sat in a wooden pew as unforgiving as my thoughts. Drew was near me, strong and stoic, a constant reminder of everything I wasn't. Neighbors filled the seats to my right and behind. They listened in rapt silence to my father's eloquent eulogy. Nodding along. Brushing away tears with furtive fingers. As he fed on their emotions, all I felt was anger and hate.

THE PEOPLE IN that church followed us home. They mingled through the rooms of my house, speaking softly and taking sips of cola and fruit juice. I moved among them, my arms limp at my sides and my throat so dry that I fought the need to cough every minute. And I stared at my brother as he strode at our father's side, chest out and eyes bright, his face a pantomime of grief.

I wandered from room to room, avoiding them as I moved among relative strangers eating sandwiches and potato salad that someone else had brought over. Having loosened my tie and unbuttoned the top of my white dress shirt, I continued to tug at the fabric like it threatened to strangle the life out of me. I moved slowly, silently. Sometimes, I would catch myself up on the balls of my feet.

An adult stopped me. I honestly had no idea who she was.

"Are you okay?" the woman asked.

"Yeah," I muttered, looking at the floor.

"Do you need . . . ?"

Then my father was there, Drew by his side. He spoke to her with gravitas. When I glanced up, I saw the way he affected this stranger. She fell under the spell and left feeling like the Brennan family would rise like a phoenix. To do more than simply survive; to conquer the world.

As he spoke, my eyes darted left and right. I searched for her without realizing that was what I did. But Marci Simmons wasn't there. She hadn't come to save me. Like everyone else's, her pity turned to indifference once she left our house that day.

When my father was done and the strangers left, so did my family. I watched as my father's hand came to rest on Drew's shoulder. My eyes burned. My stomach tightened to the point that I felt dizzy. I stared, the edges of my world fading into a bloody red haze. And I hated them both. A deep unrelenting hate, unlike anything I had ever felt before.

5

Without a word, I stand. Lauren still won't look at me. But I don't want to touch her. Not again. Ever.

"Come on," I say, my voice harsh.

And to my surprise, she rises, straightening her glasses. I grab her bag as I head to the door. Like a ghost, she seems to float along behind me, out of the cabin and down the steps. We move like halves of a long-married couple, separating without a word, Lauren going to the passenger side of the Mazda. I climb behind the wheel and start the engine. We drive away from the cabin and I know that she will never come back to this place. But I will, soon.

When I reach the apartment parking lot, I get out of the car and replace the chain. I can't have anyone finding the cabin at this point. Not after everything. When I turn back to the car, I see Lauren watching me. But her eyes are vacant. Staring past me, maybe back up the road. Back to what she saw under the tarp.

I get in and drive. She doesn't ask where we are going. And she sits as far away from me as she can. I can't care about that now. Any more than I could before. So I let the familiar roads guide me until I reach the entrance. I see her stiffen when I turn onto it and we pass the sign.

ALL SAINTS CEMETERY

I keep driving, moving along the bottom of a gentle rise. Head-stones spring from the perfectly kept grass like the fingers of the dead, all pointing up to a perfect blue sky. As I always do, I read some of the names as I pass.

MARION SMITH

JEFF LEVINSON

PATRICIA CAMPBELL

The road splits. It runs in a long one-way loop. I take the right side and follow it. A single car sits not far from the fork. I see a woman tending a grave near the tree line. She seems to be talking to herself. I drive past her, craning my neck.

At the far side of the loop, I pull to a stop. As I get out of the car, I grab Lauren's bag from where I placed it in the back. She still won't look at me. And her legs are shaking.

I stand outside the rented Mazda for a moment, Lauren's bag dangling from one finger. So many memories flood my consciousness, like a mudslide of smells and sights, colors and jagged strikes of emotion. I see the shade of my brother standing over me, fists balled and bruised. I feel the weight of my father crushing me, reshaping me to his will. I look down at my hands, large and callused. At the tattoo, at the phantom stain of blood that it has never been able to truly cover. I look up to the top of the rise, at the stone I've visited so many times. I miss her so much.

6

After my mother's funeral, the weeks passed and my rage grew. Every word my father spoke to Drew cut through me, tearing through old scars and leaving me weaker and more alone. My emotions pulled in so many directions. One minute, I would despise everything about my father, blaming him for Mom's death and for everything that had gone wrong in my life. The next, I would yearn for the attention he gave to my brother. I would pore over my psyche, trying to find what was so wrong with me, what part of my person caused everyone to shy away in disgust. I tore at myself as much as I hated them, silently crying in the darkness of my room and slamming my fist into the cinder-block walls of the basement when no one was home.

These feelings festered and burned. Simmering up but remaining below the surface for a time. Then one night, the most mundane act sent me over the edge. My father came home with a pizza. He called Drew and me down. I sat at the counter as my father lifted the box top so my brother could pull out a slice. Then he closed it without even a glance in my direction.

Of all the things that had happened in that house—all of the pain and the loneliness and the confusion—it was that pizza that broke my back. It was as if I slipped out of my own body as I leaned across my father, slamming my shoulder into his arm as I reached for the box. He staggered back. Maybe he just didn't expect the contact. Maybe I caught him off-balance. But I moved him, easily. A horrible feeling of strength surged through me. He glared at me and for the first time I saw a damaged, frail old man instead of the domineering force of my past.

Our eyes met. I swore that he felt it, too. And in that moment, maybe his anger and hatred matched mine. Even as I considered this, though, I looked to Drew. The envy I felt, though I still can't understand it, burned even darker. And maybe my father saw that, as well.

"When's your game tomorrow, Andrew?" he asked.

Drew looked up from his pizza. "Tomorrow . . . ? Three."

He nodded. "Great. I can cut out of work early. I'm looking forward to it. Understand it's a big one."

Drew looked utterly confused. His eyes shifted for just an instant, looking to me as if he was putting the pieces of a puzzle together.

"Conference rivals," he said.

My hand hit the table harder than I meant it to as I quickly rose from my seat. The sound echoed through the kitchen. It may have rattled the window over the sink. Yet neither my brother nor my father even flinched as I stormed away.

AT THREE O'CLOCK the next morning, I rose from my bed. I had not slept for a minute. My mind had raged, plotted, and fantasized, eventually settling on something I had never truly considered before.

It started with Carter. How my father had reacted that day. Then I saw him standing outside with my mother. I remembered how he had devoured that neighbor's attention. My mother's funeral. The look of hunger in my father's eyes.

Then it came back to me. I remembered the one time that my father turned on Drew. The one time he spoke to Drew the way he spoke to me. It was when I beat that stranger up. When the police brought me home. Their car parked out front. The lights flashing for everyone to see.

I told you, he screamed, *to make sure he stops embarrassing this family.*

More of my father's words came back to me then. Words from the day when I was ten and I hit Carter with a stick.

This is my neighborhood. I work hard so we can live here. And I'm not going to have the mothers telling stories about my son.

I closed my eyes again and I saw my hands wrapped in athletic tape. The vision felt so real. Like it was happening in the moment, all over again.

Why would my hands be taped?

As the question formed in my head, I felt it. I felt the first slamming into the side of my head. I felt my brain shifting, compressing against my skull. I felt the cement floor, painted blood-red and as cold as ice, striking the side of my face.

My eyes opened and the darkness was gone. My bedroom was gone. I was in the basement. Instead of looking up at the ceiling fan above my bed, I was looking at Drew's face, and that thin half smile. At his fists, taped like mine, balled up and threatening between us. The cold basement floor against the bottom of my feet. And my father's half smile as he watched.

No!

The dream, if that is what it was, flashed back into the ether. Although disoriented, I was back in my room. I rose from my bed, an eerie calm falling over me. I made no sound as I moved out of my bedroom and into Drew's. It was dark, but I could see him in his bed. I could make out his face through the gloom. His eyes were closed. He breathed with such a slow regularity that the envy flared again.

How can he sleep so peacefully?

I pushed it down and stepped up to the side of the bed. I hovered over him, my fists balling up at my sides, and I pictured my fingers wrapping around his throat.

7

Still lost in thought, I move over to the passenger-side door and open it. Lauren gets out. I dig through her bag and find her phone.

"I need your passcode."

She just looks at me. My hand reaches behind my back. She flinches. The code, 1-1-0-5-7-1, spills out of her mouth. It sits in my head, each number like a blinding light. It is my brother's birthday. I look at her and fight the urge to really see who Lauren is. For all her bravado. For all her intelligence and strength. She is no different from me. She is just another one of his victims.

In truth, it just doesn't matter anymore. So I enter the code and the phone unlocks. Then I hand her the bag. She takes it, her eyes locked on the pavement. I go into her messages and the first thing I see is Drew's name. Even now, I am tempted to open the thread, read their story. Maybe I could understand what she saw in him. What everyone does. For a second, I wonder if I could be wrong. If I've made all this up. If what I believe to be true is just more lies. How could I know if it was?

Taking a deep breath, I open a new message. I type in the number and, to my surprise, it shows up in Lauren's contacts. Seeing the name appear on her screen turns my stomach, but my jaw tightens and I just send the text.

This is Liam. It's time. Meet me at the emergency location. As soon as you can.

When I'm done, I look at Lauren. Her eyes avert, flipping back toward the ground. I slip her phone into my front pocket.

"Up there," I say.

She looks up at the stone, then back at me. Her eyes are red-rimmed and cloudy with tears. I nod, and she starts walking. I follow her close behind. A soft breeze picks up, running up the rise, blowing hair before my eyes. I brush it away and take a deep breath. It smells of pine and dried leaves. Like Halloween day, full of anticipation and a vague, unexplainable dread. I wonder, for just a second, if I would go back in time if I could. Return to my childhood, to the memories that ride that wind. Regardless of everything, how bad things were, where the years led, I think I would. Maybe just for a day. Just to feel that potential again. The chance that things could be good. Maybe.

Before I realize it, I am already standing beside her stone. I kneel, my hand running along the smooth, cold edge. I had intended to take a picture of Lauren in front of the grave. Then send it to my brother from her phone. Just another jab at him. But it suddenly feels wrong to me.

"Hi, Mom," I say.

The breeze answers me, slipping under my jacket and running up my spine. I feel at peace, in a way. But sad as well. I dig through the past, pulling at my oldest memories. It is there that I find her at her best, tall and straight, jet hair tied back in blue-and-white silk. I see her deep, big eyes, clear and bright. I see her smiling mouth, painted a shocking red. I hear my name on her lips, loving and so real that it hurts beyond belief.

A tear fills one eye. It is pain. And sadness. But also frustration, anger. I let it sit there, clouding my vision so that I don't forget. I look at the face of her stone.

VIRGINIA EVANS BRENNAN
1948–1986

Nothing else is etched on the marker. No mention of being a loving mother. A wife. A daughter or sister. My eyes lock on to that one word, EVANS, and I remember her rare but beautiful stories about a family I never knew. I should have looked for them. Maybe they would have welcomed me, taken me in as their own. I could have joined that family. Why hadn't I thought to try?

Because that's a dream. This is real. As I remind myself of that simple truth, I feel a pressure against my lower back. Something slides up against my skin, catching on the waistband of my pants.

Reality slams into me. I jerk up, spinning, and look down the barrel of my own gun.

8

That night, standing in the darkness and looking down at my brother in his bed, I didn't do it. I didn't try to kill him. I didn't even touch him. I just stood over him, watching him sleep for a time, and the pieces of the plan simply fell into place. I remembered that day I tripped him. The day I hit Carter with that stick. The police. The funeral. Our neighbors. And I knew exactly what I was going to do.

It took effort, but I pulled my attention off my sleeping brother. But I didn't leave his room. Not right away. Instead, I moved to the far corner, where I knew he kept his lacrosse equipment. As my fingers wrapped around his crosse, I thought about what my father had said at dinner. I pictured him in the stands, feeding on the sympathetic glances and the words of condolence from all the other parents like some parasitic vampire.

I pulled the stick out of his nylon bag without making a sound. With it in hand, I snuck out of his room and down the stairs. I eased the front door open. The cold night air cut through the white T-shirt I wore to sleep. It probably glowed under the moon but I guess I didn't really care. Or maybe I wanted to get caught. I just don't know.

Like a ghost, I moved through the night. I wandered down the street, looking at the dark windows of our neighbors. I imagined them waking up in the morning, having breakfast together. Talking about their days. Sharing their triumphs and fears.

As I passed each house, I stopped feeling like the specter and felt more and more like the haunted. These lives that surrounded me hurt. They seemed so perfect. So blessed compared to mine. They scraped and clawed at me every day, every smiling face, every loving hug, every look of pity. I just needed it to stop.

Up ahead, the biggest house in the neighborhood rose at the top of a steep, perfectly manicured slope. I knew that the Clarksons lived there. Their boys, Eric and Billy, were star athletes. Presidents of their classes. Their father a successful lawyer. And their mother, Mrs. Clarkson, the biggest busybody in the neighborhood.

Eric's new car, a blue BMW, sat parked against the curb. He'd just gotten it when Hopkins offered him a free ride to play lacrosse. He was my brother's rival in all things. So I smiled as I reared back and swung the lacrosse stick at the driver's-side window. It struck the glass and bounced off, barely leaving a scratch. I lashed out, slamming the stick into the glass over and over again. My mouth opened and I let out a howl like nothing I had heard before. I just kept swinging and swinging, harder and harder. I turned the stick and used the end. When the window finally shattered, I fell forward, my shoulder slamming into the frame. Beads of glass rained down to the pavement and I started to laugh. I couldn't stop. My entire body shook as the sound just crashed out of my chest, filling the night air.

The car alarm shrieked to life, harmonizing with my manic laughter. I felt so high. So invincible as I left the stick in the front seat and sprinted all the way home.

9

"Don't move."

Lauren's voice quivers. So does the hand holding my gun. But her finger slips into the trigger guard as if she's done it before. I stand frozen before her, but not for the reason she thinks. Instead, my brother's voice fills my head, not hers.

You're an idiot, Liam.

Don't be stupid, Liam.

This is why I lose every time. This is why he wins. Drew never makes mistakes. Like a machine, he does everything right.

"Give me the keys," Lauren says, her voice changing with each word.

Since seeing the bones, Lauren has looked lost. But right in front of me, I see her transform. Her back straightens. Her hands stop shaking. A smirk lifts one side of her mouth. And I realize that, at least to her, she is back in control. She's calling the shots again, and she seems to feed on that power.

"No," I answer flatly.

She takes a step back, but the look on her face doesn't change. Her voice sounds shrill and too loud, but the smirk remains.

"I'll do it, Liam. You don't know me. You don't know what I'm capable of."

"Maybe I do," I say.

She blinks. It's my turn to smile.

"Maybe I know exactly what you're capable of. Words. That's it, Lauren. That's all you have. And you use them to get what you want. Words are power. But only for so long. Then they fade away, and you're left with the truth."

"The truth?" She scoffs. "Like how you want to screw your own sister-in-law. Or how you live in a pathetic trailer down by the river. The truth, Liam, is that you're a loser. You've always been a loser. Nothing more than that. You're not some kind of tragic hero. Some misunderstood artist. You're just trash. And for some reason, your brother refuses to throw you out."

I absorb her words. They shake inside me, down to the core. I need to know if they are true. If my memories are real. I will, soon enough. That's what this is all about, really.

I take a step toward her. She takes a half step back. My head is spinning. But I don't feel angry, which surprises me. Instead, I'm just so tired.

"Give me the keys," she repeats. "And my phone."

I stare into her eyes. "Why do you let him hurt you?"

She shudders. It is slight, barely noticeable. I recognize it immediately, though. In a way, it is like looking into a mirror.

"It doesn't get better, Lauren. It never will. I know you want it to. I know you see this picture of him. He's strong and bold. Some force just draws you closer. Makes you want to stand near him. Be a part of whatever it is he's doing. That's why he makes the perfect politician. That charisma just radiates out from him like ripples in the water. But then you get too close. You get to the center. The real Drew rises to the surface, and you see the darkness for the first time. You explain it away. You convince yourself. But when the truth comes out, you're left lying there, feeling dirty and raw and empty. Like the world is staring at your shame. What is it that keeps you there? Lets you hang around until the next time?"

"You don't know what you're talking about," she says, after another shuffle back down the rise, back toward the Mazda. "Just give me the keys . . . and my phone. Or I swear, I'll—"

"Does he tell you about our father? Does he mention him?"

"Shut up! Goddamn it. Just shut up. Who do you think you are? Trying to enlighten me about the truth after all the shit you've done? Wake up. It's over. I'm going to call the cops—"

"No, you're not."

"What?"

"You're not calling the cops. You're going to run back to him. Fall down at his feet and cry. Because he's calling the shots. You aren't. He's in control." I pull the keys out of my pocket. "Go ahead. Go run back to him. You can take the car. Just go. Tell him—"

"Give me my phone," she snaps.

My eyes narrow. She's standing in front of me, pointing a gun in my face. She's been abducted. She's seen the remains. But she's going to stand here and tell me to give her the phone. She could leave. I'd let her. But the arrogance. The righteousness. It sparks the fire. I take another step toward her. Toward the gun.

"You think you're so smart. So superior. You grew up in your perfect little house. Your parents told you how great you were every day. How you could do anything you wanted to do. That the world was yours. Your dad bought you that Jetta. Probably those perfect white teeth, too. It was all so easy for you, wasn't it?"

I move closer. Her eyes widen. She starts to back up, but I notice her hands are shaking again.

"Stay back," she says.

"What are you going to do, shoot me?"

I move quickly, swallowing the space between us in one smooth thrust. I feel the barrel of the gun strike my cheek. And I keep moving. Keep pushing into it. The force of it moves her finger inside the guard. It flirts with the trigger.

"Stop!" she screams.

"Do it!" I scream back.

She stumbles but keeps her balance. I keep going. The cold metal against my skin feels real. But nothing else does.

"Shoot," I say. "Just do it. Do it!"

"I will. I'll—"

"Do it!"

I could reach out and take the gun. I know I could. It would be easy. In a way, I think she wants me to. Action isn't Lauren's game. It's mine. And Drew's.

But maybe I just want her to do it. To end this all. I can feel my mother's headstone behind me, like eyes on my back. It pulls, tugs me back off the ledge. But my momentum can't be stopped. Nothing can stop it, I think.

"Just do it," I whisper, reaching out. I grab Lauren by the front of her jacket. "Please."

"Stop! Let go!"

Her finger moves on its own this time. It touches the trigger. It stiffens. She's ready. I can feel it. My eyes close. And I see her. Her face appears before me. I try to cry out. To apologize for my weakness. For not being able to protect her. But it's over now. Finally.

"Just do it," I say. And a smile forms, despite everything.

10

Eric Clarkson's father rang our doorbell at 7:00 A.M. the morning after I smashed his son's car window. I had been sitting in my bed, vibrating from lack of sleep and a sense of what I was sure would be a raging storm. So when I heard the bell, I sprang to my feet, my entire body shaking with fear or excitement or dread. Whatever it was, whatever was to come, I think I wanted it. Like I needed it all out in the open, something real that I could confront and survive. Or not.

I thought I would just stand up in the hallway and listen. But I found myself moving to the stairs, taking each step downward as silently as I could. In contrast, my father's steps from the kitchen into the foyer seemed to rock the foundation of the house like a series of earthquakes.

He didn't see me as he opened the door. But I could see Mr. Clarkson. He was my father's height, but larger. Where Dad's face was gaunt and tightly drawn, his was prominent and full. His thick chin jutted like mine would one day.

At first, my father stood his ground. His back was straight and his shoulders back. He may have smiled, which would be typical when around the neighbors, but I couldn't see his face.

Mr. Clarkson, though, did not. His mouth was sharp and set. I don't even think Dad noticed Drew's lacrosse stick in his right hand.

My father spoke first, his tone friendly and mildly inquisitive. "Hey, Jeff?"

Mr. Clarkson did not speak right away. Instead, he lifted his arm, holding the stick between them. My father's head tilted as he looked at it. But he made no move to take it from Mr. Clarkson's hand.

"Is something wrong?" he asked.

When he finally spoke, our neighbor's voice sounded like he could barely contain a desire to rip my father's head off.

"I found this in my son's car," he said, his teeth barely parting.

"I—"

"The window was smashed in," he continued.

Like I said, I couldn't see my father's face. I imagine that moment as if I could, though. He must have been dumbfounded. Desperately wanting to think I had done it. If Mr. Clarkson had left it at that, maybe Dad could have convinced himself. But that's not how it happened.

"I'm tired of your son's shit, Patrick," Mr. Clarkson said. "Eric's been putting up with it for years. What, does he think he can bully my son out of the starting lineup? Is that it? Is that how you raised him?"

My father's shoulders slumped. He took a step back.

"I . . . I don't know . . ."

"Get him under control. Or you'll be dealing with me. You understand that?"

Mr. Clarkson thrust the stick into my father's hands. He bumbled it and it fell to the ground, awkwardly striking the threshold before hitting him in the shin.

"And you're paying for the damn window," our neighbor said as he turned and walked away.

My father didn't move. His hands hung limp at his sides. It didn't even look like he was breathing. Then, as if nothing had happened, he reached out and slowly shut the door. When he turned, I saw his face and I guess I knew. His eyes were as fiery as his cheeks. Sweat shined on his forehead. The muscle above his left cheek twitched. Worst of all, he never blinked as he stared right through me. His yell shattered the stillness, rattling my skull.

"Andrew!"

My eyes widened. I turned and looked up the stairs, every nerve in my body firing at once. I had never heard my father speak like that, even to me. For it to be directed at my brother, I can't fully explain how that felt. Maybe like a child waking up Christmas morning to find stacks of beautiful presents under the tree, only to remember that his parents can't afford all of it. That these amazing gifts, all addressed to him, will break them, break all of them.

Drew appeared at the top of the steps. He stood there and I saw the look of confusion on his face. What surprised me, though, was that he didn't look at our father. He stared at me. I started to shake, more on the inside than out. I had a second to think he would launch himself down the stairs, tear my eyes out, rend my face to strips of bloody skin, all with that thin half smile on his face.

That never happened. None of it. My father yelled his name again and Drew startled. He hurried down the stairs, his mouth agape. I think he tried to say something, maybe a question, but I don't know. Because my father went at him. He crossed the foyer to the steps as my brother reached the bottom. He never slowed. Instead, his fist reared back and he struck Drew in the face, either his orbit or the ridge between his eyes.

The back of Drew's foot caught on the step and he went down. My father kept coming. He threw himself atop my brother, grabbing the front of his shirt and screaming into his face.

"How dare you embarrass me like that!"

He shook Drew and my brother's head struck the edge of one of the steps. His eyes looked unfocused, dazed. But my father just kept screaming and screaming. He rained down obscenities and kept repeating that Drew had embarrassed him.

"Don't you think? Are you that stupid? What? You expect me to drive through the neighborhood now, with everyone looking at me, thinking how bad a parent I am, how I have no control over my own son. Is that it?"

His fist reared back, but he didn't strike Drew again. Instead, his rant ended abruptly. My father let go of my brother's shirt and pushed himself upright. He stared down at Drew for a second, shaking his head. Then he turned and walked slowly away.

I stood there, finding myself suddenly alone with my brother. I couldn't take my eyes off him. He looked battered and broken on the steps, weaker than I ever imagined he could. Our eyes met. I saw his tears. And he knew I did.

That moment stretched out. After everything, after all the years of him towering over me, beating me down with his words, with his smile, you would think I ate the moment up. I should have devoured his pain, the fear in his eyes, the shock dripping off him like a sickness. But I didn't. Instead, I felt an overwhelming panic. I fought the urge to cover my face, cower away from him. I imagined him flying off the steps, coming at me as I thought he would before. I couldn't have been more wrong, though.

Drew did get up, yet his movements were sluggish and unthreatening. He stared at me. He took a step toward me. And his hand did come up. I even flinched, but he didn't strike me. Instead, he reached out, and—I can never forget this—he touched my face. His palm felt like fire against my cheek. But that smile was gone. His eyes looked full of a pain I never expected.

"You're not alone, Liam," he said, and in my hunger, I accepted his emotions as real. I lived this moment like it wasn't just another move in our timeless game. "I promise that you're not alone. We'll stand up to him. Together."

11

---

*J*ust do it.

I'm ready. And it's okay. Maybe it's better this way. But then I hear her voice.

"Lauren."

It seems to lift up from deep inside my dreams. My eyes open and I see that Lauren has heard it, too. It's real. She's here.

It's not over. Maybe I knew it couldn't be. Not here. Not now. I stepped up to that line between life and death. I felt my will slipping away. But the truth is that I already crossed it, a long time ago. And everything since then has been a dream. Like someone else pulling the strings that move me through this game with my brother. That drag me ever forward, no matter how painful each step has been.

I look at Lauren. I see her eyes wide with shock. I think about what I've done to her. How I've treated her. I hurt her, physically. I can still feel her hair between my fingers. I can still see her skin touching those rotting bones. I can still feel the thrill of it. And it sickens me.

That is not who I am. I know that. I don't want to hurt anyone. I never have. I've just wanted to be normal. To feel smart. Strong. For so long, I looked up to my brother and just wanted to be him. But that was before I understood that I didn't have to be. I could be myself. I could be kind without being weak. I could be quiet without being soft.

As I look at her, I can feel the years behind me. They tickle the back of my neck, teasing. They shed away and I see Drew. My father. My mother. Like they are standing right in front of me. And I wonder: *Did I understand? Is it real? Or have I made it all up?*

"Put the gun down," she says.

And Lauren does. As it lowers, I reach out, gently wrapping my fingers around the barrel. Her grip loosens and she lets me take the pistol from her. I look at it for a second, the way it fits my hand, and I wonder if I could have done it. Could I have pulled the trigger? I just don't know.

Letting the air out of my lungs, I slip the gun behind my back. Lauren is staring at me. Willing me to tell her this isn't happening. That my brother's wife, Patsy, isn't standing behind her.

12

Patsy Brennan.

I look at her now, standing between the silver Mazda she rented and her black Audi A4, the sun shining behind her pale blond hair, and the moments come back to me in a series of emotional spikes. Maybe I love her. I shouldn't, but maybe I do. Or maybe I need her more. It could be as simple and as complex as that.

When I look at her, though, I can't help but think about him. Together, they appeared to be the American dream. Patsy light and pure; Drew broad and strong. The leader of men. The strong, independent woman. Like us all, though, the outside hid the core. The surface masked the poison beneath.

He's been in control for so long. For as long as I can remember. But things change. Someone else is calling the shots. There is another plan in place.

Then I turn. I see the look on Lauren's face. The blood seems to have drained utterly away as she looks from Patsy to me and then back to Patsy. I could have warned her. This moment may have been less dramatic if I had, though the spectacle is not what kept my mouth closed on the subject.

No, my silence had been complete and nonnegotiable from the start. For my entire life, Drew has seen everything. He's known things before I have even done them. He's been five steps ahead of me at all times. If he had even a hint that I had spoken in confidence to his wife, none of this would have happened. Ironically, in that case, Lauren would have been safe. Instead, Patsy and I would have been the targets.

My silence, and hers, has kept us alive long enough to reach this moment. And I had no intention of testing that any sooner than I absolutely had to.

ALL THE FIGHT seems to drain out of Lauren's body, sapped into the perfect grass under our feet, leaving her weak in the legs. I step toward her and she manages to move away. I turn back to Patsy. She stands as straight as she did the first night I met her. The light I see coming from her, pulsing out like the sun's rays, must be a trick of the moment. It cannot be real. But as I look at her, I, too, feel weak.

"Liam," she says.

Lauren twitches at the sound of my name from her lips. Her mouth opens, yet there can't really be any words for all of this. Patsy raises a hand, beckoning me. I leave my brother's paramour by our mother's gravestone and go to stand in front of his wife.

"What was that?" Patsy asks, looking both concerned and suspicious.

"Nothing," I say. "We're good."

"Why did she have a gun?"

"It . . . was mine."

"Yours?"

I nod. "Did you think I would do this without one?"

"Maybe without *her* pointing it at you, yes." Her head shakes. "You shouldn't have needed it. Right? If things had gone as *we* planned."

I nod but leave so much unsaid. Patsy watches me. Reads me. When she speaks, I can tell she knows. Not everything, but enough.

"You shouldn't have needed the car, either. That was supposed to be a worst-case scenario. That's what you told me. And now we're here. Pretty far from your trailer, I'd say."

"I couldn't risk him getting his hands on her," I say, nodding up toward Lauren. "You know what he would have done."

She nods, but I see it in her eyes. Patsy is wondering if I had any intention of going to the trailer. Following *her* plan.

"Fine. I booked two rooms in the Hilton near Longwood. We can go there and regroup. Is she going to freak out?"

I shrug. "She can't come."

Somehow, Patsy's eyes open even wider. "What?"

"I'm going to let her go."

"No, you're not," Patsy says.

"I'm sorry. But I have to."

She stands before me. "We talked about this. We agreed. Right? Or did we? Did we ever really have a plan?"

"I'm sorry," I say, and they are the hardest words I've ever had to utter.

13

S he has a plan. We had a plan. In some ways, it started the day I met Patsy for the first time. I went to O'Friel's for one of my brother's events. It was early in his reelection bid for his seat on County Council and he held a fund-raiser targeting the labor unions. I never joined the union or anything, though I was still painting houses, but my brother knew that those guys felt more comfortable with me than they did with him. And he knew how to press an advantage.

Honestly, I had a great time that night. I joined a table with a couple of guys from sheet metal, regulars at these kinds of things. We got talking about Allen Iverson. Eventually, the conversation turned to the Eagles and became some kind of drinking game. By the fourth shot, I forgot the rules exactly, but it was a blast. Bob joined us at the tail end. He already worked with my brother at Public Safety and the county. So he couldn't join in the drinking game or anything. But he brought his deadpan old-man humor to the conversation. We all laughed when he started talking about ancient football players like Tommy McDonald.

"Who?" one of the sheet-metal workers said.

"Ask your granddad," Bob said with a smile.

Another guy, maybe half Bob's age, slapped him on the back and couldn't stop laughing. Bob had that kind of effect on a group. The vulgarity slowed down a good bit, and so did the drinking, but the laughter grew. He was like a perfect father, all the wisdom without the bullshit.

Just after midnight, I walked the sheet-metal guys out to their trucks. When I got back into O'Friel's, I found Bob sitting on a stool at the upstairs bar and joined him. He sipped a Jameson on the rocks. The bartender, a buddy of ours with a giant leprechaun tattooed on his shin, poured me one, too. I should have stopped drinking hours before but I could not turn down a free one.

"Have fun tonight, son?" Bob asked, still looking at his drink.

I smiled. "I did. Those guys are a trip."

"So were their fathers," he said.

"Really?"

"Yup. I went to high school with two of them. We played football."

"Mount Pleasant?" I asked.

He nodded. "They attended my wedding."

"Oh," I said.

It was my turn to look down at a drink. Bob's wife had passed away about a year before that party, from ALS. He stood by her to the end, and everyone knew it. Some wondered if after watching a loved one suffer from a disease like that, maybe it was easier after they died. It wasn't like that for Bob. He carried her with him still, every day. I reached out and patted his shoulder.

"To Carol," I said.

"To Carol."

We drank. After a moment, Bob looked up again. His smile was back but his eyes still looked troubled.

"You okay, Liam?"

"Me? Yeah."

"I worry about you. Where are you living these days?"

"Out on Orange. My girlfriend has a place next to that big church."

"Oh," he said. "Can I ask you something?"

"Sure," I said.

I totally expected it to be about my brother. I even took a deep breath, trying to sober up a little. It didn't help, but neither did Bob go in the predicted direction.

"How old were you when your mom got . . . really sick?"

"You mean, when did she become a nonfunctioning alcoholic?"

"I guess I do," he said.

His honesty touched me. I thought about it for a second before answering his original question.

"I don't know, really. I can't remember her ever not drinking. But by the time I was ten or eleven, she got really bad. We stopped seeing her much. It's weird; I have no idea how she got her alcohol. I mean, she almost never left her room, but she was always drunk. It was like she was magic . . . in a way."

Bob nodded and then looked away. For some reason, I kept talking.

"Now, I think she was killing herself. Committing suicide. She gave up on life but she was too scared to do anything about it. You have no idea how slowly she died, really."

Bob looked me in the eyes. "I actually do, son."

"Yeah," I said. "I guess you do."

"Tell me," Bob said. "Wasn't there family you could go to?"

I shook my head. "Not really. My parents were pretty private. I think my mother's parents might have been alive still, but we lost touch."

"God, I wish I knew. We could have taken you in. Carol would have loved that. You know, we couldn't have kids. She always wanted them. Maybe it was her illness. I don't know. We tried for a while but it never happened." He shook his head slowly. "It was okay for me, though. It was enough that I just had her. Tell me, Liam. Have you ever loved anyone like that?"

I laughed. It came out so quickly that I felt immediately guilty. But Bob didn't react.

"I don't think so. I don't know if I ever will."

"You will," he said.

And that's when she sat down with us. Bob looked up first. I followed him and saw Patsy on the seat beside me. I had no idea who she was at first, but Bob got up and gave her a hug. I stared while she wasn't looking, mesmerized by her hair, the structure of her face, but most of all the way she carried herself. Sometimes, you come across someone who just doesn't fit into this world, like the grit and haze of reality suddenly part just enough for this person to stand before you. In that moment, I swear she glowed. I could feel the heat her presence radiated outward, and I had an intense desire to touch her, gently, on the arm, and draw in just an ounce of her strength. Instead, though, my head snapped down and I stared at my nearly empty whiskey.

"Liam?" I heard her ask.

I startled, slowly turning, and felt the blood throbbing in my cheeks. "Yeah."

"I'm Patsy," she said.

"Uh, hi, Patsy."

Her eyebrows raised. So did Bob's. I looked at them, confused.

"I'm your brother's girlfriend," she said with a soft laugh.

"Oh, shit," I blurted out.

They broke down laughing. It took me about five minutes for the embarrassment to lessen enough for me to speak again.

"Patsy is Frank Jackson's daughter. She used to work at Legislative Hall. That was when you were still in law school, right?"

Patsy nodded, smirking at me before turning back to him. "How are you, Bob?"

"Good," he said. "And thanks for the steaks, by the way. They were delicious."

"You need to come out with Drew and me. We'll go to Petit Poisson. They have the best mussels in town."

"I do love me some mussels," he said. "Unfortunately, I have to leave you two. It's past my bedtime."

Patsy gave him a warm hug and Bob slapped me on the back, leaving me alone at the bar with her. The bartender came up and gave Patsy a pint of Guinness without her having to order.

"Sorry," I muttered.

"Why?" she asked.

"For being such an idiot."

"No worries. So, you had no idea, huh?"

I shook my head. "How long have you two been . . . ?"

"Eight months."

"Wow," I said.

"You know we met once?" she said.

"We did?"

"Yeah, I was twenty, I think. At one of those crab-and-clam bakes in Lewes."

"Oh, yeah," I said, remembering the events, but not her.

"So I guess you and your brother don't speak often."

I tilted my head. "No, we do. But I've been working a lot. And I was down in Dewey for a couple of weekends."

In the years to come, I would start to understand that Patsy spoke with purpose. Her words were neither frivolous nor free. She had something to say that night and struck with brutal simplicity.

"He told me about your mother," she said.

"He did?"

She nodded. "I can't imagine, Liam. My heart breaks thinking about it."

"It was a long time ago," I said, my head spinning. "Did he talk about our father, too?"

"A little. Not much, though. He . . . he told me you took all of it really hard. I guess I just want to tell you that you'll always have a home with us, Liam. I want you to know that."

Us? I shook my head. "I handle myself okay."

"I mean it. You don't have to be alone."

"I'm not alone." I looked over my shoulder toward the stairway. "I have Bob."

She laughed. It was a real, unscripted burst of humor. The kind that I immediately wanted to hear again.

"Your brother loves you, Liam. He talks about you a lot."

"I'm sure he does," I said.

"Seriously. Whatever it is between you, it'll work out. I really believe that." Patsy's eyes closed for a second and her voice flattened. "I have to believe that."

I watched her, sensing this conversation had stumbled onto thin ice. That moment was like no other in my life. I sat next to her. We spoke softly, alone at the bar after closing. Celtic music played from the speakers above and we both probably nursed a couple of okay buzzes. Yet, in no way did that moment play out as I would expect. Suddenly, I felt none of that energy, no electricity.

I swear she was searching for something. She was waiting for me to let the words out, set them free. Yet, as she stared at me, I looked over my shoulder. In the corner, standing in front of a giant flag of Ireland, I saw my brother. He was talking softly with the owner of the pub, Kevin, but his eyes were locked onto mine, that thin half smile cutting through his face.

So I heard the question behind her words. Eight months was long enough for her to wonder who Drew really was. What stories lay hidden behind his silence. She was asking me if Drew was okay. Yet, as she waited for me to answer, she pushed her hair behind her ear. She did it with one long and perfect finger. The nail was painted a deep red. As I stared, I swear I felt the ground shifting under my stool.

"I got to go," I said.

I am a weak man. Even now. I wish I wasn't. And maybe if I had been stronger, none of this would have happened. We would have never gotten to this point. Maybe I would have answered her question. Maybe it would have been enough of a confirmation, something to reinforce that tiny itch I think she already felt. But when she touched her hair. When I saw the polish on her nails . . . I saw my mother. And I couldn't survive it. Not again.

So, less than a month later, Patsy and my brother were engaged. In fact, Patsy was standing by my brother's side when he asked me to be his best man.

14

A year later, I found myself sitting at a raised table looking at a little champagne flute. My callused and stained fingers seemed to violate the perfect glass. I spun it slowly, watching the drink roll up along the sides. The entire night, the night of my brother's wedding, felt at once foreign and surreal, like I'd fallen asleep and had someone else's dream.

My head lifted as I looked out at the guests, picking through them one by one. My eyes burned with the intensity of my search. There had to be someone out there. It was not as if I expected our father to suddenly appear. Nor did I fantasize that Mom would rise from her grave, drunk with love for her boys. For her new daughter-in-law. I knew we had no family, no long-lost cousins or doting grandparent. Yet I had never felt so alone looking out at the entirety of Patsy's life, painted in concentric circles of caring eyes and loving smiles. I saw her father, the past Speaker of the House. Probably the reason my brother chased her in the first place.

Then I saw Bob. He sat with a table of people from Drew's work. I knew them, too, but felt no connection, at least not in that moment.

I remember, so well, that Bob saw me, too. For some reason, his soft eyes made me feel an overwhelming sadness.

My hand hit the tabletop, harder than I meant it to. Drew's head snapped to the side. His eyebrow lifted. I turned away. At the same time, a fork sounded off the side of a glass. Others joined in. I looked back up in time to see Drew kissing Patsy. Everyone cheered.

A hand fell on my shoulder.

"Mr. Brennan?"

I turned. The man from the hotel who'd organized the event stood behind me, bent at the waist. He had spiked brown hair and a standard tuxedo. He smiled, his trimmed goatee splitting to reveal teeth that looked like they may have been recently capped.

"It's time for your toast."

I said nothing. He stared at me, his eyes slowly widening. Those sparkling teeth separated. I lifted the flute up and drained it. After that, I finished a vodka and tonic I had gotten from the bar before they called us to the table.

"I can get that refilled," the man said, looking utterly uncomfortable.

I handed him the flute and he hurried off. I watched him go, then looked at the empty vodka glass until the guy came back and ushered me out of my seat. My vision wobbled slightly as I turned toward the audience. He handed me a fork and nodded at the glass. I did as he asked, and the room quieted down. Drew looked up at me with his smile. Patsy . . .

I have no idea how long I stood there. I hadn't meant to look at her. My plan had been to get the speech out and leave, simple as that. But her eyes. I got lost in them, maybe. I really don't know. It seemed like an hour that I watched her. Not in a creepy way or anything like that. It was something so much more, and so much worse. She looked happy. And everyone in the room was happy for her. That fact tore at me from the inside out. I wanted to step away, reach out, touch her face, and convince her to run away, forever. I needed to . . .

"You're on," the scrawny little man said, trying to hand me a wireless microphone.

I startled and the audience laughed. It broke through to me, ending the charge that held me frozen awkwardly in place. I cleared my throat, tried to smile, and spoke.

"It's hard to believe I'm standing up here tonight. Not because I didn't expect my brother to get married. And not that I didn't think he would have me be his best man." I laughed. "No, I just assumed he would never trust me with a microphone."

The audience laughed. The sound took the edge off my nerves. It let me forget my true thoughts.

"If our mother and father were here today, I'm sure they would be on the edge of their seats, waiting for me to screw this up." The simmering laughter turned awkward, yet I spoke over it. "Instead, only Drew is. He's looking at his *little* brother and seeing the child I was. And the funny thing is that when I first thought about what to say, I saw Drew the same way, too. I thought of him as my big brother. The kid who became my parents. Who kept me alive after everything fell apart. My *big brother*. But somehow, I knew that wasn't right anymore.

"Tonight, Drew becomes something else entirely. Not only does he become a husband. In a way, he is free to become himself. We made it this far." I looked down at him and he nodded. The crowd stirred. I felt violently sick to my stomach, like every word I forced out was laced with some horrid poison. "Now it's time for Drew and Patsy to start the next leg of this trip. And I know without any doubt what great hands my brother is in. Everyone in this room does. Everyone who has seen them together does. There's something special, something real and . . . amazing . . . about . . ."

I felt dizzy for a second. The sight of all those people watching me, they seemed to weave back and forth, up and down. I reached out to put my hand on the back of a groomsman's chair beside me and forgot that I still held the glass of champagne. It hit the wood and some splashed over the brim and onto the guy's shoulder. Everyone laughed. I thought I might pass out, but instead, my arm came up and made a sweeping motion toward the tables surrounding us.

"About all of this. For the first time in a long time, our family is not shrinking. Instead, it grows with Patsy, and with everyone who loves her. She brings us together. Makes us . . . makes Drew whole again. I have no words for what that means. But I can say that this may be the luckiest day in my brother's life."

People clapped. I lifted my glass.

"Here's to Drew and Patsy Brennan."

Everyone toasted them with a smile. I slipped back into my chair and the guy in the tuxedo removed the microphone from my limp hand. He got the party rolling again as I leaned back and looked at the ceiling.

"Nice one," Drew whispered, slapping my upper arm.

I didn't look at him. Instead, I got up and walked along the back wall until I could slip into the hallway to the bathrooms. When I reached a stall, I pushed in and locked the door. I sat on the edge of the bowl and put my head in my hands.

I had written that speech three weeks before. I read it five times a day, doing my best to memorize every bit. Like I was afraid to forget a single word. And in that moment, more than any other, my weakness disgusted me to the core.

15

———

The years that followed their wedding, however, would become my greatest shame. I saw the signs. They lined up one by one like the guns of a firing squad. Each time, I thought to throw myself in front of her, take the bullet meant for Patsy into my own chest and let it drown the life out of me. Instead, I remained in the shadows, watching as my humanity peeled away one layer at a time.

Drew grabbing her by the wrist as she tried to leave a restaurant. Him whispering into her ear. Each word darkening her soul, though she'd never be able to explain why.

His half smile as he stood with his lacrosse buddies telling an intimate story starring her and painted in the words of a teenage athlete.

I felt her pain. In a way, I lived it over and over again. But I did nothing. Not until, of all things, my brother received his first polling response after he announced his candidacy for governor.

"Not good," he said, taking the paper from Bob's hand.

I always marveled at how my brother spoke to Bob. It reminded me of how my father spoke to our neighbors.

"It's not really a surprise," Bob said. "Johnson is sitting in the seat.

Incumbents don't lose too often in this state. When I looked at the polls, I thought it was a good start. Not bad at all, actually."

"I'd like to win this election, Bob."

"We all want that," Bob said.

The people working on the campaign talked to me, especially when Drew and Bob weren't around. All of them saw the campaign for what it was, a test of one of the party's young upstarts against an opponent who had about a zero percent chance of losing.

"So, what are we going to do about this?" Drew asked, rubbing at his eyes for effect.

I looked around the room. Along with the three of us, about half a dozen staffers stood and sat around Bob's living room. It had become the de facto headquarters. I remember thinking that Bob liked the company.

"We're going to raise money," Bob said. "Statewide elections are different. It's not as much about pounding the pavement and shaking hands. Whoever spends the most, wins the most. I've got coffees scheduled at three of our big donors next month. It'll be a good start—"

"Bob, excuse me," someone interrupted. I turned and noticed Lauren Branch for the first time. For months, I took her for an intern. There was something about her tone that night, her familiarity, that immediately put me on edge.

"I respect what you're saying and all, but Drew and I were speaking earlier. No offense, but that adage of yours is a little old-school. Raising money is great, but this election isn't going to be decided by who spends the most money."

To his credit, Bob smiled without being dismissive. "Okay."

"It's about who spends the money wisest. My friend is majoring in big data at the university. He's—"

"Big data?" Bob asked.

"Data mining . . . algorithms." She shook her head, clearly frustrated by his question. "It's a way to target our coms. We get the right story to the right people and we'll take this campaign viral. I've already got Drew up-to-date with his social media accounts. He's reaching thousands of people through Facebook. And Twitter is growing. Put it all together, and it's going to be huge."

"But it's going to take something bigger," Drew said. "Something the voters can't ignore."

Lauren walked around the couch Bob and I sat on, moving next to Drew. I swear that she almost reached out and touched him before she started to speak again.

"What I'm about to say has to stay in this room. One of my closest friends works for a PR firm in the city. They've cultivated a nice stable of trolls. We're going to start a smear campaign on Johnson, using social media. From what I understand, his campaign just isn't ready for something like that. They won't even know what's going on until it's too late."

"A smear campaign, huh?" Bob asked. "And what are you planning on smearing him with?"

Lauren laughed. "We'll make something up."

AFTER THE MEETING ended, we all moved over to O'Friel's. Bob and I walked in together with the rest of the group a dozen paces ahead.

"What's a *troll* anyway?" Bob asked.

I shook my head and pointed at Lauren's back.

"It's not going to work," Bob said. "You can't just tell lies about someone. People won't believe it."

"You're probably right," I said.

But I watched my brother open the door for Lauren. I saw the arrogance in every movement he made. And I wondered.

We settled in and ordered our second round before Patsy showed up. She stepped into the bar, so tall and light. Everyone at the table turned to look at her; everyone but Lauren. Out of the corner of my eye, I saw her move her chair a few inches away from Drew.

"Hey, sweetheart," my brother said loudly. He rose from his chair and met his wife with a grand hug. "I'll get you a martini."

Drew had *advised* her to switch drinks when the campaign started. He felt Guinness was a little rough for a candidate's wife.

"Club soda," Patsy said.

What?

I felt off-balance as she went around the table saying hello. She hugged Bob. She hugged me, too. I know I blushed. I could feel the heat on my face. And Drew watched me, that smile on his face the entire time.

Before Patsy's drink reached the table, Lauren excused herself. All of the other young staffers joined her. I could tell they were heading somewhere else for the rest of the night, one of the trendier bars down by the river. But I wasn't upset about that. Seeing Patsy watch Lauren out of the corner of her eye made me unbelievably uncomfortable.

Bob stayed with us for about half an hour. I remember thinking how much fun it was, how it almost felt like the four of us were a family. Like Bob was the father I could have had if the universe had dealt me a better hand. Like Patsy was the spirit of my mother, un-tainted by her disease. Even Drew seemed to lighten up. He laughed and the other half of his mouth rose in a true smile.

"Hey, Patsy," Bob said. "So . . . is Lauren working for you now?"

Up until a few days before, Patsy had been Drew's campaign man-ager. Bob was the only one at the table who didn't know that change had happened. To her credit, Patsy looked to Drew, her chin up and her eyes sharp. As she spoke, her voice seemed confident yet filled with an indescribable class.

"I'm taking some time to focus on being the candidate's wife."

Bob, on the other hand, remained the clown. He snorted.

"Are you serious?" he asked.

Then he looked at Drew. Saw that half smile. And had to turn away.

"Whoops," he muttered. "Sorry, boss."

Patsy saved Bob with grace. "Someone has to keep him in line."

Drew reached out and put a hand gently on her shoulder. He smiled at us all, dripping with schoolboy charm. Bob pretended to wipe sweat from his brow. And, in true fashion, spoke up again.

"What does your father think about all this talk of social media?"

She laughed. "He calls it an oxymoron."

"I knew I liked him," Bob said.

Drew leaned forward, his eyes almost predatory. "Dad's going to keep the old schoolers happy for me, right?"

Patsy frowned, just slightly. I had noticed that reaction whenever Drew mentioned her father.

"For his favorite son-in-law," she said with what looked so much like a genuine smile. "Of course he will."

Drew blinked. "Hey, I'm his only son-in-law."

We all laughed. I sat there, amazed at how Patsy could bring things around. Her presence saved the night, for a time. But then Bob left. As he walked out the door, a silence fell over our shadowed corner of the bar, like a ghost from the past slipped into the room, possessing our moods. Patsy, too, seemed affected. Even before my brother opened his mouth.

"Did you see her slip away like some kind of criminal?" he said, breaking the silence.

The change in my brother's tone seemed to dip my spine in icy water. I knew it immediately, the smooth lack of intonation, the veiled danger, like some odorless, colorless poison. And my first urge was to run. To get the hell out of there. But then I saw Patsy. I saw her stiffen, and I just couldn't move.

Patsy didn't respond. That simple fact told me that she knew, too. That she'd been there before. Like I had. My hands shook under the table.

"She sure is strutting around. Acting like she beat you out of a job." He shook his head. "Aggressive . . . Do you think she's pretty?"

And I realized that I was no longer at the table. Not only had my brother pulled some invisible curtain around him and Patsy. But my mind had slipped me back to a time I had buried long before. Drew's words seemed to change as they left his mouth, like I heard one thing and Patsy another.

"I don't see it," Drew said. But I heard, *It's not right.*

While Drew spoke to Patsy in real time, I heard his words coming back from the past. Coming back to haunt me.

"But people compare you two all the time," he said. *You shouldn't be treated like that.*

"Can you believe that?" *You shouldn't just take it.*

"I tell them that they're crazy." *I have your back, bro.*

My head spun. My vision lost focus. I felt like I was going to get sick. Drew kept speaking, kept talking about Lauren and how she hated Patsy. That she said awful things. That she had no respect for his wife. The words just kept coming and coming. Patsy and I just sat there like levies, his venom storming against our silence, threatening to wash the entire world away. As I vibrated, Patsy's hand slipped over her stomach protectively.

I stared at that simple gesture. I saw her club soda. And my entire body turned cold so suddenly that I quivered. The shaking spread from my hands up my arms and into my chest. It was like that night again, when I saw her through the kitchen window. When I realized that I had failed her so deeply. That I could have warned her so many times. And she would have listened. In fact, I think she had been waiting for it. But I had been too afraid. Too weak to even run away.

I knew I couldn't take it any longer. I knew that if I stayed there, I would snap. Maybe I would take my brother by the throat. Choke the life out of him. Drool would fall from my maddened mouth as I watched his eyes bulge, his tongue swell. I would laugh as I killed him.

I stood up so fast that my chair tumbled back, striking the wall before clattering to the floor. My vision cleared so suddenly that I startled. And I saw his face so clearly. That smile. Those flat, piercing eyes. But worse, I saw her. I saw the pain on Patsy's face. But also the anger. And it looked so utterly foreign there, like the world had turned red with fire. And my heart finally split into pieces.

I didn't speak. I didn't reach out to her, try to save her. Instead, I ran.

16

————

I ran that night. As far as I could. At first, I had no destination. Not that I understood. But something seemed to beckon to me like a siren, calling me to the darkness of the sea.

I reached a bridge over the inlet between the ocean and the Delaware Bay. The water surrounded me, buffering everything that stormed inside. Quieting the tempest.

At the next town, I turned down a narrow side street and followed it to the coast. When I got out of the pickup, I heard the faint murmur of the surf. Like a sandpiper, I followed it until my shoes sank into dry, soft sand.

The beach was wide and empty. I stopped, listening to the water and smelling the crisp, salty air. It was the exact spot where the party had been years before. A reminder of the last time I tried to run. But on that night, I was utterly alone.

Slowly, I moved closer to the ocean. A few feet from where the sand was darkened by the surf, I sat. Running my hand through the sand, I saw the tip of the moon rising over the horizon. It sent jagged light reflecting off the choppy surface like a thousand mermaids cresting and diving in the night. Calling out to me with their cloying laughter.

Then I saw my mother's finger. The light hairs of the gypsy moth vibrating as it climbed onto my young hand.

I could be free.

The thought invaded. It came uncalled-for and unexpected. I pushed it back, unwilling to believe it. But it came back with each slap of a wave breaking, with each hiss of the ocean returning into itself.

Could I?

I hung my head, resting it in my sandy hands. As my eyes closed, the sound flashed through the murmur of the waves. My brother's voice.

It's not right.

You shouldn't be treated like that.

You shouldn't just take it.

I have your back, bro.

The surf reached my feet. In an instant, the water soaked through shoes and socks. It had to be frigid but I felt nothing. The waves rolled in, crashed, and hissed up and down the sand. But I heard nothing. The salty air stuck to the heat of my cheeks, but I smelled nothing.

Mom.

That word might as well have been some primordial gear, grinding and pushing one foot forward, and then the other. I walked slowly, purposefully, out into the Atlantic. Muscles fought the push of the ocean. My heart raced and the blood pumped harder and harder. Yet the last shreds of myself, the core of me, that damaged pit hidden so deeply and darkly inside of my being, did nothing. It succumbed to the weight of it all, and my feet moved ever forward.

I did not scream out in rage. I did not pull at my hair in pain. I simply moved slowly forward, deeper and deeper into the ocean. Everything I had done in this life came back to me, and my decision—if you could call it that—made more and more sense. I was not meant for this existence of balance and order. I was chaos, like the storming ocean. I was chaos like the swirling waters. I needed to be stopped. It needed to be stopped.

The water rose above my waist and my chest seized. A wave hit my face and I staggered back, almost losing my footing. A sound pulled out of me, a keening that rose above the surf. I dug through the water with my arms, needing to keep going forever.

I don't know if I wanted to die. That desire seems simplistic. What I wanted to do was escape the truth. But that can't be done. It follows you like a dormant virus, lying in ambush. It remains inside you, waiting, watching. You can't run from yourself. There's only one way to kill that kind of virus. You have to kill the host.

The water reached my face. My feet floated off the sand. I held my breath, frustrated, paddling against the force of the water. It should have been easy. I should have been able to simply walk away and never come back. But something pulled my body to the surface every time I tried to stay under the water.

So I dove. I put my hands out in front of me and cut through the water. I reached the ocean floor. My fingers dug into the sand. I tried to hold on. All I had to do was breathe. Take water into me. Then I would sink.

I opened my mouth, ready to drown myself.

Mom!

I so wanted to be with her again. Just to sit beside her. Touch her hand. Listen to her voice as she spoke softly, sweetly to me. Her absence continued to be such a gaping wound inside me that, in the moment, only the ocean seemed to have the power to fill.

I closed my eyes. Through the briny water, I swear I felt her fingertips brush across my face, run through my hair. My hands opened and I reached for her. Willing myself to drift away from this world and find her in another.

The icy water quieted time. I found peace in that moment, a peace so foreign to me that I would never have been able to call it that. I just felt so close to her. Like I was floating slowly, gently into a future that never could have been.

My lungs burned. I opened my mouth as if the sea might douse the raging fires inside me. One breath, and it would have been over. One breath, and I would have joined my mother forever.

Then I saw her. Not Mom, but Patsy. And I saw her finger brushing away a stray wisp of hair. Her hand slipping across her stomach protectively.

No . . .

My eyes shot open. The realization pierced the cold and my fleeting peace. My brother was going to be a father.

Suddenly, I knew why I had walked out into the ocean. Why I had tried to end it all. It wasn't the anger I saw on Patsy's face in the bar. It was not the thought of her enduring my nightmare. I had so many chances to stop that, to turn her away from my brother, but I never had the strength. This time, though I tried not to accept it when I first saw it, was different.

I knew she was pregnant. I knew the second I saw her hand move. I just couldn't let it be true. I couldn't stand up to the thought of the cycle continuing. Of an innocent life stepping into my childhood shoes.

My mind had blocked Patsy's truth. It wouldn't let me face it. Yet a sliver of courage that could not be extinguished completely sent me shooting to the surface, sputtering and coughing. The cold hit me then like a stab through my lungs. My arms flailed, sending water splashing out in wild arcs.

A wave picked me up. The break caught me, pulling me under, throwing me against the ground. I took in more water when my shoulder slammed into the sand. Then I was in shallower water. I found my footing and staggered toward the shore, falling twice before a wave hit me from behind, throwing me forward onto the beach.

I crawled. Pain shot up my neck. Water poured out of my lungs. When I felt dry sand, I fell to my side. Everything left me then. I felt empty and alone. And worst of all, I was still alive. But I knew what I had to do. And I finally had the courage to do it. The next day, I would tell Patsy *everything*.

17

I lay on the beach until the sun came up. Then I drove the two hours home. As I neared Wilmington, though, I stopped at a traffic light and noticed a large art and crafts store across the intersection. I didn't think about it, really. It was more like I found myself pulling into the parking lot and walking through the doors. In a daze, I wandered around, ending up in the section with acrylic paints, easels, and pre-stretched canvases. I stared for a time, unmoving. Then something inside me snapped. I stuffed my hands with everything I could. Then I checked out without making eye contact with the woman behind the counter.

When I got back to my trailer, I set up the easel and the canvas. I laid out all the paints. Then I closed my eyes, picturing Patsy as she looked when I first saw her, before everything else happened. I thought of her the night before, the anger on her face as my brother bored into her soul. The way her hand instinctively moved to protect her unborn child.

I mixed burnt umber with water, swirling the paint with my brush until the wash thinned. I closed my eyes the second the bristles touched the canvas. The lines sprang from my heart. Sketching the contour of her neck, the angle of her cheek. The fire in her eye.

As my brush made that first mark on the white, blank surface, I thought about her life. My life that had passed. I thought about love and protection, fear and crushing truth. I painted and painted, tears running down my cheeks, mixing with the paints on my palette. I couldn't stop. The pain coursed through me, out my fingertips and onto that canvas in brushstrokes so real and firm that in the end, I swore they must have come from someone else, someone with far more strength than I had.

It took me ten hours to finish the painting. Once I was done, once I had spent the years of anger and pain, I left my trailer and found Patsy. I sat her down and told her everything. For the first time in my life, I set the story free. The truth, as I knew it would, opened her eyes. It buffered her against my brother's words.

"Is this true?" she asked me.

"Yes," I said, the word burning my throat.

Patsy searched my face. Then she nodded.

"I'm pregnant, Liam."

"I know."

"Is that why you finally told me?"

I thought about all the times we'd spoken in the past. All the times I'd sensed her unspoken questions. I felt small, weak, but I nodded.

Of all things, she smiled. It didn't come from sadness. Or repression. It was something else altogether. Resolve, maybe. But I don't know. I will never know. But the sight of it has stuck with me. It will until this is finally over.

"He needs to be stopped," she said.

"Are you sure?" I asked, trying to hide the hope that surged through my body.

"You know, don't you?" she asked.

"What?"

"What he does . . . How he does it. I think I lost myself in it. I believed him. The things he did . . . He needs to be stopped."

"What about the baby?"

She touched her stomach. "That's why, Liam. It can't happen again."

HER PLAN TRULY started that day. Maybe Drew sensed something. I know Patsy felt it. Whatever it was, his attention shifted off of her. It returned to the person whose strings he'd held for decades.

In a way, his plan started that day, too. My brother called me as I knew he would. He asked me to meet him at a large sports bar on the river. Neither of us ever hung out there. In fact, no one I knew did, either. I called Patsy right away and she told me to go and meet him.

When I got there, he was already sitting at a high-top in the corner. The music was loud and the place had a good crowd, but somehow there was space around us. I sat down and he bought me a Rolling Rock. As I sipped it, he watched me. I swore he could see it on my face, that I had finally let our secret out.

He acted nice for a while, talking about work. About how much help I was. I nodded and smiled. I felt good, but I knew what he was doing. I could see the familiar patterns now, how he filled me with pride before breaking me apart. How he broke me down and used me. Regardless, his words just seemed to be heavier than anyone else's. He was going to test me. And somehow, I already knew the stakes would be life or death.

"I went by Mom's grave the other day," he said, slipping that fact into the conversation like it was the next logical step.

I flinched, and he saw me. Drew leaned forward, his face blank but his eyes hungry.

"We wouldn't have made it if we didn't stick together." He took a slow drink and then stared at the alcohol in his glass. "It's a shame, really. Her disease. I guess it was just too much."

I said nothing, yet his words cut straight through me. I knew what he was talking about, and he knew I knew. He was reminding me of our past and the sway he held over me. He was, as always, pulling the strings. Playing his game by his rules.

As he looked into my eyes, Drew placed a folded-up piece of paper on the tabletop, slowly sliding it across to me. Hesitating only a second, I picked it up, straightening the sheet. I looked down to see a photocopy of a Delaware driver's license. Lauren Branch. 3509 Clayton Street, Wilmington, Delaware. Five four. One hundred twenty-two.

"What the hell, Drew?" I asked.

"She's trying to blackmail me."

"What?"

"She's claiming that we had an affair. It's all bullshit. You know that."

I nodded. "Yeah, sure."

"She wants me to pay her a hundred grand to stay quiet. Or she'll blow up the campaign. I don't have that kind of . . ."

"Fuck that," I said, but it was an act. I had to play along, no matter how far it went.

His smile grew. "Yeah. Who the hell does she think she is, messing with us."

"She's fucking crazy," I said.

He took a big drink this time. He looked so damn proud of himself.

"Look, can you take care of her?"

I paused, just long enough. I knew that if I agreed too quickly, he would know something was up. At the same time, my options melted away. Patsy knew the truth. That, more than anything, meant there was no turning back. His eyes narrowed and that grin dropped off his face.

"Seriously, bro. You *owe* me. You want me to . . . ?"

"No," I interrupted him. "It's cool. What do you want me to do?"

"I want you to grab her. Either late at night or early in the morning. Somewhere no one will see. I'll meet you back at your trailer. I figure I can leave my car there and no one will notice. You pick me up and we'll go to the hotel on the river, the fancy one. I have her credit card number already, so I'll make a reservation. I also have a staff pass that can get us in a side entrance, one without any cameras. I know a guy there in security, too. He'll kill the ones on the floor once we get there. We'll have to take care of him afterwards, but that's no problem. No big deal. Right?"

"Sure," I say, looking at my drink.

"What's one more, right?" He laughs. "Anyway. I'll get some pills. And liquor. We'll have some fun. Why not, right? Then it'll look like a suicide. I already have some notes from her that will paint her as crazy, obsessed with me. The story will be huge, you know. Philly media will pick it up. Huge!"

I meant to stay quiet, but the question slipped out. "Won't that look bad . . . on you?"

"Of course not. I'll play the victim. I'll act like I had no idea. The devoted married man. We'll add a platform to the campaign. Something on mental health. I'll talk about Mom. It'll be perfect."

He added bits and pieces, but I had stopped listening. I had enough, and all I could think about was calling Patsy. Once our meeting ended and I drove back to my house by the water, that's what I did.

"We can't hurt her," she said.

Her response surprised me. She was the first of the three of us to be concerned with Lauren's well-being. And she, of all people, had a right to feel otherwise.

"Maybe this is our chance," I said.

Reluctant at first, Patsy finally understood. Once she did, the conversation changed. She took control, devising the steps of her plan.

"Your trailer?" she said. "What if you got one of those surveillance systems? Could you set it up there?"

"Sure," I said.

"That's it, then," she said.

I agreed and she laid out the rest. It involved cameras and the police. Catching Drew just as he was about to hurt Lauren. Recording his orders to kill her. The authorities swooping in before someone got hurt. I could tell she put a lot of thought into it.

"It sounds good," I said, looking out my window at the black water of the river.

"Do you think it'll work? Is it too dangerous?"

"It'll work," I said.

I realized something in that moment as I stared out at the night. Patsy didn't know Drew like I did. Just like Lauren didn't, either. He was too dangerous. The truth was, anything we planned would be too dangerous. Yet every day we walked a tightrope with my brother. Maybe it would work. Maybe it wouldn't. Either way, I knew one thing for sure. Patsy, Lauren, and I were locked in. There was no turning back. Either we did something, or one of us would end up dead.

PART FOUR

MY PLAN

1

————

We did have a plan, Patsy and I. And I didn't lie to her. Not outright. I just let her think that we were on the same page. Although she knows my brother all too well, she doesn't understand him like I do. She never can. See, her idea might have worked with someone else. But if we gave Drew even an inch, he would have wiggled free. Somehow. And in doing so, he would have destroyed us all. This time, I wouldn't let that happen.

"Why didn't you follow the plan?" Patsy asks softly. "You were supposed to go to the trailer. Get him to admit what he was going to do with her on camera. It would have worked, Liam."

"You know him," I say softly.

That's all I have. I feel Patsy searching my thoughts. I blink but meet her gaze this time.

"I thought I did, once. And I thought I knew you, too." She shakes her head. "It's crazy. All my life, people have told me how smart I am. How strong. That I had everything going for me. Great education. Great job. Great family. But I let this happen. And I did nothing to stop it."

My heart breaks for her, but I also know that's not what she wants. Not right now. And not ever.

"My mom said something to me once. She said that love makes us weak. Because we stop caring about ourselves."

Patsy nods. "She's right. I knew. Not right away, but I had a feeling. It would come and go. And I would convince myself I was wrong. That I could change him. It would get worse, but I would tell myself that it wasn't so bad. That I was exaggerating. I would try harder. And he would change. He'd be different. Perfect. For a time . . . he'd be the Drew I fell in love with again."

Her head shakes and her eyes grow distant. It is as if I know what she will say next. Because, in a way, we are two sides of the same story.

"I feel so stupid," she says. "When we were dating, up until we got married, he was so different then."

"Like that lacrosse party," I say without thinking.

She looks at me like I am crazy for a second. Then Patsy nods.

"I remember that day. When we got there, I walked away from him . . . and he let me. He trusted me. He let me be myself, not just his girlfriend. So few men can do that, Liam. They want to control everything. Who we talk to. Where we go. He wasn't like that. He was so confident. So . . . different."

"When did it change?"

She shakes her head. "I don't really know. It happened so slowly. Even that night, when we got home, he started in on me. Started to pick me apart, little by little. One day, I just found myself wondering how I let it happen. I knew I should get out. But . . . I guess . . . I was so embarrassed. So ashamed that I'd gotten myself in so deep. With someone like . . . I thought I was so strong. So independent. So smart."

"That's what he does," I say. "He takes you apart, piece by piece. Just like our father."

"But why?" she asks, her voice breaking.

"I don't know. Sometimes I think that he's just like our dad. Some-times I think he's a victim, just like me. But something inside him is wrong. It's empty. I think my father saw that. He used it. He used Drew against me. And against my mother, I think. And Drew let him."

"But you were kids," she says with earnestness. "You . . ." She stops herself, but then the words come, slowly. "You're right. That's almost the worst part. I was just so wrong."

"That's because you're human," I say. "You're real. You have real feelings. Real thoughts. Drew isn't like that. He has things that he wants. And things that are in his way."

"He talked about your dad sometimes. He said that he was tough. And mean. He even told me that he was way harder on you."

I feel a moment of surprise at this, but then it clicks. "He was tell-ing you just enough of the truth to get a specific reaction. He knew you'd feel sad for us. That it would tie you to us."

"Us?" she asks softly.

I nod. "It's always been us. No matter how hard that is to under-stand. Without me, there would be no Drew. And without Drew . . ."

"What now?" she asks after a long pause.

"You know," I say.

"No, I don't," she says.

"I can still fix it."

"We can. But we need a little time to—"

"No. We can't let him have time. We need to move fast."

"Liam, I . . ."

"Just trust me, Patsy. Okay?"

She doesn't say anything for a moment. Then she looks over my shoulder, up to where Lauren stands alone, looking like a lost child.

"What about her?" Patsy asks.

"She doesn't know the truth. Not all of it. Not what Drew had planned for her."

"You're sending her back to him, aren't you?"

I nod. Patsy watches her for another minute. I notice her hand gently cupping her stomach. I feel dizzy, but my jaw clenches and I swallow the nausea down, pile it atop the rest.

"I need to talk to her," she says.

"Patsy, you can't—"

"Liam," she interrupts me. "You can't use her like this."

I look down at her hand. Her long, perfect fingers. The nails are painted red. Not fiery, like my mother's. More subtle. For some reason they make me think of something solid, something real, more like bricks than flames. And as I watch her, and as her words slip into my mind, they cut through the obsession. The frantic plans. I hear her. And I hear my mother's words once again as well. *Love makes us weak.*

I've used Lauren. I made her something less than human in my eyes. She became a tool. A weapon. Something I could fire at my brother. Wound him with. And discard without any more concern than I would a spent casing. Just like Drew would do.

Yet my brother's wife, the woman she openly betrayed, can find the compassion to consider Lauren's feelings. Maybe I am not so different from him. Maybe I never will be. I feel sick again, but this time it's not going anywhere. All I can do is scratch at the tattoo on my arm.

"I understand, Liam. I do. You're doing what you think you have to do. But you can't be him. You can pretend. You can act hard and cold. But that's not you. Don't let him make you into that." Patsy pauses. "She's a bitch. There's no doubt about that. But you can't send her back to him without her at least having some understanding."

"I know," I say softly. "But I need her to go to him. I need her to tell him what I've done."

"What are you talking about?"

"I need Drew to be angry. I need to get to him. Push him so off-balance that he makes a mistake. Just one. And maybe this can end the right way."

Patsy rubs her eyes. "We can just go to the police. Tell them . . ."

I shake my head. "His lackeys, you mean. You think they'll listen to us? Over him?"

"I know," Patsy says. I see the tears gathering in the corners of her eyes. I realize they are not for her, though. That they are for all of us. "I know . . . Just let me talk to her. I won't tell her everything. I'll give you that. But at least let me tell her that I understand."

2

———

I stand with my brother's wife and his mistress. I don't belong here.
I know that. But I can't take the chance. I will give Patsy what she
wants. What she needs. But I can't let her go too far. I can't let her
undo everything I've done.

"I'm so sorry," Lauren whispers.

She's crying. Patsy isn't now. Instead, my brother's wife stands
inches taller than her, her back straight and her eyes strong but
not angry.

I feel for Lauren, in a way. She probably thought she was so slick,
so careful. Now she stands before the wife of her lover. This is so
much bigger than her affair, and maybe she has started to see that.

"Lauren," Patsy says. "I know what you're going through, but I
need you to listen. He's not what you think he is. He's dangerous.
Really dangerous . . . Because so few people see it. But think about it.
Think about those moments you were with him. Something would
happen, something small. Like some guy at a restaurant would call
him 'boss' or 'champ.' Or maybe someone at the office would make a
joke about him. You'd see it in his eyes. You'd see the change. It

would be so quick, like a flash. One minute he is the most charming person on the planet. Then the truth would peek out. And after, you would laugh it off. But it was there. You couldn't put words to it, or even describe it if you had to. But you saw it, didn't you?"

I look back at Lauren. She is shaking now, her cheeks wet. I think to stop Patsy. That's why I am here. But I can't find the strength to do that.

"Maybe he hurt you once," she continues. "By accident . . . or you thought it was. You probably felt like it was your fault."

The words surround me. Pull me in. And before I realize it, I am a part of this. I share their pain. I know it is different for them. That he did things. Made them do things. But in the moment, we become one. We are all his victims.

"Maybe . . . Maybe he would make . . . you do something. Something you didn't want to. Something that made you feel . . . wrong."

Our wounds merge. It fills the charged air between the three of us. I feel it, too. That, and the burning, suffocating shame. I want them to stop talking. It's like Patsy's words are the beam of a flashlight, moving through the darkness, inch by inch, closer and closer to some unspeakable monster in the corner. I know that if the light shines on it, if I let it become real, it will consume us all. That's why it is so shocking that when the conversation does continue, it is my voice, my words that pass between us, melding the three of us into one.

"He'd make you do it . . . ," I say, knowing that we are not talking about the exact same thing. Knowing that only Patsy knows my truth. What I did. But I can't stop myself. "After, though, you'd . . . you wouldn't understand how he did it. They were only words. His words. But they changed you. And he would look at you after with that face, like you were the most disgusting thing in the world. But he'd be smiling, like it entertained him. Like it was funny to him. You'd look at him and feel so naked and so lost and so broken."

I feel the dampness under my fingers. When I look down at my arm, I see that I've scratched the skin off my tattoo again. Blood drips down my arm and I want to cry. But this moment feels so different. For the first time in my life, I am not alone. The three of us have been marked by our pain, eternally drawn together by our will to survive. We are a burning, burrowing force, one that moved the three of us, pushed us into the darkness, and threatened to drag us under forever. In that moment, I feel the tiniest glimmer of hope. And the sensation may be the most foreign feeling I have ever experienced.

When Patsy speaks again, I think she is speaking for all of us.

"It's the kind of broken that can't be seen. It can't be fixed. It can just be pushed down, buried; otherwise it slowly poisons everything. You hide from it. Make excuses. Worse, you lie to yourself . . . and you believe it. Your lies become this fantasy truth. And in those moments, your mind begins to adapt, to alter. In an attempt to protect you, your brain allows the most fundamental of betrayals. It allows you to survive. To *live* with it. It fractures, and pushes those awful moments into the pits that form inside your soul."

I continue. "Some days, I think about what someone might think if they knew. They'd feel bad for me, for all of us. But they'd judge, too. They'd think, 'They were just words.' To them, it would seem so easy to stand up to him. Go to the police. Vanish. But their minds aren't broken yet. They don't understand . . . because they can't, not until they are there, until their own thoughts betray . . . and they've opened their eyes to see that there are no choices anymore, no paths forward. No paths back. That someone else is pulling the strings."

Lauren is looking at me, but I don't notice at first. I can't see Patsy, but I can feel her. I blink and clear my throat, but my words are finished. I have nothing left to offer. The hope blinks out and I am only emptiness and resolve.

"He wanted you to kill me, didn't he?" she asks.

I nod.

The air seems to leave her body. "I guess I already knew that. Maybe I always did. Maybe that's just how strong he is. That I knew, but I didn't run. That I let you take me. Because . . . it was just what Drew wanted."

"We understand," Patsy says, touching Lauren's hand.

The younger woman looks at me. I see the swollen lip. Her injured wrist. I have hurt her. Badly.

"You saved me," she says.

I swallow the bitterness and shake my head. "Not yet. Patsy's going to drive you to the office. Go back to him. Tell him what I did to you. Tell him what you saw in that cabin. Everything you saw."

All Lauren can do is nod. I watch her walk down the rise, down to Patsy's car. I know what she will do. And I know what my brother will do once she tells him about the bones. Because this has been my plan all along.

3

_____

As I watch Lauren walking down to the Audi, Patsy touches my hand. I turn and there are tears in her eyes.

"He . . . did that . . . to you?"

"What?" I ask.

"Everything you just said. Did he . . . ?"

I thought of Marci Simmons and how I reacted when she thought the same thing. This time, I just shake my head.

"But is it so different?" I whisper.

I immediately regret what I said. But Patsy surprises me when she says, "I don't know."

I think about what I did. What Drew and I did. And I see that Patsy is thinking about the same thing. Trying to understand. She has probably done that a million times since I told her. But I know she never will. And I'll never fully understand her pain, either. That's the horrible truth of abuse. It shackles you alone, in the dark, no matter how much you talk about it. Or don't.

That's why I changed the plans. That's how I finally figured it out. How I knew that I was the only one who could end this.

"Liam . . . Come back, okay?"

"I will," I say, looking into her eyes. "I promise."

We watch each other for a moment.

"I need you to hide out," I say. "Stay away until this is over. I had meant to send Lauren away before you got here. I just . . ." I glance back at my mother's headstone. "I just got distracted. But he knows you're involved. If I mess this up, he'll come for you. You need to be ready, okay? Promise me that."

"Look, we can still figure this out. My father knows the federal prosecutor. We can go to him. Maybe—"

"It's too late for that, Patsy. You know it is."

"It's . . ."

"Don't forget what he's done. What he's capable of. You want him thinking your family is involved, too? That they're against him? Do you want to take that chance?"

"If it—"

I grab her arms. "Patsy, just trust me. Please." I force myself to smile. "I'm not as stupid as he thinks."

The corners of her mouth turn up, too. "I never once thought you were stupid, Liam. Far from it."

I look down to her Audi. I can just make out the outline of Lauren sitting in the passenger seat now. Patsy looks down, too. Her head shakes slowly.

"So I guess I'm supposed to just drive her to my husband, huh? That seems wrong. On many levels, Liam. But . . . I'll do it. Because I do trust you. More than I trust anyone else right now. Just . . . Promise me. Promise you'll be careful. And that you'll come back. Okay?"

I look her in the eyes. "I promise."

Patsy's arms wrap around me. Part of me has dreamed of this moment. Wished that one day I could feel her against me. But it is like all dreams; when my eyes open, I know it isn't real. I realize that I never wanted it to be. That it was never close to being about that, no matter what my brother said. I pull back and see everything so clearly now.

"One other thing," I say. "Can I borrow your phone?"

"My phone?"

I nod. And she hands it to me without hesitating. We look at each other for a moment. Then she hugs me again. I let her hold me. I smell her skin. I feel her warmth. I wish I could bury myself in them both, but not as I am now. Instead, I wish, for a second, that I am just a little kid again. And I could let her hold me, shield me. Protect me from everything that is to come. Everything that already has come to pass.

4

———

Patsy's Audi winds along among the dead. I watch until they are out of sight. Then I turn and walk slowly up the rise. Back to my mother.

When I reach her, I kneel down in the grass. My hand reaches out and I slowly trace a finger along the engraving of her name.

"Mom," I whisper to her cold gray stone. "I should have stopped him."

My hand reaches down. It is shaking as I touch the ground under which she is buried.

"I was a kid . . . I didn't . . . I didn't . . ."

I kneel there, clutching the grass like I might be hurled away at any second.

"I didn't know what to do," I whisper.

"I think about you every day. I think I remember it right. That you loved me. And I loved you. That we would never hurt each other. I tell myself that over and over and over again."

My hair hangs in my face, sweat dripping off the ends. My chest is so tight. Every breath hurts. I find it so hard to take air into my body. It's like my energy simply melts into the ground. Pulling at my most basic instincts.

"They did this. I know they did." My voice rises in anger. I pull a handful of grass out at the roots. "They hurt you."

I throw the clump of grass and dirt over my mother's headstone. Soil rains down on the cold granite. My hands are shaking but I gulp air like I did that night in the ocean. Like my pain had tried to drown me once again.

As I catch my breath, a strange calm falls over me. My eyes focus, back onto the path forward. When I reach down to the ground again, my fingers caress the blades, running along the tops like I am running free through a field.

"It doesn't matter anymore," I say. "Either way, I'll know the truth. Either way, it will be over."

I push up to my feet. Then bend and touch my lips to my mother's stone.

"I'm sorry, Mom."

5

—————

I leave her then. But the question doesn't leave me, no matter what I do. No matter how many times I try to tell myself it doesn't matter anymore. The truth is that it guides me as I walk back to the Mazda. When I pull out of the cemetery, I should turn right. That would take me to the cabin. Back to where it will all end. But that's not where the wheels take me. Not right away. Instead, I head in the opposite direction, driving until I reach the short line of office buildings. My truck is gone, but I'm back. This isn't part of the plan. But, like an addict, I can't stop myself.

The tires howl as I bank into the parking lot. There are four or five cars in the lot, but that doesn't matter. I barrel into a spot and get out. Without slowing, I push through the entrance. A woman sits behind a sliding window. I ignore her and walk straight back.

"Sir," she calls after me.

I throw open the first door I pass. The room is empty, so I go to the next. In that one, two men sit across from each other. One looks on the verge of tears. I keep going and find her in the fourth office I check. Marci, her name was . . . is Marci. She sits across from a man who stares at me with the eyes of some hunted herd animal. The years have changed her but the eyes that widen at my sudden entrance are the same ones that I looked into as a teenager.

This moment has played through my thoughts for over a decade. I dreamed of storming into this woman's presence. Demanding that she answer this one question that has poisoned my life.

Yet, as I stand there, with those eyes locked on to me, I realize something is horribly wrong. I expected those eyes to flash a heart-breaking recognition. Instead, Marci Simmons stares back at me with shock, and nothing else.

For a second, I can't move. I hear the woman from the front desk. She is yelling. Talking about the police. The man in the chair cowers. Marci, to her credit, slowly rises. Her hands come up, palms out.

"Sir," she says in a soothing tone that sounds nothing like I remember. "I need you to step back into the waiting room and have a seat. I'm in the middle of an appointment right now. When I'm done, I'll come out and speak with you."

It is hard for me to accept the moment. I look at this woman, and she has changed, but not as much as I have. Her unkempt long hair may be a little grayer. She wears her glasses instead of leaving them dangling from a chain. But she is, otherwise, frighteningly unaltered. I have an out-of-body experience. I seem to float outside myself. I see the tightness of my jaw. The deep lines of my face. Gone are the easy smile of my youth and the wide-eyed innocence I can't even remember having. It is almost as though I can see right through myself, as though I wear the years like camouflage, hiding so much that I might as well not even exist. Maybe I wish I didn't. Wish I never had.

Yet here I am. Right back to the beginning, in a way. That's when I realize that time definitely stood still, just not for her. Or for anyone else. Just me. I have been trapped in this endless circle for so long, numb to the pain of biting my own tail.

"Was he evil?"

The question slips out before I know that I am going to ask it. Her head tilts, just slightly. I wait, needing the answer now that the question has been asked. When she speaks, her tone has changed. There is a quiver at the end of her words. For the first time I think that maybe she does remember. "I'm sorry," she says. "I don't know what you're . . ."

In that moment, my resolve cracks. Although I need to know, it just doesn't matter now. The wheel is rolling. The answer is imminent. There's no getting out of the way. I'm just afraid, but I am done being a coward. I take a step back, looking over my shoulder at the doorway.

"I'm Liam . . . Brennan. You came to my house . . . when I was thirteen. You couldn't have done anything," I say, my voice cracking. I can't make eye contact. "There's nothing you could have done."

"I remember you," she says, barely above a breath.

I back away. She follows.

"Wait."

But I can't. I won't. I'm out of the office and through the lobby. I push open the outer door. When I see the Mazda, the weakness that brought me here dries up to nothing. I am a husk. A shell. I have one purpose now. One path. And I just need to take it.

"Liam," she calls out behind me. "Liam Brennan. I remember. Something happened back then, didn't it? I tried. I did. I went to the police when I heard. I told them about that day. I told them that they needed to do something. But . . . Liam!"

I get into the rental car. The engine ignites, wanting to move. She stands across the hood from me. I see her mouth moving, expressing her regret, and all I feel is guilt for coming to this place. For seeing her again and allowing myself to believe that anything could have been different than it was.

6

_____

Clouds darken the afternoon as I turn into the apartment complex. I stop on this side of the chain blocking the access road. When I get out of the car, I decide to leave the keys inside. Then I remove the chain, leaving it on the dirt across the entrance. A cold, wet breeze blows out of the east, slipping under my shirt. My teeth chatter, maybe from the chill. Maybe not. I pull out the phone and dial Bob's cell number. He answers and the sound of his voice nearly breaks my heart.

"Patsy?"

"No, it's Liam."

"Liam?" He pauses, as if trying to understand why I would call from Drew's wife's phone. "Oh, man, what is going on? Everyone's freaking out here. They're saying that you . . . you have something to do with Lauren Branch's disappearance."

"She's fine," I say.

"How do you know?"

"I just do, Bob."

There's a silence before he continues, his voice guarded.

"Thank God. Was that . . . her? In your car?"

"Yes."

"Oh, jeez. Where are you? Are you looking for your brother?"

"No," I say. "I need your help. But you have to promise me you won't tell anyone about what I am going to ask you to do."

Bob does not speak at once. Instead, I just hear his breathing.

"This is about you and Drew, isn't it?"

"Please, can you trust me this once?"

"Son," he says softly, "I would trust you more than once."

For some reason, his words make me cry. I try to hide it, but I know he hears it in my voice. There's nothing I can do about that now.

"I need you to wait exactly half an hour and then call the police. Tell them that you got a call from me and that I told you I had Lauren at the old swim club behind the Arundel Apartments."

"That's it, huh?" he asks.

"That's it."

"Hmmm." He pauses again. "Just promise me you'll be careful. Don't let him hurt you."

"Him?"

"Your brother, Liam. I'm old but I'm not blind. Promise me you won't do anything stupid."

I think about everything I have done so far, taking Lauren to the swim park, ditching her car in the middle of traffic, driving through our childhood neighborhood, my truck at Marci's office. He'll know them all by now, all of the steps I've taken. And I'm counting on that.

"I won't do anything stupid," I tell Bob. I just hope my brother does. In fact, everything counts on that happening.

7

The first raindrops of a coming storm send tiny clouds of dust up in the air. The droplets dampen my hair, run down my face and my arms. I look up at the sky, opening my mouth. The water tastes so pure, so fresh, that I am left wanting more. As if I have never caught a raindrop on my tongue before.

I don't have much time. He'll be here soon. So I keep walking, moving deeper into the darker shadows under the high oaks and maples and beeches. The smells bring me back, damp leaves and musty soil, pine sap and rotting wood. I walk with my eyes closed, my hands open palms out. I let the air surround me, enter me. It feels so new, so different, so alive. I let it carry me. I let it bring me back to that night one last time.

I FIND MYSELF in my room again. Drew stands by my door. He is seventeen now. Not the man I am destined to face. He has the same line to his mouth, though. And the same way of looking through me. For days, I had expected retaliation. For what I'd done to Eric Clarkson's

BMW. I'd expected Drew to turn my father's attention back on me. But it hasn't happened. It never happened.

Instead, he stands there looking at me. The bruise that surrounds his eye has started to yellow. His mouth opens and the words slip into me like the tip of a needle.

"Do you know how Mom got the alcohol?"

I don't say anything. He takes a step closer to me.

"He bought it all. He brought it home with him. He carried it up to her room. Did you know that?"

"Dad?" I whisper.

"Jesus, Liam, are you that stupid? Yes, Dad."

I close my eyes, picturing the empties on the table beside her bed. I can feel her cold skin against my fingertips as if I relive that moment layered atop this one. Then an older memory returns. A neighbor offering help to my father. And him returning home with a paper bag, glass bottles clattering inside.

"He took me with him a couple of times. In the car, he kept telling me that if he didn't do it, she would. She'd get herself killed driving drunk. He told me he was keeping her safe as he pulled bottle after bottle off the shelf."

The corner of my brother's mouth hovers as a deep pain throbs behind my forehead.

"You know when he brought me to the liquor store the last time?"

I close my eyes.

"After she came home from rehab. When she wasn't drinking anymore. It was that day, Liam. After she brought home that kitten."

"What kitten?" I ask stupidly.

Drew just rolls his eyes. "I skipped the last three periods that day. I got home just before Dad. He had dropped off Mom already. For that meeting. He had me go around the house and pick up all of the stuff she bought. I had to carry it out to the car. He grabbed the cat, though. Right by its neck. And he threw it into that cardboard carrying box."

Finally, the smile slips from his face. He looks troubled, exactly as he would the night he tried to turn Patsy against Lauren.

"He told me to get into the car and he drove over to that apartment complex, the one at Arundel. That thing screeched the entire drive. He drove around back, near that trail that goes into the woods. The one that goes to that creepy pond. There was a dumpster back there. He parked next to it and told me to throw all that stuff in."

My eyes open. I don't want to hear this. I don't want to listen to him.

"Then he threw the cat in, box and all. I couldn't believe it, really. The funny thing is, Liam, he closed the lid of that dumpster so softly, like he couldn't hurt a fucking fly. Isn't that funny, bro?"

He actually laughs. But I hardly notice that. Instead, I see my father. What he did. But it's not about the cat.

"When we got back into his car, he drove to the liquor store. He didn't lecture me that day. Not at all. He never said a thing. Nope, he just bought a case of vodka. He had me carry it into the house. Up to her room. He wanted me to be a part of it, Liam. He wanted that. You know he did."

I slam my fist into the wall. The sheetrock rends as my fifteen-year-old hand passes through it. White powder sprinkles the carpet and covers my knuckles as I pull my hand out of this new hole.

I hear my brother laugh. I look and see his smile. I boil from the inside out, like my skin might suddenly peel away. My shoulder strikes him, hard, as I pass. He staggers back into the wall, laughing outright now. And I race down the stairs.

I tear through the kitchen, past the laundry room and the family room. I throw the door open. And I see him at his workbench. He is tall, straight-backed. His graying hair is full and slicked back. His forearms are tan and wired with muscle as he works on another of his models. But when he turns to me, when he looks at me . . . I . . .

He has no face. It is blurred, like someone has hurriedly erased his features. But no, that's not right. That's not how I saw it then. It is how I remember it now. I press fingers into my eyes. I squeeze until it hurts, trying harder to pull up a memory of his face. Instead, he stares back at me through time, through an empty soulless void. I see him but I can't see him. I need to see him.

8

M y memories fail me. My childhood double binds my adult mind, turning every thought into an endless, convoluted knot. I was in the garage. I was in my bedroom. My brother was there. He's gone. Both are true. Both are false.

I walk through the rain to the cabin at the end of the trail. Even in the growing gloom, the silver padlock sparkles like a beacon. It draws me to it, like I hear the song of the siren once again. I know where it leads. I know the doom. But I walk nonetheless.

As I stand before the door, I reach back and touch the grip of the pistol that rests against the small of my back. It is there still, as I knew it was. Nodding, I remove my key and unlock the door. The hinges creek as it swings open. A smell washes across my face. Not death, not really even decay. Instead, it is the aroma of nature's relentless force, ever pressing to reclaim what was once hers. What will be again, regardless.

The inside of the cabin is dark. I pull out Patsy's phone, switching on the flashlight. A harsh beam cuts into the corner, shining on the crumpled blue tarp. I move to it, kneeling down reverently. The light pans and I see the human skull still lies among the pile of blackened bones. The empty darkness of its eyes stares at me, pleading with me to let the past rest in peace, as I have for so many years. But that isn't going to happen. I am ready to face it now. Nonetheless, I can barely breathe as I snap a photo and text it to my brother.

9

_____

I stand at the edge of the water, staring out at its darkness. The rain disturbs the surface, making it jagged and harsh. I feel him out there. He is coming for me. I can see the arch of his shoulders so clearly. The bend of his knee. The strength of his back. I see his hand, large and dry. But his face is a void.

The emptiness enrages me, both now and then. The anger builds, merging the smells of the forest with those of my father's workshop. Glue and oil. Acrylic paint and dampness. They swirl like a tornado around him, around us.

"You killed her!" I scream at him, and I hear the voice of a fifteen-year-old in my head.

Strangely, I can hear his voice. It is clear and loud in response. It roars from the emptiness that is his face, my father's face.

"What did you say?"

"You killed her, you bastard!"

My father stares at me. Slowly, he rises off his stool. His steps are like torture. His hand, open, rears back. And he slaps me across the face with enough force for me to falter backwards, my ear ringing and my vision a flash of pure white light.

"Get out of my house," he hisses.

I stagger back, tasting blood in my mouth. My head spins. My back touches the doorway to his workroom. I can barely see through tears that burn with my shame, which grows with each shuffling step I take away from him, out into the basement, toward the steps. Where could I go? How could I be free?

But I'm not alone. As my bare feet shuffle across the cold red concrete floor, my brother appears in front of me, a ghost out of the darkness. That smile is on his face, but I can't notice that. All I can think is that he will see the burning red mark on my face. The thin trickle of blood at the corner of my mouth. And worse, my tears.

"You can't let him get away with that, Liam," my brother whispers.

I try to step around him but his hand against my shoulder is firm. His words in my ear are a bitter, unimaginable poison.

"Mom needs to rest in peace."

10

_____

Where am I? My eyes are open. I am looking up through a canopy of branches that sway and whip in the rising wind. Rain falls on my face, heavy now. I reach up and touch my skin. It is there. It isn't empty, faded. It is the face of a man, not a fifteen-year-old boy. I take in the air. I know where I am. I am at the old swim park. I know what it means.

Drew has not responded to my texts. Maybe he hasn't seen them. Maybe I wish it could be true. Even if he did, if he saw them and understood, he might not come alone. He could bring half of the state police force. He could arrest me, blame me for all of this. He could paint one of his stories: I am the jealous little brother trying to bring him down. Or worse, Patsy and I are having an affair, and Lauren found out. That's his game. And he never loses.

But we aren't playing his game. I've made sure of that. He's spent hours being unsure. Where am I? Why would I leave her car like that? My truck at her office? How could I have Patsy's phone? Where is she? Where is Lauren? How much could they know? The bones?

I have him off-balance. I feel it to my core. He'll come, and he'll come alone. He will race here to confront me. He will, once again, underestimate me. He needs to. He can't admit that, for the first time, I have defied him. Patsy has defied him. And for all his power, he can't be prepared for that.

TIME PASSES SLOWLY now. I stand on the bank of the pond. The wind causes a light current to lap up on the black sandy beach. I reach down and pick up a stone. As the rain falls in sheets across the surface, I throw the rock out into the center.

A flash of lightning illuminates the park for the quickest of instants. It is like time stops, like I stand in the middle of some fading picture watching the splash. I imagine the stone sinking into the depths. I picture it falling and falling until it comes to rest on the roof of a rusted-out Ford Explorer, one that remained in peace for far too long.

"Liam."

His voice is flat and hard, just loud enough to be heard over the storm. I turn, my eyes still adjusting to the sudden flash. At first, all I can see is a shadow. He towers between two of the cabins, his hands in the pockets of a long overcoat. I freeze for a second, because his face is so shrouded in darkness that I can't see his features. I can't see his eyes, his mouth. I need to see his face. To know it is real. To know all of this is real.

For an instant, I think to run away. Get out of there and never look back. For so long, I saw him as something above human. A god with the power to warp reality to his will. Since I saw him turn that power on Patsy, though, something changed inside of me. The years came crushing back. The torture. The fear. The disgust and guilt and pain. Everything that was broken inside me. I pictured it all being laid at the tiny feet of that unborn child, my brother's future son. I saw the cycle so clearly in that moment. I saw my life repeating over and over and over again. No one could deserve that. I thought about everything I had done. And, for one shining moment, I found the strength to take a stand.

But his face. Trying to blink the rain away, to see him, I close my eyes. In that instant, instead of Drew, I see my father. He stands in his workshop, the light from that tiny lamp shining on his hard, sharp profile. Slowly turning toward me. But his face remains a void, a splash of nothing.

When my eyes shoot open, my brother is still wrapped in darkness. His face is still hidden. I need to turn away, to run away. Or the shadow will simply swallow me whole.

A jagged bolt of lightning crackles overhead. In the flash, I see. It is Drew's face, his piercing eyes and flat mouth. He is real. He has always been real. And he is not the emptiness. And he is no longer smiling.

"I know you brought her here," Drew says. "You can't stay away, can you?" He laughs. "Maybe I couldn't, either, if I did what you did."

My head shakes. I hear my fifteen-year-old voice when I say, "I didn't do it alone."

Drew finds this even funnier. He is practically in tears.

"Liam, we both *know* you didn't."

My eyes widen. It is the first time my brother has said this to me. His words rock my fragile hold on reality even more deeply. He takes a step closer to me. His features, even in the storm, begin to emerge. I can see his eyes clearly now. They are sharp and deadly.

"But who cares about that?" he says. "We can't take it back. You can't change it."

"No," I whisper.

He walks up to me. He puts his hand on my shoulder. I can smell him, clean and sharp. I swear I can feel the heat of him through the cold rain. His fingers grip me, dig into my muscle.

"We're in this together, brother. We always have been."

11

ightning flashes once again. The moments of the past roll by in reverse. We are here and we are there, like the endless loop of time, the snake eating its own tail.

I stand in the basement, my brother in my ear.

"You need to avenge her. He *killed* her."

My head spins. "What?"

"I saw it. He took a pillow and held it over her face until she stopped breathing. Then he had me lie about it. To everyone. Even to you."

Everything turns as red as the floor. Years of crushing anger. Years of veiled abuse. Years of being the toy stuck between two sets of claws. It all crashes down on me in that moment, this moment. I think to avenge my mother. But I am the weapon of his revenge. I am as good as the gun in his hand.

My brother's hand opens. I see a shine of metal, the blade of one of my mother's pristine kitchen knives. A set my father bought for her years before. A set that sat on the counter, unused, as her life slowly wasted away.

"Take it," Drew says.

With a smile, my brother places the knife in my hand.

"Stand up to him," he whispers.

The words bounce off my skull, flashing through my mind over and over again. He touches my face, his fingers tender but firm. He tilts my head, looks deeply into my eyes. He is close to me. His eyes are sharp. His breath is hot.

"It's okay, little brother," he says, so softly. "He hates you. I tried to tell him, but he won't listen. He's always hated you because . . . you aren't like me, Liam. You're weak and small and you cry all the time. He thought Mom babied you. He's ashamed of you. He wants to send you away so that he doesn't have to be seen with you. He doesn't have to explain to people. That's why he's always leaving. It's either him or you. Either he goes . . . or you do."

His hands move to my shoulders. Gently, he turns me, guides me back toward the open workshop door.

"You need to stand up to him," he whispers, or maybe the words just repeat again.

It's not right.

You shouldn't be treated like that.

You shouldn't just take it.

I have your back, bro.

He does not push me, not physically. My father's back is to me. His thick fingers work with a delicacy that seems impossible. I am there and not there. He is there and not there.

The rage lashes out like a storm. It crackles and burns inside me. But there is something else, too. Fear. Revulsion. I don't know. But it makes me shake. It makes time fold in on itself. It makes the knife so heavy in my hand. My feet so cold. My legs stiff and awkward.

My father turns. He looks at me. But his face is gone. It is nothing. It is emptiness.

"Liam, what are you doing? Where did you get that?"

I expect him to rise in a flash. Lunge at me. Rip the knife out of my hand and beat me to a single second from my death. But he just sits there and looks at me like I do not matter. Like I might as well not exist.

My heart races. My body tingles. My father sits in front of me. Looking at me. Judging me. *Embarrassed. Ashamed.* And I swear someone stands behind me, whispering.

"Do it," Drew says.

Or maybe I just hear his voice in my head.

Do it do it do it

12

_____

What happens next . . . I don't know. Was it rage? Or worse, was it calmness? Did I move with intent? Did I stumble? Was I even there? Really there? I just don't know. Even today, I'll never know.

I stood in my father's workshop. He sat on his stool, still holding on to his model, a ship or an airplane or something else. His face was there. It had to be. But I still can't see it, no matter how hard I close my eyes.

Nor can I see the moment that I finally moved. One second I just stood there, staring at him. The next, I felt the resistance in my wrist as the knife's blade plunged into his back. It caught for an instant, maybe on a rib. I remember that. But my momentum, the abandon of it, pushed past that, diverting the blade. With a hitch, it sank deeper into my father's body.

He lurches to his feet. The harsh light of his desk lamp flashes off the knife's handle like a lightning strike. The gurgling sound that rumbles from his chest sounds so much like the driving rain. His hands, like talons, grasp for the handle of the blade in his back, just out of reach. A blossom of blackness stains his work shirt like a flower opening after some dreadful storm.

"Dad?" I whisper. "Dad?"

And all I hear is the sound of his pain.

13

As the rain falls in sheets between us, I stare at my brother.

"Why do you keep coming back here?"

I don't say anything.

"When you didn't show up at the trailer, I knew you'd be here. And I knew you'd be back. I just don't understand why. You would have chickened out that night, left me to handle everything. I did, though, didn't I? I took care of everything. I took care of you. You didn't trust me. You thought we'd get caught. But guess what, we didn't. When I told them that Dad ran off, left us, they didn't even care. It's crazy. As long as you give them a simple truth they want to believe, people will believe it."

He watches for my reaction. I try not to give him anything. But his words tear at me, chipping at every wall I've ever built. I feel the emotions raging inside me. I know I can't afford any of them, not now.

"It was an accident," I whisper.

Drew barks out a laugh. "Accident? Are you kidding me? It was an *accident* that you stabbed our father?"

"I . . . it was once. I didn't . . ."

"Once?" Drew's laughter fills the space between us, harsh and thunderous. "I guess that's true, bro. You stabbed him once."

14

———

D ad?" I whisper again and again.

He wriggles and shakes, trying to reach the knife. The stain on his shirt grows, spreading vines down his back, droplets slipping off the edge of the stool, splattering on the red concrete.

The chair tumbles behind him. He turns and his fear fills my mouth with bitterness. He tries to speak but instead he shrieks in pain. Or rage. I don't know. I don't know what to do. I want to take it back. Turn back time. Instead, or maybe because, I lurch forward, my fingers wrapping around the handle of the knife. His hands slap at it but can't reach as I yank the blade free of his body. Blood sprays through the air.

"Oh, shit," my brother says behind me.

My father calls out to his son, the one who doesn't *embarrass* him.

"Help me. Do something . . ."

Drew doesn't move. I can hear him breathing behind me. My father's voice rises in panic.

"He did this to me . . . Goddamn it, do something."

Drew's laughter is so cold.

"Drew," my father moans. "Do something. Stop him."

"You have to finish it now," Drew says in my ear. "If you don't, he will."

"Drew . . ." His word ends in a wet, drowning sound.

Maybe that moment is the first time I truly see my father. He has towered over my life, a suffocating force. But standing before me, cursing me and pleading with my brother, he looks so fragile. I feel so confused. How could I have been so afraid of this man for so long?

"Do it," my brother says. "Do it."

"I can't," I whisper.

15

_____

You went in there?" Drew asks, pointing through the sheets of rain at the pond behind us. "You brought *him* out? What is wrong with you?"

I blink, and it is as if this moment, his words, what I have done, it all merges to lift the veil. I see my father's face again. But his eyes are not flat and piercing. No, they are wide and bulging. And his mouth is not thin-lipped and pursed. It gapes so widely that I swear I can see his dark soul deep in the pit of his being. I feel the warmth on my hands. Up my forearm.

And I see the fingers, bloodstained, wrapped around his throat. Tightening. Squeezing the life from my father.

"Maybe you're not as weak as I thought."

Drew's words tear the image from my mind. I blink and see him just as clearly. He means what he says. He looks at me with a respect I have never seen before.

"You dove down there and brought him back up, huh? I assume

the Explorer's still at the bottom. What about the knife? You bring that up, too?"

"I didn't do it," I say.

He laughs again. "Shut up, Liam."

My eyes close. I see the fingers choking my father to death. But they aren't mine. They weren't mine.

16

"You can't do anything right, can you?" Drew says. He said, as we stood together in my father's workshop.

He pushes past me and gets in our father's face.

"You're going to hit me, huh? You piece of shit. That was a mistake, wasn't it? Wish you could take that back now, don't you?"

Drew pushes him to the ground. He screams and my brother falls on him. His fingers, not mine, wrap around my father's neck. He squeezes the life out of him. He does. I didn't . . .

I blink, and I see the blood. It pools around my father as he convulses on the floor. It seeps up the side of his shirt. I feel a dampness on my forearm again. When I look down, I see his blood staining the paleness of my own skin. The emotions strike like lightning. My teeth grind together and my vision tunnels. My other hand tears at my father's blood, clawing at it, trying to rend the stain from my skin. But it won't come off. Ever. No matter what I do. No matter what I have done.

I didn't . . .

Drew grunts with the effort. My father's feet kick out. Then they shudder. And the blood keeps coming. The pool getting wider, a darker red against the floor. The smell, tinny and surprisingly sour, touches my nostrils. I cough.

And Drew is standing before me. He is grabbing my shirt. Shaking me. Laughing over the body of our dead father.

THE NEXT MORNING, I wake up and think it is all a dream. I wander through the house. Down to the basement. I creep into my father's workshop. I find the stool upright. The floor pristine. Even his model on the table, waiting for him to come home.

I move back up the stairs. His keys, with the Ford logo key chain, are gone. Clutching the wall, I look out into the garage. My father's car is gone. The space it had taken shines stark and empty. He's at work. He will come home and return to his hobby like nothing ever happened. I smile before reality returns like it always does. I back up, sliding down the wall. My hands cover my head. My body shakes as I remember Drew dragging me into the bathroom. Together, we cleaned our father's blood away. Afterwards, I sat on the floor, my sleeve up, just staring at the stain that still would not come off my forearm.

Together we rolled him up in the carpet from the foyer, one we would replace the next day at some cheap store by the airport. We lifted him awkwardly up the stairs, into the back of his Explorer. Drove to the access road. I got out and lowered the chain, jumping back in as my brother rolled slowly over it. He sent me to find the rock that would hold the gas pedal down. We stood together, side by side, as the car rattled across the dock, splashing into the water and sinking out of sight far faster than I thought it would.

"I cracked the windows so it would fill up with water," Drew said, emotionless. "Not enough for him to float out, though. That would have been stupid." He laughed. "Like something you would do, bro."

As my father's lifeless body sank to the bottom of the pond, into the depths of the long-dead swimming hole, my brother moved to my side. I felt his hand atop my shoulder. A loving squeeze. So much like my father did to Drew the day of our mother's funeral.

"I love you, Liam," my brother softly said. "It's just you and me now . . . Just you and me."

We did everything together that day. Everything except touch my father's keys. Only Drew did that.

17

——————

The past shrinks in around me. Every breath feels like glass in my throat. I close my eyes and try to see his face. I try to remember. But instead of the void, I see his bulging eyes. The rictus of his mouth.

"You needed me to clean up your mess. Like you always do. I've protected you forever. Can you imagine what would have happened to you if they found out what you did? And no matter what I do for you, you betray me. Over and over again, you betray me. You . . . really? You're still doing that?"

At first, I don't know what he's talking about. Then I feel the burn on my arm. I stop scratching at the tattoo, the Celtic knot that never truly masked the stain.

Drew's head tilts slightly. "Do you still see the blood?"

I don't answer. But I do let my hand fall to my side again.

"You do, don't you? Grow the fuck up, bro. Why the hell did I ever trust you?"

I stare at him. My hand moves up my leg to my waist. I slide it around and under my shirt and feel the cool handle of the gun move against my back.

"I went to the trailer," he says, his voice merging with the rumble of the storm. "I saw it. I saw what you did. I saw your fucking painting. Look, this can all go away. We can get past this." He pauses. "Think about it. Think about everything we've overcome. Everything we've done together. It'll be okay, Liam. Just tell me where she is."

I blink. "Lauren?"

"Jesus," Drew snaps. "Are you serious? I don't give a shit about her."

I see the change on his face. It is subtle but slow. He is getting angry. This place. Patsy. Me. He is on edge. He is, maybe for the first time in his life, feeling the strings slipping from his fingers, just a bit. Hopefully, just enough.

"Patsy knows," I whisper.

He has pinned everything to me. He's hidden behind me. I know this now. I need to take that away. I need my brother to feel exposed, naked in front of the truth. Only then will he slip up. Only then do I have a chance.

"There's nothing to know," Drew says.

"She knows I didn't kill him," I say.

His laughter is cutting and harsh. "Yes, you did."

No, I think. "She knows what you *made* me do."

"I made you stab your father? Seriously."

"She knows you choked him, Drew."

"That's a lie," he says. "Who do you think she'll believe, you idiot? You or me?"

I don't know the answer to that. I don't even know who I believe. Not yet.

"She knows about Lauren," I say.

"Who cares?" he shouts.

"She's leaving you, *bro.*"

"Yeah . . . right . . . she is."

It is the first time I have heard my brother stammer. I say nothing, watching him, trying to let the fear I feel show on my face. Just enough for him to suspect nothing.

He rubs the rain from his eyes. "She's using you, Liam. Can't you see that? Patsy hates you. She always has. You scare her. But look, it's done between us. That's why the whole Lauren thing happened. Patsy and I are finished. I'm done with her. Don't let her ruin everything."

This is it. My last card. "I have the keys, Drew."

And he blinks. For the first time in all our games, he blinks first.

18

———

My brother's eyes widen. I swear, even through the pounding rain, I see the calculation behind them.

"What keys, Liam?"

"The ones to Dad's Explorer."

Drew shakes his head. "So what? Even if you do, so what!?"

"Did you forget? I never touched them. Only you did."

This time, he laughs. It is too fast. Too loud.

"You're lying," he says. "Besides, even if you did have them, they've been under the water. Any fingerprints would be gone."

"You're wrong," I say, smiling. "I've been paying attention. I've been waiting."

"What are you talking about?"

"A few years ago, I found an article. It was about identifying fingerprints on metal after it's been in stagnant water. They have new methods now. Ones that can pull prints from metal that has been in the water for weeks."

"Weeks! It's been *years*!"

I look him right in the eyes. "No, it hasn't."

He recoils. It is slight. Less than a step, but I see it. I feed on it.

"I went back, Drew. I went into the water. I saw him, before he was just *bones.* The keys were under the water for less than a week. I've been holding on to them. Keeping them safe. But when I found the article, I went to someone. An expert."

"No, you didn't," he says. "I would have known."

"Not to the police," I said. "To an investigator. He took the prints. He has a whole report."

Drew snaps. I see the control breaking. His hands curl into fists. I take a step back and I pull the gun from my waistband. I raise it between us, my hand shaking. He looks down the barrel and then into my eyes. His head cocks to the side.

"You're going to kill me?"

I take another step back. My finger slips into the trigger guard.

"*You're* going to shoot me?"

"Shut up," I say.

I make my voice shaky. The gun waves wildly. I stagger back a third step. I see his eyes narrow. His mouth set. He steps toward me.

"You can't do it," he says.

"You know I can," I say.

He laughs again. "You can't finish it. You couldn't then. And you can't now. You don't have it in you. We both know that."

I want more than anything to put a bullet into his face. I think about my life, every moment of it. I see the knife. The blood. I see their faces . . . because I never stood up to him. Never stopped him.

But he's more right than he knows. I can't hurt him. No matter how hard I try, I can't do it. It is the easy answer. I could shoot him, kill him, and it would be over. Patsy would be safe. I would be free. It would finally be finished.

Every muscle in my body tenses, except that finger. It remains frozen, paralyzed by years of lies. I try. I do, but even before this all started, I knew I couldn't. If I did, it wouldn't really be over. The cycle would just continue. And it would swallow every shard of innocence now and forever forward. That is the emptiness. And that is the cycle I will break, whether anyone can understand or not.

On the fourth step, I slip on the muddy bank of the water. For a second, the gun points to the sky. That's when Drew moves. His hand shoots out. He grabs the barrel. The handle slips from my hand. I fall back, throwing an arm behind me to break the fall. I sprawl with one leg folded below me and one jutting straight out between Drew's feet. One arm is free. The other is pinned behind me, sinking into the mud.

I find my gun in my brother's hand. The barrel now, finally, pointed at me. I look up into his face. He thinks it is over. He thinks he's won.

"Get up," he hisses.

"No," I say.

His head jerks. "What? What did you say?"

"No," I say calmly.

For just an instant, I see myself through my brother's eyes. I lay prone in the dirt, but my eyes are soft. My jaw is lax. The fear is gone. So is the pain and even the numbness. I look up at him with the eyes of truth. I see him. And he sees me.

"Get up!" he screams.

"No," I whisper.

He kicks me, hitting the inside of my thigh and my groin. The pain fires through my stomach, into my chest. I fight to find my breath. But I do not move. I will not do what he says.

"I'll . . ."

"No," I say again.

I know my brother. In a way, I am him. We are, and always have been, mirror images of one another. I have pulled the trigger for him his entire life. I have done what he needed to have done. And he has done whatever it took to keep his hands clean of it. The last thing he will do is pull the trigger himself. For he stands alone out here, no one to point to, no one to blame. No story to build up that portrays him as the hero. And me as his bumbling villain.

For my brother to pull the trigger, he needs to see no choice. He needs to have no story. I need to take that from him. I need to leave him naked and exposed, with only one choice moving forward.

I look him in the eyes. "I'm going to confess."

He scoffs. "You don't have the guts."

"I do," I say, a half smile creeping up my face. "I am going to tell them I stabbed him."

"You're right," he says. "You did. You stabbed him. Not me."

"I'm going to tell them everything. I've already talked to Lauren. And Patsy. I'm sorry, Drew," I say. "I have to do it. I have to end all the lies."

"They won't believe you," he says.

"I have proof now, Drew."

"You can't," he says. "We're family."

"I know," I say, closing my eyes. "You were right. I couldn't shoot you. I couldn't hurt you. But I can't let anyone else be hurt now, either. Not anymore. Never again."

It is the only way *we* can be free. That's what I realized that night watching Patsy fall victim to my brother's will. It is the only way to end this loop. To cut it clean and true.

The rain falls around us, between us. The sound fills my head as my brother says nothing. Slowly, I open my eyes again. I see his face. I see his pain.

"No, Liam," he whispers.

"I'm sorry," I say.

The gun shakes again, but this time in my brother's hand. "I can't let you. You know that."

He is pleading with me now. But I say nothing. I just look up to him, up into the rain. It's time.

"Liam!" he shouts.

"It's over," I whisper.

It's funny, in a way. I swear I can see the weakness he must have seen in me all those years. But it is not written on my face. Not anymore. No, it is painted brightly within my brother's wide eyes.

"I love you," I say, but not to him. To her. "But you're just like him. You can't do anything yourself. You just sit there with your job like he used to sit there playing with his model. But he wouldn't have pulled the trigger, either."

"No!" my brother yells.

I smile, something full and pure. "You're just like Dad."

That's when everything changes. His eyes seem to refocus. That thin smile returns to his face. It's like my words remind him. Maybe he was born into it. Maybe my father made him. Nature or nurture, it doesn't matter. Drew is my father now. He has been for a long time. And just like my father, he can't let the secrets out. He can't let people know the truth. He can't let a light shine on the monster inside. No matter what.

I stare at that smile. And I know I've won. I did it. It took me so many years to finally understand. He's just like my father; there was no beating him at his game. Unless you played his game better.

My hand moves slowly. I reach into my pocket and pull out the keys. There are no prints. Time swallowed them years ago. There is no detective. There is just a lie, just my final move. The endgame.

He sees the *evidence*. The *truth*. And Drew believes. Everything I have done leads to this. My question will finally be answered. Either he will walk away, and I will know the depths of my weakness. The decades of lies I've told myself. Or he will pull the trigger. End this. And I'll finally know for sure. I will finally be free.

My smile burns brighter than the lightning in the sky. And then my brother pulls the trigger. I hear the gun fire before pain flares just below my breastbone. The force drops me the rest of the way to the ground. My head hits the pond's edge and I look up through the branches, at the slate-gray sky.

"Good-bye, Liam," my brother says.

Faintly, I hear the sirens before the gun fires again. And I am still smiling.

"Thank you," I whisper.

19

---

hear voices like they speak under the water. I feel a chill rising in my legs, passing my hips and slipping into the core of me. I close my eyes even tighter, willing just one last moment to appear. I paint her face with the little strength I have. The colors blossom with each stroke of the brush. She comes to life in that moment, all swirls and blends of light and innocence. I see her. I see her, just as I painted.

She's free, I think. After it all, she's free. And the cold overtakes my chest. Hands touch my body, but not me. It starts under my breastbone, a gentle pull. I move toward it, into it. I let it take me. My eyes open, or maybe they did. Through them I see the sun now shining between branches thick with bright green leaves. I hear my brother's words.

"You got it," he says.

My fingers, so small, tighten the laces of my shoes. I look into his face. He is young and fresh and full of life, full of truth and innocence. His smile lifts me, warms me more than the sun.

"Come on," he calls, running through the woods ahead of me.

My legs are short. My muscles young. I try to keep up, but the distance between us grows. I call out to him, begging him to stop. And I hear his laughter as he passes out of sight.

I am alone, lost in the woods, the sun shining down on me through the timeless branches. I feel the pull again, starting at my chest. I call out one last time but there is no answer. So I slip slowly, peacefully into the cold darkness, for once in my short life knowing that everything will be okay.

EPILOGUE

Patsy cups her stomach as she stands outside his trailer. The weather is warm and the sun shines across the bleak, unkempt landscape as a slight breeze plays with her light blond hair. Through large, dark sunglasses, she takes in the house, the sprawling field beyond it, and the silent emptiness. She remembers their hopeful plans, and she wonders how it all went wrong.

Slowly, she walks along the gravel path to the front door. The yellow police tape drapes in a loose X. Her finger traces it without touching the plastic. She looks around once before gripping the tape and pulling it away. She opens the door and the putrid smell of rotting food rolls out of the trailer.

Patsy pauses then. The pain and confusion war within her as she relives those moments as if they run on an endless loop. She first saw it on the news. She watched the grainy footage of two bodies covered in white sheets. And she learned that they were both gone, forever. Liam shot by Drew. Drew shot by the police after a violent standoff in the woods. She tried to return home, only to find a swarm of reporters outside the house. Everything after that was a blur, running, hiding, and eventually giving in to the crushing reality. She gave an interview and was blindsided by the reporter, who had somehow found out about her pregnancy. She became the victim. The press lauded her as they tore Liam and Drew down. An anonymous source reported that bones were found at the scene, and that their father's death would be reopened as a murder investigation. More and more stories of the Brennan brothers leaked. Some she knew to be true. Others, she might never know.

Days passed. Eventually, the pull grew too strong. Standing outside the trailer, though, Patsy can't put into words what has drawn her to this place. Her family urged her to move away, run from the story before it identified her and the life of her child forever. She would do that, too. Without regret. Yet she could not leave, though. Not without understanding.

Holding her breath, she walks into the trailer. The air is thick and still. The furniture has been moved. She assumes the place has been searched by the police. Whatever she hopes to find would most likely have been removed. Yet something draws her inside.

As she passes a stained, threadbare couch, her hand runs along the top. Her head turns, and she sees it by the back window. The painting hangs on an easel, a pile of brushes and paints on the counter. A ragged hole pierces the right corner. The fabric folds over itself, blocking her view of the picture.

Slowly, through the crushing pain, she takes her first step. Then the next. She reaches the painting, standing at arm's length, staring. Patsy reaches out, lifting that corner, exposing Liam's final work of art.

The painting is overwhelmingly beautiful in the raw pain that marks every inch. Thin, umber strokes outline a face. The iridescent skin. Gaunt cheeks and bright red lips. Shades of blackness fall out from under a blue-and-white headscarf. Long, skeletal fingers, tipped with perfectly manicured nails a fiery red, reach out as if they might tear free from the canvas and touch her cheek. The deep lines of an exposed collarbone. The perfect 1960s movie star.

And the eyes. They stare back at her, full of life. The sharpness of the color, the line of her lids, the deep and sharp contours, the play of shadow and brightness. She feels the strength, the power that now seems to fill the room. In the clarity of those eyes, his mother's eyes, she sees Liam anew.

She lets go of the canvas. It's not what she's here to see. Patsy looks above the door, the space over the cabinet, everywhere they had discussed putting a camera. There are none. She searches through the trailer, hoping to find just one. But there is nothing. No cameras. No surveillance. Nothing to hint that Liam ever intended to follow their plan.

Patsy holds her stomach. She imagines she can feel the baby growing inside her. And all she can do is pray her son will take after his uncle, not his father.

Acknowledgments

To Michelle, we've made it this far and I certainly wouldn't be me without you.

To Ben and Lily, teenagers rock!

To Stephanie Rostan, the Tom Brady of literary agents.

To Jessica Renheim, you made this book so much better than I thought it could be.

To Christine Ball, John Parsley, and Jamie Knapp, thanks for letting me visit so much. You're fun.

To Kayleigh George and Marya Pasciuto, thanks for not judging my silly questions and mindless e-mails.

To everyone at Dutton, serious thanks for everything you do!

To Jen Moffa—who was so mad at me that Eric Maney was mentioned in the last book—maybe we can all meet up for dinner. How's 2023?

Most important, to Tyler and Austin Hofmann-Reardon. Your conversation on the beach led me to change the professions of the two main characters, the politician and his muscle.

And to everyone who reads more than the internet, keep the torch burning. It's getting pretty dark out there.

About the Author

Bryan Reardon is the *New York Times* bestselling author of *The Real Michael Swann* and *Finding Jake*. Prior to becoming a full-time writer, Bryan worked for the state of Delaware for more than a decade, starting in the office of the governor. He holds a degree in psychology from the University of Notre Dame and lives in West Chester, Pennsylvania, with his wife and kids.